MURDER
AT THE
MENA HOUSE

MURDER AT THE MENA HOUSE

ERICA RUTH NEUBAUER

KENSINGTON BOOKS
www.kensingtonbooks.com

KENSINGTON BOOKS are published by

Kensington Publishing Corp.
119 West 40th Street
New York, NY 10018

Library of Congress Control Number: 2019953568

ISBN-13: 978-1-4967-2585-1
ISBN-10: 1-4967-2585-9
First Kensington Hardcover Edition: April 2020

ISBN-13: 978-1-4967-2587-5 (e-book)
ISBN-10: 1-4967-2587-5 (e-book)

10 9 8 7 6 5 4 3 2 1

Printed in the United States of America

For my Dad.
I miss you every day, Chief.

CHAPTER ONE

Egypt, 1926

When selecting an exotic location for travel, it's advisable to choose one where the air isn't trying to kill you. I would try to remember that for the next time.

"Jane, you look terrible in this heat. You're practically dripping." My aunt Millie's mouth puckered, but also slipped into a smug little grin at the edges. She looked as fresh as linen off the line, without so much as a glisten.

I sighed inwardly.

"I didn't realize how hot it was still going to be this time of year." I eyed the long, wide blades of the fans as they turned lazily overhead. I decided they were more for appearance than actually moving any of the heavy air around.

Millie sniffed and went back to surveying the bar, whiskey highball firmly in hand, lipstick now slightly askew with a matching plum-colored scowl on the rim of the glass. My aunt's first order of business upon our recent arrival at the Mena House Hotel had been a drink, any drink, as long as it was a step above the bathtub rot being churned out at home.

Prohibition was my aunt's archnemesis.

With Millie sorted out, I excused myself to go in search of

a drink of my own. I threaded through the thin crowd to the bar and leaned against the polished wood. It felt good to stand after hours of travel, and I surreptitiously stretched as I waited for my gin rickey.

Within moments, the young bartender appeared at my elbow with my drink. I hoped the cool lime and refreshing fizz would wash the sandy grit of travel from my mouth. My aunt had barely let us settle into our rooms before bustling me down to the bar.

It hadn't even been enough time to catch a glimpse of the Great Pyramids I knew were just outside this hotel.

I surveyed our fellow travelers at the bar, stopping myself from slugging my drink back in one go. I was more parched than I had thought.

"Mrs. Wunderly, I presume?" The low, pleasant rumble interrupted my gawking at the scene around me, nearly startling me out of my skin.

I turned and faced the broad-shouldered owner of the posh British accent that addressed me. As my hazel eyes met dark chocolate ones, a frisson of electricity traveled down my spine before I tamped it down. Hard. Handsome men were not my concern.

He nearly towered over me, and I was not a small woman by any standard. I eyed him, one eyebrow cocked, wondering how he had discovered my name before any introductions had been made. Perhaps he had some magic at his fingertips. Another shiver tickled my spine.

"Well, you've pulled my name from a hat. Will you be performing any more tricks this evening? Pull a coin from my ear, perhaps? I could use one to pay for this drink, frankly."

One corner of his mouth turned up. "Your aunt mentioned you when she introduced herself to me just now."

"That was fast," I muttered, and cursed my inattentiveness. I wasn't at all surprised that my aunt had sniffed him out and then sent him over—especially once she realized he wasn't wearing a wedding band. Which I cursed myself for noticing also. I was just surprised she had managed to do it so quickly.

"I'm afraid no further tricks will be forthcoming."

"Well, that is a disappointment."

"All I can offer you in exchange for your loss is another drink."

"I suppose I will have to make do."

A full smile lit his already handsome face, and I gave myself a small shake and a stern lecture on the perils of men while he turned and gestured to the bartender. He ordered another gin rickey for me and a glass of water for himself.

This time, when my drink appeared, it was generously poured. Too generously. I would have to take it slow or I would find myself zozzled and lying beneath a table.

"Not drinking?" I eyed his water, tiny drops of condensation making their way to the bar from where his long fingers rested on the glass.

"I had a long day in the sun," he said. "Sticking with water seems a safer bet."

"I see." I paused and studied him for a moment. "And what line of work are you in, Mr. . . ." I suddenly realized he hadn't introduced himself.

"Redvers. Call me Redvers." He revealed a roguish grin as both of my eyebrows headed north—was that a given name? A surname? It seemed I wasn't going to get any clarification on that point.

"And what is it you do . . . Mr. Redvers?"

"I'm in banking."

I'm embarrassed to say I burst out laughing. He looked slightly alarmed, as if he had suddenly come across an unbalanced relative out in public. More than a few heads turned our way.

"My apologies." I got hold of myself, mentally kicking

myself for my rudeness. "You simply look too dangerous to be a banker."

And he did. His suit was of fine linen and perfectly fit his athletic frame. Even my untrained eye could see that it was tailor-made and expensive. His dark hair was slicked in the current style, but the thick waves were giving him a great deal of trouble in taming them. He was all energy and movement. And the wolfish grin he was now giving me, along with the sparkling intelligence in his brown—nearly black—eyes, gave the impression of someone who was most definitely not trapped behind a desk counting money.

We continued chatting amiably before a brief lull in the conversation prompted me to offer him an out. "You know, Mr. Redvers, if you have other obligations this evening, I very much understand. I know my aunt can be persuasive, but I would hate to keep you."

It was his turn to study me. "I admit that it was your aunt's suggestion that I introduce myself, but I'm quite happy where I am."

I shrugged. Against my better judgment, I found myself enjoying his company and didn't entirely mind prolonging it. But I also didn't want to give him the wrong impression. Even though I was past what society considered my prime, I had done my fair share of shooting down offers since I had been widowed, and depending on the man, they didn't always take the rejection gracefully. I was not looking for anything outside of a pleasant conversation.

As I kept reminding myself.

But Mr. Redvers had a sharp sense of humor—something that I had sorely missed back home. The society circles that Millie moved in were stuffy, to say the least. My father's family was solidly upper-middle-class, but with Millie's high society marriage, and then my own at the tender age of twenty, it was impossible to avoid being dragged into the upper echelons of society alongside her. Just the thought of those proper circles made my eyes cross with boredom.

Redvers' eyes caught on something behind my shoulder, and he suddenly looked apologetic. "But I'm afraid I do need to excuse myself for a moment. I shall return shortly."

I raised my eyebrows, but excused him gracefully. I wondered what—or who—could have called him away as soon as he had announced he was staying.

I returned to my perusal of the room.

Within moments, I felt a presence behind me and turned to find a moustachioed gentleman, leaning on a wooden cane. As he readjusted his broad hands, I caught a glimpse of the brass lion head perched on top of the dark mahogany stick. It looked both fierce and substantial.

"Good evening, my dear." He smiled graciously. "Having any luck getting a refreshment?"

I smiled at him, immediately put at ease by his demeanor. "I'm all set for the present, but the bartender has been quite attentive."

"Excellent." He caught the young man's eye. "A sherry, if you would." He turned to me, extending his hand. "Colonel Justice Stainton, at your service." His clipped British vowels and upright bearing would have given away his military background, even if his title hadn't.

"Jane Wunderly." I gave his hand a firm shake. His gentle blue eyes widened slightly at my grip, and my smile widened in response.

He cleared his throat. "What brings you to the Mena House, Miss Wunderly?"

According to social mores, the proper address would have been Mrs., but I didn't bother to correct him. I would rather eat hot coals than discuss my widowed status with friends, let alone perfect strangers. And I was tired of facing the pity that comes with losing one's husband in the Great War. Of course, even more dreaded were the questions from people whose false concern masked their desire for proximity to drama. I didn't get that sense from the colonel, but sleeping dogs and all that.

"My aunt and I are traveling together." I gestured with my free hand to Millie, who took no notice of me, but appeared quite pleased now that her hand was holding a full drink again. Quality liquor and a warm climate had been Millie's only two requirements when she had suggested that I accompany her on a trip—at her expense, no less. And while I also relished the idea of enjoying some gin without the threat of going blind, I was beyond thrilled to fulfill a lifelong dream to see the pyramids. "And yourself?"

"I wanted to show my daughter, Anna, that there was more to the world than parties in London and young men with money." A wry smile curled the edges of his bottlebrush moustache as he nodded in Anna's direction where she stood nursing a drink, eyeing the crowd.

Her brassy blond bob glowed in the gentle bar light, although it had that brittle quality that comes with too many applications of peroxide. Her boyish figure was perfectly suited to display the current fashions. Even from a distance, I could see that the young lady's heavily beaded—and short—navy blue dress was nothing short of couture.

Looking her over, I had to admit to a small stab of jealousy. My figure was far more suited to an era that appreciated padded curves—it's been mentioned by Millie (more than once) that perhaps I should consider one of the lightweight corsets to bring my curves into a more fashionable line. The current trend in drop-waist dresses looked terrible on anyone who was not built like a lollipop—or willing to constrict themselves into the shape of one.

I enjoyed breathing far too much to try.

I turned back to the colonel and returned his smile. "She's

lovely." His face lit with pride. "And rich young men are better than the alternative, I suppose." He chuckled, and our small talk quickly turned to our mutual interest in local historical sites and current digs.

"I'm happy to share with you what I know about the area." The colonel's eyes danced. "We've been here for several weeks already, and I was stationed nearby during the war. Were you planning to do some touring soon? It would be my pleasure to offer my services to you and your aunt."

"I was planning on giving myself a day or two to get acclimated to the heat and then take a tour with a local guide." As anxious as I was to see the pyramids, I knew that I would enjoy them more if I gave myself a chance to get used to the weather first. "But I would love to take you up on your offer. It's very kind of you."

"Excellent. Let's plan on it, then." His gaze drifted over my shoulder and his left eye twitched ever so slightly.

I turned my head and quickly located the source of his irritation. Anna had found a group of three fashionably dressed young men of varying degrees of attractiveness. Her giggles carried down the bar like brittle bubbles, breaking over us as the gentlemen jostled each other for her attention. The tallest of the bunch bent to light her cigarette, and I could see her fluttering her lashes.

"If you will excuse me, Miss Wunderly." I smiled graciously as the colonel moved down the bar toward Anna.

A voice rumbled in my ear almost immediately. "Hello again."

CHAPTER TWO

I had been entirely caught up in the scene Anna was creating and was startled once more. Hand to my heart, I turned to find that Redvers, true to his word, had returned.

"Are you certain you're not a magician? That was an excellent reappearing trick."

"Simply the gift of stealth."

"I've known tigers with less stealth than you, then."

"And you're acquainted with many tigers?"

"Only my fair share."

Redvers paused for a moment, glancing down the bar. "Who were you chatting with?"

"Colonel Stainton. He introduced himself." I studied Redvers for a moment, but his face remained impassive. It seemed entirely too convenient that Redvers had disappeared when he saw the colonel coming, and reappeared just as quickly. But what reason could he have for avoiding the man? With a mental shrug, I went on to explain what I had told the colonel about our recent arrival and travel plans, and soon found myself once again discussing my interest in archeology and its modern relevance.

It wasn't long before our polite discussion dissolved into a heated debate of the current political climate and I was taking pointed jabs at the British.

"But don't you admit that the continued occupation of this country is outrageous? They declared sovereignty three years ago, but the British government is still running interference."

Redvers laughed. "That seems awfully hypocritical coming from an American. Do you know how many colonies *you* have? Besides, without our interference, the current system may well collapse entirely."

He made an excellent point. My own position was largely due to naiveté about nuanced world politics, so I changed courses. "Is that why you're here? To bring a better banking system?"

"Oh, my. You're a banker? Does that mean you have a lot of money outside the bank as well?" Damn the man, I had failed to notice that I was being flanked—this time by Anna Stainton herself. I was annoyed at the interruption, but managed to smooth my face into a pleasant smile long before she bothered to flick a glance my way. Redvers, much too observant, caught me and seemed amused.

"Well, it's not as simple as that." He turned to face Anna fully. "Miss Stainton, I presume?"

"Oh, please call me Anna."

She put her hand on his arm and I just barely managed to keep my eyes from rolling. Instead, I turned back to the bar to ask for a glass of water. Two large fizzy drinks had obviously played havoc with my self-control, and it was time to get my equilibrium back. As Anna continued to coo questions in Redvers' direction, I considered excusing myself. I was not going to fight for a man's attention—any man. But I especially did not want to battle with a woman nearly ten years younger than I, and obviously on the hunt.

Farther down the bar, I spotted a caramel-skinned man wearing a pristine white linen suit. He was now staring in our direction, and for a moment, I worried that I was the object of his intense gaze.

Then I realized it was Anna's back he was burning holes in.

I turned to ask whether either of my companions knew the man when I felt a sudden deluge of cold liquid down the front of my dress, and heard the tinkle of a few stray ice cubes fall at my feet. I sighed as I looked down at my now-soaked chest.

It was no accident. I had seen Anna's hand tip her glass while she watched me out of the corner of her eye. In fact, it was quite a feat as I stood nearly a head taller, and yet she managed to hit me directly in the chest. My initial shock turned briefly to rage, and just as quickly, I tamped it down. I refused to be upset by this young woman. In fact, I almost had to admire her—it was a very efficient way to rid herself of competition for Redvers' attention. He was, after all, the most attractive man in the room.

It was merely an observation. Not an interest.

I would never admit it, but the cold seeping into my clothing felt rather good—it was still a warm evening. I was, however, relieved that I had changed into darker attire before dinner. Sheer fabric and liquids are not exactly a recipe for modesty.

"Oh, I'm dreadfully sorry," Anna said without a trace of sincerity.

"Not a problem," I said. "I'll just pop back to my room to change."

"I hope I haven't ruined that . . . charming blouse."

I nearly laughed. A cat with claws embedded in my leg couldn't have been more obvious. Instead, I smiled widely. "If it makes you feel better, I'll send the cleaning bill to your room."

I was about to excuse myself when I saw a flash of white linen pass by us, bumping Anna's arm from behind, causing her to lose her grasp on the silver beaded clutch she held there. The clasp broke open as it made contact with the floor, and both she and I immediately bent to retrieve her things. Backed against the bar, Redvers couldn't bend to assist us, but he helpfully pushed some items toward me with his neatly polished wingtips. I gathered the items nearest me—a tube of lipstick, a compact that miraculously seemed intact, and some stray coins. As I passed her items back to her, she quickly stuffed everything back into her bag. Then she gave the clasp a decidedly firm click, pressed her lips together and glared at me.

We could have stared at each other all evening long, but a "thank you" was never going to pass those ruby lips.

I decided it was the perfect time to make an exit, and I bid them both good night. As I wove through the crowd, I kept an eye out for the white linen suit that had collided with Anna, but he had disappeared just as quickly as he had appeared. I was sure it was the man I had seen staring at Anna, but I couldn't imagine why he would have purposely spilled Anna's purse. And it had certainly looked intentional.

Selfishly, I felt a twinge of relief that it hadn't been my own public display this time. I was not a stranger to embarrassing myself with clumsiness.

Aunt Millie was chatting with two young women at a table as I passed by. I waved a hand at my soaked shirtfront. Millie gave a quick, exasperated glance to the heavens and continued with her conversation. I had no idea how many drinks she had under her belt, but I wasn't worried about her. I knew she could manage on her own.

The majority of the guests had either retired for the evening or were peppered around the bar, leaving the moonlit hallways empty as I passed through. The heels of my shoes clicked conspicuously against marble and echoed slightly in the quiet, and I acknowledged to myself that the sound made me a little jumpy. The hotel was an absolute maze and I didn't know where the gentleman in the white suit had disappeared to. Empty doorways opened onto dark and mysterious paths and I found myself hurrying a bit as I passed each one.

I could see the intersection where I needed to turn toward my room. But as I passed yet another dark doorway, a hand shot out and touched my arm.

I shrieked and stumbled forward.

CHAPTER THREE

"Oh, my dear Miss Wunderly, I'm so sorry to have startled you." The colonel's brows furrowed. "I saw you passing by and thought I would catch up with you. I would like to apologize for my Anna—I heard what happened in the bar just now." He managed to keep his eyes on mine and away from the damp lake of my blouse. A true gentleman.

Hand to my chest, I could feel my heart racing, but I smiled and reassured him that I was fine. "I'm certain she didn't mean it. It was just an unfortunate accident." A small lie on my part, but an innocent one. There was no sense in stirring up trouble with Anna's father. I dropped my hand and surreptitiously wiped my damp palm on my skirt.

He smiled, somewhat sadly. "I'm sure it was. She seems difficult, but she has had such a rough go of things since . . . Well, she is easily wound up." He failed to elaborate, and I didn't press him. It was an easy assumption that their family had suffered some sort of loss, most likely during the war. Everyone's lives had been affected in some way.

"I'm certain it was just an accident. And truly, Colonel, no harm done." I paused. "I'm sure I will see you at some time tomorrow. Please have a pleasant night."

He smiled, obviously relieved, and patted my arm clumsily as he turned to go. I watched for a moment as he ambled down the long hallway, cane tapping, before I headed on my way. The wet shirt I wore was becoming more than a little uncomfortable in the rapidly cooling night air. I prayed I could make it back to my rooms without running into anyone else—carrying on a conversation while wearing a soaked blouse was . . . awkward, to say the least.

Once in my room, I stripped off the soiled clothes and rinsed them in the adjoining bath. Whatever Anna had been drinking was strong enough to leave a lingering odor, and I didn't want either my clothes or my rooms to smell like a speakeasy. Once I was confident the smell had disappeared down the drain, I hung them over the edge of the tub, making a mental note to have them taken to be cleaned properly. Fortunately, whatever Anna had been drinking was light in color, so I felt confident it wouldn't stain.

Instead of changing into another set of clothes for the evening, I decided to turn in for the night. Several days of travel, the excitement of the evening, and the mystery of a very foreign country left me barely able to keep my eyes open. I collapsed onto the soft bed and fell into a dreamless sleep.

The next morning, I awoke early and dressed in what I supposed would become my Egyptian uniform—a light cotton sleeveless blouse and loose-fitting skirt—and headed down to breakfast alone. I figured Aunt Millie would be sleeping off the effects of last night, so I didn't bother to check with her. I felt certain the first I would see of her would be sometime around lunch.

I walked slowly on my way to the breakfast room, pausing to admire the architecture as I passed through arabesque doorways, dark and light marble alternating to form striking stripes around the rims. I ran my fingers over the cool marble, the smooth surface rolling beneath my fingertips. In the daylight, the same doorways had none of the menace from the night before, and I laughed a bit at myself—the hotel was nothing but beautiful. As I continued on, I noticed the potted palms scattered throughout the hotel, bringing warmth and life to the marble surroundings.

Within moments of my arrival at the dining room, I was greeted by a dark-skinned man with raven-black hair just beginning to show the signs of gray at his temples. He wore the customary long white robes of the hotel staff, but his ensemble was topped with a round felt hat in a rich red, a gold tassel hanging merrily along the side. His large dark eyes were warm and creased at the corners, framed with the kind of eyelashes a woman would kill for.

"Good morning, ma'am," he said in beautifully accented English. "My name is Zaki and I am the head waiter here at the Mena House. Please come this way."

As he showed me to my table, I couldn't help but gape at the dining room I was being led into. It was a sight to behold—designed to create the impression of a mosque's interior, it was unlike anything I had ever seen in a hotel. Or anywhere, for that matter. Numerous lamps of pierced metal hung from the high-domed ceiling, casting fascinating shadows on the white linen tablecloths and sparkling silverware below. The walls, windows, and ceiling were covered with stunning fretted woodwork carved in intricate designs. As we passed, I could see Arabic inscriptions worked into the patterns.

"Zaki, what are these beautiful wooden panels?" I asked, gesturing to the walls. He held my chair for me, then pushed it in gently before handing me the morning menu.

"Ah, you have excellent taste, madame. They are called *mashrabiyas* and were hand-carved by very fine artisans. They were popular many hundreds of years ago. The panels you see here were saved from a nearby town by the new owners of this hotel." He beamed at me. "If you have other questions, I am always happy to help. I will send someone to take your order right away. Please enjoy your breakfast."

"Thank you, Zaki."

I decided on a simple breakfast of eggs and toast, handing over my menu and my order before taking in the rest of the room. There weren't as many people as I had expected, even given the relatively early hour—but it was late September and the end of the off-season. The warm weather in winter and spring would surely bring more tourists from both the States and the Continent, but for now few had found reason to escape their own reasonable climates. I wondered if we had been right to come so early in the season, but I comforted myself with the hope that the tourist sites would be less clogged with visitors.

After my quiet breakfast, I settled myself in the shade of a large palm on the wide terrace behind the hotel. A postcard scene of the pyramids floating above the trees stretched out before me, and I found myself distracted by the view and the possibilities. I looked forward to exploring the pyramids and perhaps even some of the archeological dig sites in the area—I made a mental note to ask the colonel later if he had any special recommendations.

I had just picked up the book I'd brought along, when my aunt Millie appeared before me.

"Aunt Millie!" I was unable to hide my surprise. "I didn't expect that you would be up yet!"

"My dear girl. One can't lie about all day. I realize we're spending a fair amount of time here, but it would be a waste to spend it in bed. These ladies are going to accompany me for a round of golf."

I was so startled by Millie's early appearance that I'd completely failed to notice two things—that my aunt had dressed in something resembling athletic wear, and the two young ladies from the evening before were trailing in her wake.

"This is Miss Lillian Hughes." Millie indicated the tall, trim girl with auburn hair, who smiled a greeting at me, but seemed preoccupied, her eyes straying toward something beyond the tree line. "And this is Miss Marie Collins." Marie briefly raised a hand in greeting, but her eyes barely strayed from Lillian.

"How do you do, ladies? It's a pleasure," I said. "I didn't know you played golf, Aunt Millie."

"I suspect there are a great many things you don't know about me, Jane." Millie gave a playful smile, and threaded Lillian's arm through her own. Lillian smiled at Millie, and the pair migrated in the direction of the golf course, with Marie trailing slightly behind. My mouth was still agape as they disappeared from view. I had never seen Millie so physically affectionate with anyone, and I could not begin to imagine what Millie had in common with two young British women barely into their twenties.

Except golf, apparently.

Once I stood, I could see the green grass of the course lying in striking contrast to the gold sand all around. I hadn't realized that there was a golf course at the hotel. It never occurred to me that something so green could survive in the middle of the desert, even though I knew logically that Egypt wasn't entirely sand. It had the Nile, after all.

"Not one for golf, Mrs. Wunderly?" I started, then realized that Redvers had appeared at my side, stealthy as per usual. I truly needed to work on my powers of observation if I was going to survive the barrage of surprises.

"I've never been one for sporting pursuits."

"Of any kind?"

I could feel a red stain creeping up my neck. I ignored it as I sat back down, gesturing for him to join me.

"Would you like some coffee, Mr. Redvers? The local brew is quite good. Or would you prefer a cuppa?"

He cocked an eyebrow at the British colloquialism.

"My mother was English," I explained.

"Ah," he said. "But you failed to acquire the taste for tea?"

"I'm afraid it's fine for the afternoons, but I require something a bit stiffer in the morning. You never did answer my question. Can I order something for you?"

"No, I'm afraid not, Mrs. Wunderly. I have business in town this morning and was just passing through. Although I would like to continue our conversation over a drink this evening, if you're available. I was disappointed when you didn't return last night."

As much as I shouldn't—*didn't*—care what this handsome and somewhat mysterious man thought of me, I was pleased that he had noticed my absence. Of course, I was also somewhat appalled at my forward behavior the previous night.

"You enjoy having a woman argue politics with you?" I hid behind my cup as I took a sip and avoided looking at him.

"I prefer an argument with an intelligent woman over two minutes in the company of a simpering one."

"Well, I can assure you that I never simper."

"No, I can't imagine that you would."

I smiled at him, despite myself.

Redvers retrieved his bone-white Panama hat from its place on the table and made to leave. "Until tonight then?"

I realized I had never answered his initial question, and lost a brief internal struggle over whether to turn him down. I didn't want to give him the wrong idea, but it also appeared that my aunt had her own agenda and I might find myself more at loose ends during this trip than I had expected. It couldn't hurt to have a few friendly faces in the crowd.

"It would be my pleasure, Mr. Redvers. Until tonight," I said.

He rose and gave a slight bow before disappearing into the

cool shadows of the building. I pretended to return to my book as I discreetly watched him over the top of the pages.

But as soon as he disappeared from view, my mind turned back to Millie, a woman I would have wagered could not surprise me.

I would have lost that bet.

CHAPTER FOUR

I spent the remainder of the morning on the terrace alternately enjoying the spectacular view and reading Agatha Christie's *The Man in the Brown Suit*. I came up for air after a particularly riveting scene and realized that I was developing a slight headache. The unseen birds, which had earlier called to each other from their shady perches, quieted as the sun moved higher overhead, and the day was now beginning to swelter. Escaping to my darkened rooms suddenly sounded glorious.

An hour later, I emerged from my room to join Millie for a quiet lunch on her private terrace.

"Are you pleased with your rooms?"

Millie's suite with its private verandah faced the pyramids themselves. My rooms were several doors down and on the opposite side of the hall. They had a lovely view of the gardens, but nothing compared to her spectacular panorama.

Millie gave a careless glance around. "They are sufficient."

I resisted the urge to roll my eyes, although I had been surprised my aunt suggested the Mena House for our stay—in my experience, she was more likely to prefer the more socially positioned hotels in Cairo itself, like Shepheard's or the Continental. But I was delighted with the location. Flat roofs at multiple heights broke up the long white façade of the building, and the numerous balconies gave it a distinctly Arabian feel. Not to mention, it was directly in the shadow of the Great Pyramids.

It was also the only hotel in Egypt with a pool, which definitely added to its appeal. If the weather continued in this vein, I suspected I would be living in the pool before too long.

We settled ourselves in the padded chairs on the terrace. Mind-reading mystic that she was, Millie brought up the very subject I was hoping to avoid.

"Well, Jane. How was your little chat with Mr. Redvers?"

"It was fine."

She fixed me with a disapproving glare. "I would hate to see you ruin this opportunity. I'm afraid there don't seem to be many other eligible men here, Jane."

"Well, it's a good thing I'm not looking for any." I turned my attention to the lunch menu. I caught her disapproving look over the top.

"It's been plenty of time since Grant passed, Jane. Time to move on."

I kept my eyes pasted on the menu and prayed she would drop it.

She didn't drop it.

"If only Nigel's dear nephew had survived the war. You wouldn't be"—she lowered her voice into a whisper, as if discussing a sin in church—"in your *thirties* and still alone. And surely you and Grant would have had children by now." She sighed dramatically. "To be widowed at only twenty-two and left childless. You're running out of time to have them, Jane."

Tension crept up my spine and took root in my shoulders. I rolled them back, one at a time, before searching out an alternate topic of conversation. "Will you look at this menu. So much to choose from. What do you think you'll have?"

Millie grumbled—noisily—but allowed herself to be distracted. Unfortunately, there was no doubt in my mind she would return to this particular battle. I knew Millie—she would never lay down her sword for good. She made her choice and I phoned our order to the kitchen downstairs.

While we waited, I tried to draw my aunt out about her morning playing golf with the girls, but she was unusually reserved on the topic, refusing anything but the briefest answers. I finally gave up and hoped that whatever was bothering her would resolve itself. I spent the remainder of the time soaking up her view.

After lunch, I returned to my rooms and my novel, but after a time, I became restless and ventured out again. A slow wander through the hushed halls soon brought me upon the colonel. He was dressed in what my mother used to call short pants, with a khaki shirt and a pith helmet, looking for all the world like he was going on safari. His cane was at the ready.

"Good afternoon, my dear Miss Wunderly." He tipped his hat to me. "Have you spent a pleasant day?"

"I did, although I had to escape from the heat for a bit."

"It's the best thing. The only thing, really, until you get used to it. Once that sun is directly overhead, it really gets cooking." I agreed and we walked companionably toward the lobby.

"Where were you headed just now, Colonel?"

"I was just going to take a stroll out to the stables. Wanted to see what kind of horseflesh the hotel keeps. Anna has been raving about the riding here."

I wondered if it was the horses or the stable hands she was interested in, and then immediately chastised myself for thinking such uncharitable thoughts. It was true she was a flirtatious young woman, but I needed to take the high road. Even though the young woman had been rude to me the night before, I had no real reason to dislike her.

"Would you like some company?" I asked.

"I would be delighted!" He beamed at me, and we took off at a leisurely pace in what I assumed was the proper direction.

The grounds were extensive, and I hadn't gotten a good sense of the place yet—I was glad for the excuse to do some exploring with the colonel. We chatted easily about Egypt and travel in general as we moved away from the hotel, my companion cheerfully acknowledging the various groundskeeping staff with a tip of the head.

"Do you ride?" The colonel's stick tapped along beside us, the sound muffled in the grass as we moved out onto the well-maintained paths.

"I know how, but I'm afraid there isn't much riding to do back in Boston." My mother had insisted that I learn as a child, but I hadn't mounted a horse since her death. While there were surely stables in the city, I had never maintained the interest.

He chuckled. "I suppose not."

"I didn't even know the hotel had a stable."

"Do you know they also . . ." Thunder drew up from behind us.

I never found out what else the hotel had, because at that moment, Anna Stainton pulled up beside us on an enormous chestnut gelding. As it snorted and danced in place, I had to give her credit for being able to handle such a large horse. She made it seem effortless.

"Hello, Father," Anna drawled, reins clutched tightly in hand.

"Good afternoon, my child. You remember Miss Wunderly."

"Of course." Her lip lightly curled as she looked me up and down.

My own casual outfit qualified as rags compared to her short red riding coat, which covered a silky ivory blouse. The coat came just below the waist of her close-fitting taupe pants, and a pair of tall black boots in smooth leather hugged her calves, matching the black leather riding crop in her hand. She tapped the crop against her boot a few times, causing me to physically flinch. She looked as though she would like nothing better than to hit me with it.

She turned her look of disgust to her father. "Your taste in company hasn't improved any, I see."

"Anna!" A mottled red stain spread across the colonel's face as my own eyebrows shot up.

Without another word, she gave a tug on the reins and a kick to the side of her mount. The horse turned tightly and took off at a gallop, leaving a cloud of dust in its wake. I had begun to sweat lightly on our walk, even though we were moving at a leisurely pace, and the storm Anna left behind stuck to my exposed skin. I felt as though I had taken a bath in sand.

Coughing, the colonel turned to me, his face red and sputtering. I shook my head and smiled.

"It's fine," I said. "She's young."

"I'm so sorry, Miss Wunderly." He wiped a bit of sand from his own face. "She . . . Anna had a difficult childhood. We didn't always have much when I was just starting out, and the other children . . . Well, children can be cruel. And then we lost her mother . . ." His voice trailed off.

"I understand."

The colonel was obviously struggling in his effort to give me some kind of an excuse. And while there were certainly reasons behind Anna's behavior, I wasn't terribly interested in hearing them at the moment, uncharitable as it was. My enthusiasm for a walk to the stables had been well and truly spoiled. All I could think about was going back to my rooms, having a bath, and scouring the dirt from my skin.

I also dreaded the idea of spending the rest of our walk listening to him apologize for his ill-behaved daughter, only to arrive at the stables and have yet another potentially unpleasant encounter with her.

"If it's all the same to you, Colonel, I think I'll head back. The heat might still be too much for me and I need a chance to clean up before dinner." I smiled and met his eyes, doing my best to convey that I didn't hold him responsible.

For a moment, he looked as though he would argue, but he relented.

"I understand, my dear. I do hope we can continue our conversation later." He returned my smile, although a bit sheepishly.

I briefly patted his arm. "Of course."

We parted ways, and I retreated back the way we had come. The return trip went much quicker, not least because I had the incentive of a nice, long bath at the end.

But I could not help wondering what Anna meant. She obviously disliked me, but who else had the colonel been keeping company with that she disapproved of?

CHAPTER FIVE

I barely made it back to my rooms before Millie stopped by and told me that I was meeting her for a drink before dinner. Rather than argue, I sighed and briefly lamented that I would not be able to take the long, luxuriating bath I had been looking forward to.

I stripped off my sandy clothes and piled them in a corner of the room, hoping to corral the dirt and sand in one small area. I crossed my bedroom into the private bathroom, and as my bare feet padded softly across the cool tile, I took a moment to appreciate the room. While I didn't have the spectacular view, the bathroom nearly made up for it. The gorgeous cobalt blue tile covering the floor was unlike anything I had seen at home, and I found the color quite soothing.

A gentle breeze came in through a high window carrying a touch of mint from the eucalyptus trees in the garden. As I turned the gold taps on the large claw-foot tub, filling it with lukewarm water, I regarded the basket of heavenly perfumed toiletries that had been provided. I selected a jasmine-scented soap and promised myself that I would put some of the exotic bath salts to use later—when I had the time to truly enjoy them.

After my too-short soak in the tub, I dressed in a simple plum silk dress with sheer cap sleeves and brushed my hair until it gleamed. I didn't wear much jewelry, but I thought that the little scarab brooch Millie had given me would be the perfect touch with the dress. I searched for a few moments, but it wasn't with my other jewelry or lying out anywhere that I could see. Spinning slowly and surveying the room, I tried to recall if I had worn it the night before, but a glance at the clock told me I would have to continue my search later. Millie would not be pleased if I kept her waiting any longer.

By the time I joined Millie in the lounge, she was installed at a small table in the corner, several empty glasses before her. Either she had been early, or my search had taken longer than I thought. The bar was a small but comfortable seating area off the main lobby. Tall ceilings complemented the gold-flocked wallpaper that adorned the walls; an exquisitely carved wooden canopy hung above the horseshoe-shaped bar. Without the height of the vaulted ceilings, the room may have felt incredibly closed off. Instead, it had an air of cozy exoticism. Tall windows with widely spaced beaded hangings decorated a glimpse of the closest pyramid. I still couldn't help but smile at the sight.

"I can't seem to get proper table service, Jane. Why don't you head to the bar directly and get me another highball," Millie said before I had even pulled out a chair.

I crooked an eyebrow at the empty glasses on the table, but without a word, I followed her suggestion. It was hard to believe service was slow, since the hotel staff had been very attentive so far. Of course, Millie's idea of slow—especially where alcohol was concerned—was probably different than the average guest's.

I brought Millie her whiskey highball and took a seat as she gulped at it greedily. I placed my own sidecar on the table and decided to broach the subject of her acquaintance with the young British women again.

"How do you know Lillian and Marie, Aunt Millie?"

She took her time in answering, peering around the lounge as though she might be able to find a more interesting topic to distract me with. Finally she pursed her lips.

"I knew Lillian's father back in England. You were rather young, so you wouldn't remember, but your uncle and I traveled there for his work and spent nearly two years in London. I told Lillian's father I would keep an eye on her while we were here together." Millie took a long drink and avoided meeting my eye.

"I didn't know you had plans to meet anyone here."

Millie's brow drew low and her face darkened. "I don't need to tell you all of my plans, Jane."

My spine stiffened at the rebuke, and I said nothing. In the awkward silence that followed, I gazed around the room. The caramel-skinned man entered and headed straight for the bar. Beside me, Millie sat upright, her eyes locked in his direction. Her reaction surprised me, especially since I didn't think she had seen his run-in with Anna the night before.

"Have you met him, Aunt Millie?" I kept my voice light. "I've seen him several times, but I haven't been introduced."

Millie didn't respond, but shifted in her chair several times before picking up her drink and pushing back from the table. "Let's go in to dinner, Jane." She moved toward the dining room without looking to see whether I would follow.

My mouth hung open for a moment before I rushed to join her.

I caught up with her as she marched through the doorway to the dining room. Not only had she ignored my question and taken off, but a new awkwardness hung in the air. While we waited for the host to return to his post and lead us to our seat, Redvers appeared, looking dapper in a brown tweed suit, breaking the continued silence between us. Air puffed out of my lungs in relief at the interruption.

"Good evening, Mrs. Wunderly." He inclined his head to my aunt. "Ma'am."

"Mr. Redvers, I believe you already know my aunt, Millicent Stanley."

As I remade the introductions, Millie eyed him up and down, her face brightening. Her relief at the interruption of our little twosome was almost palpable.

"Mr. Redvers, it's a pleasure to see you again. Will you be joining us this evening?" Millie flashed him a wide smile as I looked at her in disbelief. She typically hated dining with strangers. Apparently, I had underestimated her desire to avoid talking with me this evening.

And there was her usual goal of marrying me off.

"I would be delighted." Redvers continued with us to our table.

Talk over the meal centered on Redvers and his childhood. I wasn't surprised, as Millie was driving the conversation train and was keeping the tracks as far from my earlier questions as possible. At least that's what I assumed. In any event, we learned all about Redvers as a youth—that he had an older brother he rarely saw, he'd had a brown-and-white spaniel named Mr. Jones, who died tragically when Redvers was ten, and that the boys spent summers in the small seaside town of South Shields.

"Remind me where that is exactly, Mr. Redvers?" Millie asked.

"It's near Newcastle upon Tyne, ma'am. In the North."

"Your accent doesn't sound as though you are from the North of England, though."

I glanced over at her with a cocked eyebrow. I had no idea Millie was so familiar with the various accents of the British people.

Redvers also raised an eyebrow. "Yes, I was sent to boarding school quite young, and then attended Eton."

Millie gave a little "hmm" of approval and nodded as though this made perfect sense. "Is your family from that area? Near Newcastle?"

For the first time, Redvers seemed uncomfortable. "Not . . . exactly."

I was surprised that Millie let his evasion go. But then I understood why.

"And are you married, Mr. Redvers?" Millie asked, lips pursed and face openly anticipating his response.

As much as I hated to admit interest in the question, I was also very curious about the answer. He wore no ring, but that wasn't always an indicator with men, especially men traveling abroad.

Redvers paused and cleared his throat.

The man certainly knew how to build suspense.

"I am not, Mrs. Stanley. With my line of work, I never found the time. Or the right woman who could handle the hours."

"*Banking hours?* A woman who can't deal with banking hours?"

He leveled a stare at me and I shut my mouth, but it took quite a bit of effort.

"She's right, Mr. Redvers. Whatever can you mean?" Millie wasn't going to let that pass by, either.

There was a long pause as we looked at him expectantly.

"There's an element of travel with the bank I work for, and I'm frequently away from home. As you can see." Redvers spread his hands and smiled.

Millie seemed satisfied with the explanation, but I was still suspicious.

The dining room had filled while we ate, and the other diners now appeared to be finishing their meals as well. I declined the offer of dessert, choosing instead to order my usual glass of after-dinner port. Millie waited for her next drink, and once it was in front of her, she pushed her chair away from the table, readying to leave.

"I think I'll just see what my charges are up to." Millie took a long pull at her drink before hurrying off, careful not to spill a drop. I wondered if the girls were her actual goal, or if Millie was just scheming to leave us alone together.

"Your aunt can certainly hold her alcohol." Redvers watched Millie disappear into the crowd without a hint of a stagger. I'd lost track of the number of glasses she downed over the course of our meal. But I had long ago stopped counting.

"Do you know . . . she's always been such a heavy drinker that I'm afraid I barely notice anymore." My brow furrowed for a moment. "Although she does seem to be drinking quite a bit on this trip. Maybe because the alcohol here is so much better than what we can get at home right now."

Redvers nodded. "Have you always been close?" he asked.

"I can't say we're that close now, to be honest."

Millie was my father's only sister, and I spent a fair amount of time with her as a child, and also as an adult—both before my marriage and after. But despite all the years spent with the woman, I still knew very little about her personally. Millie kept her private affairs *very* private.

I realized that Redvers had directed his attention toward the stream of people heading for the terrace instead of the saloon.

"The dinner crowd seems to be heading outside. Do you know what's going on?" I asked.

"I believe there's going to be some live entertainment tonight. Shall we?" Redvers stood and offered his arm. I paused for only a moment before I accepted and we moved down the hall and out onto the terrace with the others.

CHAPTER SIX

We took up a post on the far side of the curved bar. It was an excellent vantage point for watching our fellow guests as they came onto the terrace and started to mingle. A band was setting up near the stage and a bevy of workers was clearing the majority of the tables from the terrace floor. I felt a moment of panic over the thought of Redvers asking me to dance. I loved to watch, but my feet were incredibly uncooperative in the actual act. I started thinking of polite ways to turn him down. Firmly. But then I glanced at his handsome face, strong arms, and broad shoulders, and the sudden thought of him holding me close on the dance floor made me feel quite . . . warm. A tingle crept up my spine and tickled my neck.

Redvers gave me a strange look. "Are you well?"

I cleared my throat. "No, I'm quite fine. Thank you."

Just then, Anna and the colonel came through the open French doors. Anna was quite the sight, and nearly every head turned in her direction—rightfully so. Her scarlet red dress was fine gauze and nearly see-through, exquisite silver beading just covering any . . . personal . . . areas that would have otherwise made the dress obscene. Her father seemed mortified—glancing at his daughter and just as quickly looking away, moustache twitching—but I could imagine how any argument about the dress would have gone. If I was honest, she wore it well.

"Well, that's certainly . . . eye-catching." Redvers gave Anna a cursory look and turned back to me.

I felt my own small swell of triumph, even though I wasn't nearly as done up or well turned-out. I also reminded myself that I shouldn't—*didn't*—care.

The colonel spotted us from across the room and gave me a friendly nod, his eyes coolly sliding over Redvers and away. Then he and Anna moved in the opposite direction, nearer to the band setup. That friendly nod had not included Redvers, nor did Redvers acknowledge the colonel, which struck me as odd. Colonel Stainton seemed friendly and congenial with everyone, staff included. And Redvers . . . I didn't yet know about Redvers. But the interaction, or lack thereof, was intriguing.

I continued to watch as Anna disengaged from her father and headed for a somewhat rowdy table of young men. The colonel fumed, but instead of going after her, he gazed about until his eyes locked with the caramel-skinned man seated alone at a table nearby. There was a brief acknowledgment between the two men, but the colonel did not join him. Instead, he headed for the bar, using his cane to push his way through the bodies pressed there.

"Do you know that gentleman?" I indicated the man who had bumped into Anna the night before. He sat alone now, swirling a delicate glass in his hand. The light caught on his large cuff link, gold with some sort of jewels encircling the rim.

Redvers cast his eyes in that direction. "The gentleman seated by himself?" At my nod, he continued. "That is Mr. Amon Samara."

No further information seemed forthcoming, and I raised my eyebrows in question.

"I know him only by reputation." He didn't seem inclined to continue. Again.

"What kind of reputation?"

"You know." Redvers waved a vague hand. "Not the kind to be discussed with young ladies."

I rolled my eyes, winning me an amused grin.

Temporarily giving up my line of questioning, I watched as Anna whipped up activity among the increasingly boisterous group of young men. I could see Mr. Samara looking on also, a bemused expression flitting across his face as he sipped at his drink. I was glad to be able to put a name to the man. It was interesting that Mr. Samara and the colonel seemed to know each other, and I wondered if it meant he also knew Anna. It was hard to imagine why he would have bumped so purposely into Anna the night before, especially if he knew her, but I kept my musings to myself.

Soon the band started up and the Bright Young Things swarmed the dance floor and started swinging about wildly. I wasn't the right age to be part of the flapper generation, but I did enjoy jazz, and I took a moment to let the music soak through me. Several numbers into the first set, the band began playing "I Wish I Could Shimmy Like My Sister Kate," a favorite of mine, and I couldn't stop my feet from tapping along—without any sort of rhythm, of course.

"Would you like to dance?" Redvers' tone was unfailingly polite, but he didn't seem terribly interested in actually heading to the dance floor. Which was just as well.

"I'm fine here. But thank you for asking." He looked more than a little relieved, and I found myself hoping that his relief was simply because he didn't care to dance and not that he didn't care to dance with *me*. It was a question I doubted I would ever learn the answer to.

Before long, it was too loud to carry on a conversation and we moved to the far end of the terrace. We found a small table on the very outskirts of the scene where we could still hear the music quite well, yet far enough away to be able to hear each other speak.

"Where did all these young people come from?" I asked. "I haven't seen nearly any of them around the hotel before."

"The Mena House advertises with the other high-end places downtown, and they run special transportation on the nights there will be live entertainment," Redvers said. I imagined that it helped the hotel bring in additional revenue when the rooms weren't completely filled. The guests were certainly keeping the bar and waiters busy with drink orders.

It wasn't long before I saw Anna and a lanky young man in a smart pinstripe suit tumble past, low murmurs and breathy giggles following in their wake. I didn't get a clear look at the young man's face, but I was fairly certain that I hadn't seen him before.

Redvers noticed the pair also—that scarlet dress was hard to miss. Our eyes followed the pair's progress across the lawn, until they were swallowed up by the darkness. Redvers raised an eyebrow, and I shrugged delicately. It was not my place to judge.

Our drinks dwindled, and Redvers offered to head back to the bar in order to refresh them, since the hotel staff was overwhelmed. I requested water this time.

I watched the crowd for a time and saw the familiar form of the colonel breaking through the crush of dancers. I gave a small wave when he glanced in my direction, and he threaded his way toward my table, using the head of his cane to push aside flailing limbs.

"Miss Wunderly, I see you have situated yourself away from the melee." He seemed slightly out of breath as he gave me a brief, distracted smile and continued to glance about.

"I did indeed." I turned in my chair to face him more fully. "Are you looking for someone?"

"My daughter. You haven't by chance seen her, have you?" His pale blue eyes finally settled on my own.

"I did actually." I paused, considering how much to relate

to him. It seemed impolitic to tattle on Anna for escaping with a young man. She was of age, after all.

"I think everyone in the hotel saw her this evening in that getup," he muttered, staring into the dark distance beyond.

As I tried to come up with a tactful response, he gave a sigh.

"She wasn't always so much trouble, Miss Wunderly. We . . . Well, I might have mentioned that we lost her mother unexpectedly when Anna was young. Things have been difficult since." I nodded my understanding. "I hope you don't think me impertinent, my dear. You're just so easy to talk with." I smiled, and the colonel continued on. "In fact, I rather wish you were my own daughter."

"That's kind of you to say, Colonel." I sought a new subject before he could continue along those lines. While I found him to be a kindly man and enjoyed his company, I cherished my own father back home.

"Are you still in the service, Colonel? I have been wondering whether you were simply on leave or . . ." I hoped he could be distracted by talking about his career.

He bit. "No, Miss Wunderly, I was able to retire after the last campaign." He chuckled. "My time is my own now."

"How wonderful that you can now travel where you please, instead of where you are sent."

"It's true, it's true. Although," he said, his voice dropping conspiratorially, "I had been thinking that when I return home, I might try my hand at the stage."

My face must have betrayed my surprise, because he straightened to his full height and assumed a pose, hand on chest. I couldn't help but think that he resembled an overgrown Napoleon.

"I was born for the theater, my dear girl," he projected in a camp voice, and I forced a smile through my astonishment. It was truly the last thing I had expected to hear from Colonel Stainton.

"Well, that's wonderful, Colonel. I think you should absolutely try your hand on the stage. I'm sure you would . . . cut quite a figure."

"Thank you, my dear." His eyes moved back to the crowd, and his broad smile dimmed. "I see your companion is returning. I shall leave you to it." He patted my shoulder and trotted out into the darkness.

I realized that I had never answered his question about Anna, and I was relieved that the choice had been more or less made for me.

Redvers passed me my water. "Was that the colonel?"

"It was indeed," I said.

"Hmm." He regained his seat. "Now, what were we discussing?"

"I think we were discussing whether you knew Colonel Stainton. From your work in banking, perhaps?"

Redvers' lips quirked. "And I'm certain that is not what we were discussing."

"But it's an interesting topic anyway." I waited for his answer, knowing the chances were slim that I would get one.

Redvers leaned his elbow on the small table. "You ask an awful lot of questions."

"It's a habit of mine."

"Well, I think it's my turn to do the asking."

And he did, peppering me with questions about my interests and my life back home, until the colonel and his daughter were completely forgotten.

After a time, I was no longer able to hide my yawns, and I had begun to shiver. I didn't account for how cool the evenings would become after the sun went down, and I noted that I would need a wrap for nights on the terrace. Redvers escorted me back to my rooms, where we bid each other a polite good night. It was so proper and reserved that we may as well have been two chaps shaking hands over a business deal. Closing the door, I felt an unreasonable amount of disappointment.

But as I prepared for bed, my disappointment soon melted into anger at myself for being disappointed at all. Feelings toward a man were precisely what I was looking to avoid—and disappointment was definitely a feeling. One I couldn't afford.

I fell into bed, but sleep was still a long time in coming.

CHAPTER SEVEN

The next morning dawned brightly as my eyes squinted against the light pouring through the cracks in the louvered wooden blinds. I could have easily slept for several more hours, but I didn't want to waste the entire morning. I forced myself to roll out of bed and wash up, deciding that a splash of cold water to the face followed by a pot of coffee would have to prop me up. I snagged my book on the way out in case I decided to move out onto the terrace after breakfast.

As I meandered down the hall, I heard steps coming up quickly from behind and turned to see the colonel and a member of the staff hurrying up the corridor. The colonel saw me and stopped, slightly flushed and fidgeting with his cane.

"Miss Wunderly. Excellent. Would you be so kind as to accompany us? I've been trying to raise my daughter with little success. And, frankly, it might be better if . . . well, if a woman was to enter her room first."

"Have you looked for her on the terrace? Or the stables?" It was possible that Anna was up—although I doubted it— but she may have decided to take an early morning ride.

The colonel fidgeted with the head of his cane. "We've looked everywhere. Frankly, I've had the staff combing the place. Everywhere except her room. As I said, I think it would be best if a woman went in first." His voice dropped. "Someone we know." He glanced at the staff member and I interpreted his meaning. He didn't want to enter her room and see his own daughter in an embarrassing state of undress or in a compromising position with an overnight guest. But he also didn't want a member of the staff to enter, thus risking the possibility of gossip about whatever they might find in there.

"I'm glad to help. You knocked already?" I increased my stride to match their hurried pace. He grunted his assent and I tried to reassure him. "Well, she must have been out late last night. The band was still playing when I turned in. Perhaps she's just having a lie-in." I sincerely hoped that I would find her alone in her bed, regardless of whatever kind of lie-in she was having.

I remembered his search for Anna the previous evening and wondered if this was somehow related. "Did you ever find her last night?"

The colonel stumbled slightly, cane missing a beat, before continuing on. "Ah, yes. We arranged to meet for breakfast. She always manages to bounce back quickly from her late evenings, but she failed to join me this morning."

I remembered those days, myself, but they were more than a few years behind me. Even still, it was hard to imagine Anna as an early riser; I couldn't remember seeing her at breakfast with her father the previous morning, either.

We came to Anna's door, and the young man produced a master key from somewhere in his robes. I made a mental note to find out if those robes had pockets—merely for curiosity's sake.

The colonel raised a hand. "Let me try one more time." He banged on the door—loudly—leaving no doubt that if Anna was inside, she would have heard the noise.

I was certain that none of her neighbors were sleeping anymore, either, and I wasn't surprised when the door to our right opened a crack. A man's sleep-rumpled face peered out, but one murderous look from the colonel sent the door closing quickly.

Yet there was not so much as a peep or a rustle from behind Anna's door. The colonel waved a hand at the lock, and the young man with the key moved forward. He fumbled for a moment before finally unlocking it, pushing the door open slightly and then taking a large step back. I was tempted to do the same.

Instead, I passed my book to the colonel for safekeeping as I slipped through, leaving the men shuffling their feet outside.

The room was absolutely still. I paused for a moment inside the door, holding my breath and listening, my eyes closed tightly as though it would help me hear.

Nothing. No sounds but those from outside.

It was dark in the room, the only light coming from the cracked door. The warm rays illuminated the sparkling litter of dresses and accessories scattered at my feet. I had to kick more than a few discarded garments aside on my way through her sitting area. In fact, I was practically wading through sequins, little flashes erupting around my feet as the light caught them in motion. It was an astonishing amount of clothing, and I couldn't even begin to imagine the cost, based on what I had seen her wearing already. An unpleasant aroma reached my nose, and I thought to suggest that the colonel have the room aired out.

When I reached her bedroom, it was even darker. Tiny shafts of light stole around the closed blinds and I could only just make out shadowy lumps on the bed. I assumed one of the motionless mounds was Anna. I fervently hoped none of the other lumps would reveal themselves to be a young man in some state of undress. I hadn't yet had my morning coffee, and it would take several cups to deal with that sort of thing.

I wrinkled my nose. The unpleasant smell was stronger here—a sharp smell of iron and a whiff of something unfamiliar.

"Miss Stainton," I called out. No answer and still not so much as a flutter. Hesitantly I put my hands out and shuffled to the windows through the darkness, hoping my shins would make the trip unscathed. I pulled the shutters aside, allowing the morning light to stream in. I turned and saw that she was alone after all.

She was also very dead.

CHAPTER EIGHT

"Merciful heavens," I gasped aloud.

Anna's body was splayed across the beautiful four-poster bed with one pale leg hanging limply off the end. A thick puddle of blackest red spread across her chest and spilled more brightly onto the white linens beneath her. She was still wearing her scarlet gown from the evening before, the sparkle of the silver beading dulled and matted with blood. It didn't take a trained member of the medical field to know that she was long past help.

There was a sudden watering in my mouth and I felt my gorge begin to rise. I clutched one hand to my gut and clenched my eyes tightly, willing my body not to be sick, swallowing rapidly and repeatedly. My deep-breathing exercises wouldn't work here, since every breath I sucked in brought the fresh smell of spilled blood deeper into my sinuses. I moved the crook of my left arm to my nose, breathing in the faint smell of jasmine soap, and stayed like that. After a few moments, the feelings of nausea passed.

When I was sure I was not going to be sick, I glanced again at her lifeless body, and found myself absently wondering about the feathers spread about the room, brushing at one that had become attached to my skirt. I kept my other arm where it was, lifted to my nose.

I closed my eyes again. I would have to break this to the colonel. Anger and resentment that I had been put in this position warred with pity for the man and sadness for Anna. She was not the most likable person, but she certainly didn't deserve to die like this.

I briefly considered using the room's balcony as an escape route, but dismissed the plan. That kind of cowardice had never suited me. Instead, I stiffened my resolve and took a moment to sort out what words I would use to tell a father that his daughter had been murdered. Then, back straight, I slowly retraced my steps. I didn't lower my arm from its position until I had passed well into Anna's sitting room, as though the safety of my own elbow could protect me from what I had just seen.

As I lowered my arm, my eyes fell on Anna's room key lying near her handbag on the writing desk. I thought the colonel might need the key later to retrieve her effects, so I palmed it, intending to give it to him. It would occur to me later that the plan didn't make much sense, and that the police would have preferred if I hadn't taken anything from the scene, but my brain was moving in a thousand directions at once. The body on the bed didn't make sense to me, either.

I hesitated again at the door before slipping back out into the sunshine, my eyes squinting against the sudden brightness. The colonel looked at me expectantly, and he must have read something in my face because his eyes registered panic.

I paused, and the colonel's ragged voice filled the silence.

"What is it? What's happened?" he asked.

"I'm afraid there's been an accident." I moved in front of the men to block the door with my body, knowing full well what I had seen was no accident. "She's been shot."

"Can we . . ." He moved toward me.

"There's nothing that can be done for her," I said, reaching out and placing a restraining hand on his arm.

He nodded, accepting my verdict. His back stiffened, and I

marveled at the famous British resolve to maintain a "stiff upper lip." He blinked back tears and nodded again.

"I would like to see her just the same."

I paused, but finally stepped aside as he quietly pushed past me into the room. I then looked to the hotel employee, who had watched our entire exchange with wide eyes. I whispered to him that he should fetch the hotel doctor, as well as the police. He nodded and nearly ran down the hall.

Once he was gone, I realized that I had been clutching Anna's room key so tightly in my palm that it had left deep grooves in the skin, so I absently slipped the key into my pocket and rubbed feeling back into the area. My book had been discarded next to the railing, and I picked it up, awkwardly waiting for reinforcements to arrive. I didn't want to stay there, but I also didn't think it would be proper for me to leave. I shifted from foot to foot. After a few minutes, the colonel rejoined me.

"I hope they find who did this," he whispered hoarsely.

I patted his shoulder and watched as the hotel doctor came sprinting down the hall. We both knew it was a wasted effort, but the colonel seemed to appreciate the attempt. The doctor passed into the room, and the colonel retrieved a handkerchief from his pocket and wiped surreptitiously at his eyes.

It wasn't long before the police descended in large numbers to the scene. The colonel and I were separated, and I was secretly relieved—I wasn't entirely sure what to say to the man. There were few words that could give him comfort, as I had learned during the war, and we had waited for the police in uncomfortable silence.

Then I was kept busy retelling my story and answering the same handful of questions asked repeatedly by a revolving door of officers. I was annoyed that they couldn't elect one officer to take my statement once—it looked like a problem of disorganization rather than an interrogating technique.

Over and over, the same questions, the same story.

I was shamelessly eavesdropping while waiting for yet another round of repetitive questions, and overheard the house doctor—in his obviously Australian accent—giving his final verdict on the cause of Anna's death to the head officer, an Inspector Hamadi.

Gunshots.

It came as little surprise to me after having seen the wounds. I also learned that Anna's body would be removed to the local morgue in Cairo for an official autopsy as soon as the police were finished looking over the scene.

Finally, weak from hunger, I begged the nearest officer for release. There was a brief conference between several of the men milling about, and I was told I could go, but not far. The inspector himself would want to interview me soon. I almost shook my head at the idea of answering more questions, but instead I told them that the inspector could find me at breakfast downstairs.

I headed directly to the dining room, but as I had expected, I was too late to catch breakfast. Cursing my luck and the entire day, I changed course to the terrace, hoping they would be able to scrounge up some leftover pastries or stale bread. I was not too proud to resort to begging. My head was beginning to throb from the lack of caffeine and the overdose of adrenaline.

It turned out that begging was unnecessary. The hotel was already abuzz with word of the death, and once the waiters realized I had been detained by the police—and had found the body—I had no lack of attention or food. They kept my coffee topped off and my pastry basket full, as though by serving me they were part of the drama unfolding. This was a scenario I was very familiar with, and while ordinarily I would have been annoyed, I was grateful for a full stomach and the buckets of coffee they were lavishing on me.

Aunt Millie and Redvers converged on my table at nearly the same time, just as I finished the last pastry and wiped my buttery fingers on the white linen napkin. Aunt Millie wasted no time in demanding to know what the police had told me. Redvers quietly lowered himself into a chair. Millie hovered near one but never settled, choosing instead to stand, her hands gripping the rolled wicker back.

"Well, they haven't really told me anything," I said. "I suppose you could say I was the one doing the telling."

"How did you even come to find her?" One of Millie's hands released the chair and fluttered near her neckline. News of my discovery had spread, but apparently not the why. "I thought you couldn't stand that woman."

I grimaced. "Please don't share that opinion with the police." I hoped I wouldn't need to count on Millie as a character witness.

I explained how Colonel Stainton had come upon me in the hall and asked me to enter Anna's room in case there was anything . . . unseemly . . . for a staff member to find. Millie's mouth flattened into a disapproving line, and I wasn't entirely sure of the cause—my being caught up in the sordid affair or the likelihood that Anna was engaged in something inappropriate.

"Well, thank heavens." Millie's back straightened ever so slightly. "Then they can't possibly think you had anything to do with this." She paused and assessed me with narrowed eyes. "You didn't, did you?"

"Aunt Millie!" I was shocked that she considered me capable of a cold-blooded killing. Redvers' eyebrows had gone up, but he looked amused.

"Well, my dear. You never know." She eyed Redvers, then turned back to me. "Answer their questions and send them on their way. We don't want the police loitering about. Now, if you'll excuse me, I'm meeting the girls for some golf."

"That's a lot of golf, Aunt Millie. Twice in two days?" I tried to keep any hurt or accusation out of my voice, but she leveled a glare at me, just the same.

"If you must know, Lillian is practicing to go semiprofessional."

"I didn't know women were allowed to do that." Sports had never held my interest.

"The U.S. holds a Women's Amateur Championship every year, Jane. It's quite prestigious. I would think you would be more interested in the achievements of your gender." With that, Millie puffed off in the direction of the links.

I looked after her thoughtfully. I was hurt that my aunt had abandoned me to play golf without any concern over whether I was all right, but I was equally curious about her reaction. Redvers gave me a moment before gently interrupting.

"What are you thinking?"

"Does it seem odd that Millie wasn't interested in how Anna died? Or what I told the police?" I asked him. "She only seemed concerned that the police might be spending any time near me." It made me wonder if she had some reason to avoid the police, but I dismissed it as overly fanciful and suspicious. Millie was secretive, but I couldn't think of any reason she would need to fear the police.

"It does seem strange, but perhaps she simply didn't want to hear any upsetting details."

"I suppose." Although I doubted even the most gruesome story would have an effect on my aunt. I took another sip of my now-lukewarm coffee. The cup rattled back into its saucer as I noticed where Redvers' attention had landed.

A small, grim-faced man with caterpillar-thick brows and dark skin was making his way toward us. He was small and wiry, his dark uniform hanging slightly from his frame. I could see the bulge of a cigarette case in his pocket, just below the white belt with a polished gold buckle. Reams of ribbons, the kind you would expect to see on a military uniform, clung to his chest beside the brass buttons that marched down the crisp jacket. His tarboosh was dark as well, set precisely on his head.

Inspector Hamadi, in the flesh.

Chapter Nine

"Mrs. Wunderly?" Hamadi's voice was low, with the heavy rasp of a serial smoker. I noticed that he barely spared a glance for Redvers.

"Yes." I glanced between the two men. "And this is Mr. Redvers."

The inspector flicked a glance at Redvers, briefly inclining his head. "Redvers."

"Inspector," Redvers replied.

The whole exchange left me with the distinct impression that my introduction had been most unnecessary. The inspector pulled out a vacant wicker armchair without invitation and settled himself in it.

"Can you go over the events of this morning for me, Mrs. Wunderly?" he asked.

"I told several of your officers more than once," I started, but as the inspector's caterpillar brows crawled south, I quickly assured him I was more than happy to tell the story for him. I took a drink of water then went over the events of the morning for the inspector. Again.

"Feathers?" was Redvers' only contribution.

The inspector looked at Redvers, mildly annoyed, and as I opened my mouth, he cut me off to answer. "Yes, we found a pillow that had been shot through several times. It appears the killer used it to dampen the noise of the gunshots."

I had been about to tell Redvers that the room was covered in feathers, but I took in the reason for those feathers with great interest. Redvers nodded at the explanation, and the inspector continued with my interrogation.

"When was the last time you saw Miss Stainton?" Even seated, the inspector was a surprisingly imposing force for such a slight man, his words simple but heavy with meaning.

"Last night. Here on the terrace. Mr. Redvers and I were sitting on the far side, over there." I pointed in the direction of where our table had been the night before. "We both saw her leave the party with a young man. It looked like they were headed out onto the grounds—maybe out to the stables? Like I told your officers, I didn't recognize the young man she was with."

"Yes, there were a number of guests from other hotels at the party last night," Hamadi said. "It is possible the young man is staying elsewhere." He paused, reached into his pocket and pulled out a handkerchief wrapped around a small object.

"The problem is this, Mrs. Wunderly." He pulled the item free from its wrapping and I could see that it was my brooch—the one I had misplaced. A small scarab beetle, bedecked with green and blue jewels set in gold.

"But that's my brooch. Where did you find that?" I was shocked and somewhat disturbed that the police might have been going through my things. And absolutely baffled as to why he would have taken it. "Have you been in my rooms?"

"This was found in Anna's room, in her handbag. It was identified as yours. Do you know how it would have gotten there?" Hamadi's black eyes glittered, and I glanced at Redvers, who now wore a slight scowl.

"I haven't the faintest idea." But the wheels in my mind

were turning and I immediately contradicted myself. "Wait! Miss Stainton dropped her bag the other night, and I helped her pick up her things. It must have fallen off then and was accidentally put into her bag."

"But you didn't notice it was missing?"

"I did, but—"

The inspector cut me off. "You had plenty of time to ask for it to be returned, Mrs. Wunderly. Well over a day, in fact."

I didn't have an explanation for that, and instead sputtered uselessly.

"What she says is true, Inspector. I witnessed the whole thing." Redvers had struck a casual pose, one arm draped over the back of his chair, but his gaze on the inspector was sharp and focused.

The inspector shot him a dark look, but let Redvers' remark pass.

"May I have it back?" Despite the uneasiness in my stomach, I wanted my brooch back in my own possession.

"No." Hamadi rewrapped the brooch and secured it back inside his jacket pocket. "It is part of a murder investigation, Mrs. Wunderly. Where were you this morning at five a.m.?"

My eyes widened at the insinuation. I tried to take a few breaths to get my heart rate under control as I had been taught.

"Where were you, Mrs. Wunderly?" Hamadi was impatient.

I explained that Redvers had escorted me to my room at the end of the night, and I had been asleep in bed at the time of the murder.

Hamadi gave the two of us a long look, and I found myself flustered at the unspoken insinuation. "I see." He cleared his throat. "I heard you had an altercation with Miss Stainton the night before last."

I explained that it had all been an accident—the spilled

drink and then her dropped bag. But even to my own ears, the protests sounded weak.

"All reports point to a feud between the two of you, perhaps over this gentleman." The inspector nodded his head at Redvers. I couldn't even answer the charge. My mouth was slightly agape and my cheeks burned. I was too appalled to look at Redvers, but from the corner of my eye, I could see him shaking his head in disgust.

"My men are searching your room, even as we speak. So we will soon know if you have anything else to hide." Hamadi's face was difficult to read.

I started to splutter about warrants, but Redvers put a hand on my arm and I quieted. The food I had just eaten sat like a boulder in my stomach, and then started to churn. For the second time that morning, I worried that I might be sick.

I had no idea how to fire a gun, or where I would even get one, but these facts seemed to fall on deaf ears. My panicked voice was reaching ever-higher octaves as I tried to explain my innocence to the police inspector.

"Please don't make any plans to leave the hotel, Mrs. Wunderly." Hamadi's mouth twisted into a nasty smile as he rose from his chair. "I'll be in touch."

I knew that I had nothing to hide and that they would find nothing incriminating in my rooms, but that knowledge did nothing to still the roiling nausea in my stomach. The very thought of being considered a suspect terrified me. It occurred to me that they probably believed in capital punishment, and a feeling of panic started to claw its way up my throat. I had no idea how effective their justice system was or if it was rampant with corruption. I took several long breaths to force my panicked thoughts to slow.

But the inspector's insinuations about Redvers and me— and that I might have killed Anna over him—also hung in the air like a foul cloud. I didn't have the slightest idea how to go about addressing that issue, so I signaled the waiter hovering at the edge of the terrace and ordered more coffee, hoping to buy myself some time.

Luckily, I remembered that I had some questions about how Redvers knew Inspector Hamadi.

"You two seemed to know each other from somewhere." My voice was shaky, a match for the rattle in my hands.

"We've met before, on another matter."

"That hardly answers my question."

"It wasn't really a question, was it?" He quickly changed course. I knew exactly what he was doing, but I didn't have the presence of mind to object. "Did you recognize the young man with Anna last night?"

I shook my head. I had not seen him around the hotel; but then, most of the young people from the night before were new faces.

"I didn't, either. The police will look for him, though. And the other partygoers as well. Perhaps someone saw something that will clear you of suspicion."

I sat up straight in my chair. "I just remembered something. Mr. Samara is the one who bumped Anna from behind and made her drop her bag. It looked as though it was on purpose. He could have had something to do with all this." It was probably a stretch, but I was feeling desperate enough to grasp at any straw within my reach.

Redvers' eyes narrowed. "Did you see him do it?"

"I'm pretty certain I did." I went over that night again in my mind, the flash of white linen before the bag hit the floor, but now doubt crept in and made me question my earlier convictions.

"Are you absolutely sure it was him? How did it seem intentional?" His voice had taken on an edge, and now I slumped back in my seat a bit. Perhaps it was too silly a notion to mention to the police, after all. But it also meant I was still on the hook for a murder I hadn't committed.

As if he could read my thoughts, his dark eyes grew warm and concerned. "Even if you only think you saw him, it's probably worth mentioning to the inspector. And don't worry too much. The inspector is just trying to get a rise out of you. I'm sure he has other suspects."

I wasn't so sure myself, but I appreciated the sentiment.

I *was* certain the police would want the matter wrapped up quickly. The murder of a foreigner is never good for tourism—especially the murder of an attractive young socialite. But if the police thought they were going to close this case with my taking the fall for a crime I didn't commit, they were sadly mistaken. After the disaster known as my marriage, I would never fail to stand up for myself again.

It had only taken a few weeks after the vows were spoken for me to realize that my girlish dreams of a marriage built on trust, love, and a true partnership between equals were nothing but that—dreams. My husband had been able to slip on a façade of charm as easily as his bespoke suits. I was still ashamed that I hadn't been able to see beneath that façade to the depravity simmering just below. But then, our courtship had been a whirlwind—as soon as my aunt introduced me to her husband's nephew, I became a trophy for Grant to win. And break.

I took a deep breath and pushed the past behind me. This crime would be solved with the actual murderer behind bars, even if I had to do it myself.

CHAPTER TEN

Redvers stayed with me for a time, and I appreciated the concerned glances he kept sending my way. At least one person seemed to be concerned for my well-being, and for that, I was grateful. But soon enough, I decided I could use some time alone with my thoughts, so I shooed him off. He admitted to having some business in town and excused himself with a final worried glance. For once, I was far too distracted to wonder what that business might entail. Instead, I found myself pondering who at the hotel had both a gun and a motive to kill Anna Stainton. She wasn't the most likable of characters, but I was having a difficult time conjuring up a motive for murdering the young woman.

Suddenly I remembered the inspector's instructions to stay on the hotel grounds and I groaned. I had been so looking forward to my trip to the pyramids, and now it looked like that excursion would be postponed indefinitely. Lovely as the Mena House was, the notion that I might be restricted to the grounds made me feel stir-crazy, and it did nothing to ease my anxiety.

I was lost in my own thoughts when I heard a not-so-subtle clearing of the throat at my elbow. I looked up to see Amon Samara before me.

"I am so sorry to interrupt your thoughts, madame." His

cultured, lightly accented voice washed over me. "But I couldn't help but notice you."

I forced a smile that I hoped looked genuine—I couldn't imagine choosing a worse time for him to introduce himself formally. Brushing him off crossed my mind, but I hated to be rude. And I was deeply curious about whether he had any connection to Anna.

I held out my hand for a handshake. "Mrs. Jane Wunderly." He took my hand and instead turned it over in his own soft palm to give my fingers a gentle kiss. The entire process made me recoil, despite its gentlemanly nature.

"Amon Khanum Samara." He returned my hand to me. "But you must call me Amon." I grimaced a smile and ducked my head, but failed to offer the same familiarity in return.

"Well, Amon, can I offer you something to drink?" Perhaps my lot in life was to offer men refreshments, after all. And here I thought I had escaped that indignity once I became widowed. Recalling my husband's demands to wait on him hand and foot while he lounged indolently, my hands shook with anger and I twisted them together in my lap. Failure to obey Grant's demands came with a price—a price I'd paid only once before deciding the cost wasn't worth the pain that followed. His cruelty had quickly shattered my innocence.

"Madame, it is I who should do the offering." He caught the attention of my hovering waiter and spent enough time speaking to the young man in Arabic that I began to suspect he was ordering far more than a simple cup of tea. My suspicions were correct. Soon the table had been cleared of my coffee things, and a host of pastries and drinks appeared. I found myself annoyed at his presumption.

"Where are you from, Amon?" I asked, more to cover my irritation than out of genuine interest. After the events of the morning, I couldn't believe I was having such a mundane con-

He gestured to the creamy

versation. I wondered if he could be that oblivious to the events unfolding around him—the entire hotel was in something of an uproar.

Or maybe he was here to learn something from me.

"I am originally from Egypt, although I have been traveling these last few years. My sister was once married to the current king, a puppet of the British government."

This seemed like a lot of personal information to share with a stranger upon first meeting, and I felt my eyes narrow.

"I am a revolutionary at heart. I am here to meet with my fellow countrymen to find a way to free our great country." His polished voice began to drone as his story dragged on.

And on.

As I listened to him further, it occurred to me that Amon's tale sounded more like a practiced recital than anything else. For a man who claimed to be a revolutionary, he sounded remarkably dispassionate. Those willing to die for a cause were normally lit from within by it, but Amon could have been discussing the weather. So, what was his endgame with this sordid tale?

Perhaps I had been wrong to be suspicious of his intentions—he seemed entirely disinterested in the hotel gossip.

At the end of his recitation, he gave me what he probably assumed was a very winning smile, and I feigned one in return. I decided to change the subject to a more neutral one. "How are you finding the hotel, Amon?" It took some restraint to keep myself from asking whether he had heard about the murder, but I wanted to see if he would offer the topic himself.

"It is luxury itself, is it not? The king himself often attends garden parties on this very terrace. And now, you must try some of this *Jawafa bil-Laban*." He gestured to the creamy orange drink on the overladen tray before us. "It is very refreshing. I think you call the fruit a 'guava' in your language."

"One would think it is your language, too, Amon. You speak it flawlessly." I reluctantly sampled the drink and had to admit that it was quite tasty. Cool, creamy, and refreshing, the drink had a calming effect on my still-nervous stomach. It disappeared quickly.

Amon paused for a moment, then recovered. "I have studied it for many years."

I watched in mild disgust as he continued sampling various pastries, slathering them with butter and honey. Despite his impeccable dress, I noticed that he had failed to put on cuff links, and his shirt cuffs flapped slightly beneath his coat sleeve. I wondered what had happened to the eye-catching pair he had worn several nights before.

"You'll forgive me. I missed breakfast," he said around a mouthful of food.

"Not at all." I suddenly felt uncharitable for my annoyance. I hated to be hungry.

"And are you currently married, Mrs. Wunderly? A woman so attractive as yourself . . ." His voice trailed off as he eyed my naked ring finger.

"I am widowed." My voice was clipped and an angry flush crept up my neck. I hated his eyes on me, assessing my availability, looking me over as if I were a prize mare and he was deciding whether I was worth his investment. It was too similar to how Grant had regarded me when we first met. If Amon Samara was in the same category as my deceased husband, he didn't deserve any part of my story or another second of my time. "And I really must be heading back to my rooms. My aunt will be looking for me."

It wasn't true, but I had no intention of continuing this discussion.

"So soon, Mrs. Wunderly? Just when we were getting acquainted." His lower lip jutted out in a slight pout, which I found immensely off-putting. I wondered if this act worked on other women. I decided it must, as ladies of all ages around the garden were eyeing him like a fresh slab of meat at the butcher shop during rationing.

"I'm afraid I must." I rose and retrieved my book, nearly lost under the plates on the table. "I'm not quite used to the heat yet, and I'm developing a bit of a headache." I felt like leaving it at that, but forced myself to remember my manners. "Thank you for the conversation and the drink. I'm sure we'll chat again soon." I doubted I could hide from him for the entirety of our stay as I had begun to hope—he would no doubt force another conversation with me.

As I left, I noticed some ladies preparing to move in on my vacated seat—Amon Samara wouldn't be without company for long.

In my haste to leave, I had missed the chance to ask whether he knew Anna Stainton. I kicked myself, but there was no way I was turning back. I would have to find out later whether he had heard about her murder.

Or what he knew.

CHAPTER ELEVEN

I was feeling far too restless to stay in my rooms, so I decided to head for the pool. The day had become well and truly hot while I was on the terrace. Sitting in the shade of an umbrella with a book and taking occasional dips in the water to cool off sounded like an excellent distraction. My mind kept circling around the fact that I was a murder suspect, and I couldn't stop seeing Anna's lifeless body whenever I closed my eyes. I optimistically thought a swim might wash the images away.

I headed back to my rooms, hoping the police were finished violating them with their search. I reached into my pocket and pulled out a pair of room keys, instead of the one. Realizing what I held, I gasped out loud, and then immediately checked the hallway to make sure I hadn't been seen or heard.

I was alone.

I had completely forgotten about pocketing the key to Anna's room. I felt relief course through me that the inspector hadn't had me searched—if he had, I would surely have been carted off to jail.

It was too late to give the key to the colonel as I had planned. And now that I was a suspect, it would look suspicious if I tried to give it to him. I quickly decided the best course of action was to hide the thing—but secreting it any-where in my room was not the wisest plan, especially if the police decided to give my rooms another go.

I stared at my door for a moment, and then turned to the hallway. A potted palm sat inconspicuously halfway down the corridor. I considered it and decided it would make an ex-cellent hiding spot for the pilfered key. I checked the corri-dors again—several times, in fact—and once I was sure I wouldn't be seen, I hid the key under a thin layer of dirt in a corner of the ceramic pot.

Breathing a small sigh of relief, I continued into my rooms. The police hadn't been destructive in their search, but I could tell that my clothes and personal items had been rifled through. I took a minute to straighten things up, hoping it would lessen the feeling of violation. That done, I pulled out my bathing costume. It was a modest navy blue wool affair, but it hugged my curves well and completely covered my back down to the tops of my thighs. I had been pleased with the find during my shopping excursion before we left.

But that pleasure was lessened as I changed into it and found myself glancing around the room. I knew the police of-ficers had gone, but that didn't stop me from feeling that the room was no longer my own and that I would find someone standing behind me. I wondered if I should request a move, but ultimately I decided to stay put. Changing rooms would only give the police a reason to look more closely at me.

I added a loose-fitting pair of white pants and a lemon-yellow blouse as a cover-up, changed into some low-heeled sandals and headed poolside. I made it to the door before I remembered I also needed to grab my swimming cap.

As I came into the pool area, I paused to survey the area. A white stucco building ran crosswise to the pool, and a long row of marble columns before it cast shade toward where I stood. There was a small row of changing cabins—I hadn't been sure if it was best to change in my room or if changing space was provided, but it looked as though either was an option. White lounge chairs were crowded all around the pool, colorful bathing costumes and striped umbrellas dotting the scene, the smell of tanning oil heavy in the warm air. Most of the lounge chairs were already occupied, either by bodies or with the towels and personal effects of the numerous tourists splashing in the water—I obviously wasn't the only one looking for a cooling swim. Shielding my eyes from the sun, I spied an empty chair next to a couple that appeared close to my own age. The woman was lying in the sunlight, but the empty chair next to her had the benefit of an umbrella, so I headed in their direction.

"Is this chair taken?"

They both looked up and smiled easily.

"No, not at all! Please join us." The young woman gestured to the free chair. I had intended to drag the chair and umbrella away to find a quiet spot to read, but I could hardly do so now, without seeming rude. I smiled, put my book down, and readjusted the chair so it was more fully in the shade of the red-striped umbrella.

They introduced themselves as Deanna and Charlie Parks. Deanna was bareheaded, and wearing the absolute latest in bathing costumes: a striped navy blue and white number, showing entirely more skin than I was comfortable with displaying. Instead of avoiding the sun, she appeared to be reveling in it, and I wondered how she could bake in the open without becoming a lobster. In fact, her long, shapely legs were already a pleasing golden brown.

"Jane," I replied. "It's a pleasure to meet you."

"Likewise," Deanna said, and Charlie cheerfully smiled his agreement. The young couple seemed completely at ease with themselves and with one another. Within moments, I felt the same sense of serenity easing into my bones, despite the horrific events of the morning.

Charlie was tall and lanky, but even though he was thin,

he was muscular. In fact, something about his build reminded me of someone, but I couldn't place who, like a word on the tip of your tongue you can't quite bring to mind. His long face was topped with sandy brown hair that stood up slightly at the back in a small plume I found endearing. His hand went to it and smoothed it down frequently, although it never did anything but pop right back up.

"Where are you both from?" I could have turned to my book and ignored them altogether, but I was curious about this pair.

Deanna explained that she was originally from Iowa, and that Charlie was from the South, although he came from a military family that moved around a lot. Mississippi was merely the last place his family had landed before he left home. It explained why he didn't have the Southern drawl one would otherwise expect.

"But now we consider ourselves citizens of the world," he pronounced with a grand sweep of his hand.

Deanna rolled her eyes, but gave him an affectionate smile. "We're in vaudeville." Deanna pushed up onto her elbows as she explained. "The last place we played was in New York State, but we'd like to hit the other coast when we get back. Stick to the warm air and sunshine." She heaved a happy sigh and tipped her face back to the sun.

I didn't know much about vaudeville actors, although my father had taken me to see a show when I was a teenager. It was billed as a family-friendly matinee; otherwise, I'm sure my aunt would have forbidden my exposure to such racy entertainment. As it was, my father had never repeated the outing, despite my begging to go again.

"What act do you do?" I asked.

"Charlie's sort of a jack-of-all-trades. Some acting, comedy, and card tricks . . ." Deanna trailed off and shot a look toward Charlie. He shifted in his seat a moment, but his easy smile burst forth again.

"And Deanna here started out in the chorus, but now she is the mystical snake charmer." Charlie wiggled his fingers dramatically. "She's brilliant—really knows her onions." They gazed at each other with secret smiles.

Deanna glanced over at me. "Sorry. We're on our honeymoon."

"And how!" Charlie's eyes gleamed.

"Congratulations! That's wonderful." The sentiment was entirely heartfelt. They not only seemed well suited to each other, they also appeared to enjoy each other's company.

Although I couldn't help but wonder how a pair of vaudeville actors could not only afford a trip to Egypt, but stay in luxury accommodations as well.

I found myself studying Deanna. She had thick honey blond hair, but she wore it long and pinned up. It surprised me, since short hair was all the rage, and she appeared so otherwise avant-garde. She saw me looking at the bun pinned at her neck and smiled.

"It's for the stage. You really need nice, long hair to get done up for the act. Otherwise, I'd have to wear a wig, and I just can't stand 'em. They make my head itch." She scratched at her scalp as she said it. "So I just keep it long." She shrugged. "Besides, Charlie thinks it's copacetic."

Charlie wiggled his eyebrows at her lasciviously, and we both laughed. He had a face for comedy—I imagined it worked well for him in his act.

"Have you been here long? I'm embarrassed to say I don't remember seeing you before today."

"We've been here about a week already," Charlie said. "But we've been doing a lot of day trips with a local tour guide . . . a dragoman, they call 'em. He's great. Speaks six different languages, if you can believe it." That would explain why I hadn't run into them during the day, but I couldn't imagine that this fun-loving couple would miss out on time in the bar.

On the other hand, they were on their honeymoon. I decided not to press the issue.

"I'm not surprised you didn't see us." Deanna laughed. "I doubt anyone saw anything besides Anna last night. I'm sorry she's dead, obviously, but that dress was something else." I couldn't help but agree. Then I grimaced as I remembered that I was a suspect in that murder. I probably needed to be careful about what I said to other guests.

Charlie lowered his voice. "We heard about the murder from the staff. I managed to convince our waiter to give us the goods."

"The police haven't talked to us yet, but I'm sure they will. They're probably talking to everyone who's staying here." Deanna lit a cigarette and gave a wave with her hand. "Whenever they get to us. Unfortunately, we won't have anything to tell them."

"It's too bad, really," Charlie said mournfully. "I could do with some excitement."

Deanna laughed and playfully swatted his arm. "Stop. Like this trip with me isn't excitement enough."

Charlie grinned back at her.

"Did you know Anna?" I felt it was safe to ask the question, since they had opened the topic.

Charlie gave a little shrug. "I saw her at the card tables. I gotta say, she was no dope. She was giving some of the best players a run for their dough." This surprised me, since I had assumed Anna was all looks and little substance. And I never would have imagined her playing cards—and winning, no less.

"I never met her. I just know what Charlie told me about her. And, of course, I saw her around the bar—you couldn't help it." Deanna gave a mischievous grin. "Good thing I wasn't looking for some male company, because Anna was working every one of them." I couldn't help but return her smile.

I was enjoying their easy exchange. They seemed not only like they were very much in love, but they also had fun with one another. I couldn't imagine a marriage like that, mostly because my own had been such a far cry from what I had initially hoped for. My parents had had an easy affection for each other, built on love and respect, and I'd hoped for much of the same in my own marriage. Instead, my days as a married woman had been about mere survival. But then my thoughts drifted to Redvers and the easy patter we seemed to share. He seemed the type of man who knew how to enjoy himself. With a shake of my head, I quickly returned to the conversation at hand.

The rest of the afternoon with Charlie and Deanna passed swiftly. At one point, she and I took a dip in the water—it was not as cool as I had hoped it would be, but it was still refreshing. When I finally parted from them, it felt as if we had known each other for years.

I completely forgot to recall who Charlie reminded me of.

Chapter Twelve

Aunt Millie stopped by my room after teatime to check on me, but after hearing the news that I now appeared to be a suspect instead of a mere witness, she quickly made her excuses and hurried off. I heaved a sigh. This probably meant I would be on my own for dinner as well, but I wasn't entirely upset about the prospect.

Deanna had invited me to join them at dinner, but I promised that we would have dinner another night instead. It had been a lovely afternoon, but after finding a body, a police interrogation, and then several hours chatting with new friends, I was utterly exhausted. I needed some time to myself to process the day.

I decided to take dinner alone on my own small balcony. I stopped by the front desk to make the arrangements and headed back to my rooms.

I spent a long part of the evening staring into space, replaying the events of the day. I wondered if the police were making any progress in their investigation and heaved a sigh as I realized that they weren't going to share that information with me.

My dinner was delivered as promised, and I ate it at the small wooden table overlooking the extensive garden. But even the delicious meal and the lovely breeze couldn't keep my thoughts from the murder. I went over everything I knew about Anna repeatedly, but I still could not conceive of a motive for her killing. The best I could imagine was a jealous lover; although it seemed unlikely that someone had become so infatuated with her that he would be driven to murder. She had only been in Egypt for a few weeks.

Could someone have followed her from home? I shook my head. It was a possibility, but I hadn't noticed anyone lurking about, and with Anna gone, I had no easy way of finding out.

All in all, it was unlikely that I would be able to come up with any answers.

It had already been dark for some time, so I changed into my light cotton nightgown and tried to sleep. I tossed and turned and spent several more hours staring at the ceiling, unable to stop the parade of thoughts in my head.

The key. I had actually stolen—no, *borrowed*—the key to Anna's room. I punched at the soft pillow beneath my head, making virtually no difference at all, and put my head back on it. I worried that the hiding place would be discovered. Did the staff water those plants regularly? It might wash the dirt away, leaving the key shining brightly against all that dark soil. That would certainly get the police involved. Then I began to wonder what the police had found in Anna's room during their search.

Or what they had missed.

I finally decided that if my brain wouldn't let me sleep, the least I could do was put the pilfered key to good use.

I waited until the last sounds outside died away and the hotel felt entirely still. Truthfully, I didn't have long to wait as the wee hours of the morning had already crept up on me.

I threw the bedclothes aside and pulled out my dress from that day, but then decided that it would be a far better idea to put on my darkest garb to blend into the shadows. I rifled through my clothing until I came across a navy dress—I had packed quite a bit of light-colored garments to reflect the sun away, but had some dark pieces I'd thought to wear once the sun had set.

I listened at the door to the hallway and, hearing nothing, crept outside and down the hall to the potted palm. I dug around for a few seconds, glancing furtively about while I retrieved the key and brushed it off with my fingers, making sure more dirt went back into the pot than on the floor. Luckily, the moon was bright, and I was able to make my way along the corridors with little trouble while still keeping to the shadows. I had yet to meet another guest, and I hoped that most of the staff would be gone as well—it was rumored that they only ran a skeleton crew overnight in case of emergencies.

When I came to the last turn, I stopped and pressed myself against the wall. I realized that my pulse was racing with the fear of being discovered—a master criminal, I was not. If a policeman had been posted outside Anna's door, there was a possibility he would recognize me. After all, nearly the entire force had interviewed me that morning. And I didn't have a good excuse for being in this part of the hotel.

The hall was quiet, so I crouched down and popped my head around the corner to see if anyone was outside Anna's room. Not a soul. Apparently, the police had not felt the need to leave an officer at the scene, and a little breath of relief escaped me.

My hands were shaking with nerves, but there was no turning back. I had already come this far, and I was determined to get a look around her room. I stood and made my way to the door, trying to keep my footsteps as quiet as possible, attempting a tiptoe on the balls of my feet. I had never given any thought to what type of shoe would have a quiet sole, but I would have knocked someone down for a pair just then. Heels were very inconvenient for creeping around hotels with hard floors.

Of course, when I packed my bags, I hadn't anticipated creeping around the hotel. Or breaking into anyone's room.

My hand was on the doorknob and I was about to put the key to the lock, when I felt someone grasp my elbow. I jumped, jabbing back with the elbow that had suffered the assault, narrowly avoiding a full-out scream.

Redvers.

I put my hand to my chest where my heart was doing its best to make an escape.

"What do you think you're doing?" His low voice was a whisper as he massaged the place on his side where I had caught him with my sharp elbow. I would have apologized if he hadn't startled me so badly.

"What am *I* doing?" I whispered back fiercely. "You nearly killed me with a heart attack!" Blood was still pounding madly in my ears. "How did you manage to sneak up on me . . ." My voice trailed off as I saw he was standing there in his stocking feet.

"Aren't you supposed to be a banker?" My eyes narrowed at him.

"And I thought you were a proper young lady."

At that, I snorted.

"I don't remember making that claim." I went back to unlocking the door. My life of crime appeared to be off to a rocky start.

"You shouldn't do this." His whisper was close to my ear, stirring my hair. My pulse quickened again, for an entirely different reason, which irritated me nearly as much as his attempt to tell me what to do.

"Do what? Use this key?" I jabbed the key into the lock, twisted the knob, and pushed the door open just wide enough to slip inside. I didn't care that I sounded childish— my nerves were strung too tight.

The idea of being caught in Anna's room and having another charge leveled against me had my stomach churning, but now my nerves steadied and I simply felt determined. Being told not to do something nearly always had the opposite effect—it made me want to do it more. And besides my mulish nature, I needed to find some evidence that would clear my name. Or at least find something that would point me in the right direction.

I tried to close the door behind me, but it was pulled from my hand as Redvers slipped in silently behind me.

"Fine. You may come, too." As if I could stop him. "But try to be quiet." He grinned and I wrinkled my nose at him.

Redvers took a few pieces of the scattered clothing and pushed them against the bottom of the outside door. I immediately realized he was blocking the crack so that any light we used wouldn't be seen outside. I hated to admit that it was a brilliant move. It was sad to see exquisite clothing abused in such a way, but I knew firsthand that their owner was beyond caring.

We kept our voices low, but Redvers shuffled to the bedroom and flipped on the electric lights. "What are you looking for?" he asked.

"I could ask you the same question." I was feeling prickly, but I quickly deflated. "Something to clear my name. Or just give me an idea of where to start looking for answers. I doubt prison life in Egypt would suit me."

"I think you would be running the place in very little time."

I didn't think that deserved a response.

"I'll start over here." Redvers indicated the left side of the bedroom.

Hands on hips, I stood near the doorway and simply looked around. I wasn't really sure what I would come across that the police hadn't already found, so I simply let myself take in the scene for a moment. Her bedroom setup was similar to my own, although hers was much larger, and much less tidy. I looked at the clothes strewn about and the blanket of feathers that covered the room. There was a higher concentration of them around the bed where Anna had been shot, and a mere scattering of them at the farthest reaches of the room. I flicked a glance at the bed, and just as quickly looked away. Red-brown stains where Anna's blood had pooled and dried covered the sheets and bedcovers. I would be concentrating my search elsewhere.

As Redvers methodically searched the dressers on his side, my eyes fell on a needle and thread that had been pulled from a small sewing kit and carelessly tossed aside on the dressing table. It was unusual that Anna would have such a thing—a girl from Anna's social set would have a maid to take care of any mending that needed doing. Or she would send things out for repair. So, what would Anna need with a sewing kit?

"Were you planning on doing any searching? Or simply supervising?" Redvers had paused in his search, and his voice was mildly amused. Without answering, I waved for him to continue what he was doing, and went back to gazing around the room.

My eyes fell on the wardrobe and the clothing that still hung there. A long frock dangled awkwardly from its hanger beside its tidy companions, and I tiptoed through the mess on the floor to reach it. Pushing the other clothing aside, I ran my hands over the dress. It was heavy and quite expensive, with many layers and an exquisite beadwork overlay. I gave a small sigh—money really could buy some extraordinarily beautiful things.

Redvers stopped and came to stand at my side, this time without any snide comments. My fingers had covered all the obvious hems. Frustrated, I paused, then turned the garment inside out. I felt along the thick bodice where the heaviest of the beadwork was centered, and I felt two hard lumps that were out of place. I smiled triumphantly and dug through the many layers of gauzy fabric until I found the right layer. A small area of the seam had been stitched down, and poorly.

"She must have sewn this not long before she died."

"What makes you think that?"

"The needle and thread are still lying out." I gestured to the dressing table. "I would have tidied them up if I used them to conceal something."

"I don't think tidying up was her strong suit." Redvers did make an excellent point.

I gave a tug to the end of the thread and it came away easily. Poor Anna hadn't been terribly good with a needle, but she had been clever in her choice of hiding spots. The police had obviously overlooked her clothing. It was understandable, given the vast quantities.

A pair of gold engraved cuff links fell out into my hand. The initials read *DH,* and there were small sapphires encircling the rim. The initials were wrong, but the unusual size and shape were the same as ones I'd seen previously.

"*'DH'?*" Redvers asked.

I looked up at him. "I think they belong to Amon Samara." Redvers raised his eyebrows in question. "I saw him wearing them earlier—the night of the dance. The stones kept catching the light, and I remember thinking they were unusual, although I couldn't see the initials, obviously." I recalled something else. "The morning I found Anna, Amon joined me on the terrace and he wasn't wearing any cuff links at all. This would explain why."

Redvers held out his hand to me, and I passed him the cuff links. He bent his head over them. "What do you suppose Anna Stainton is doing with them?"

"That's an excellent question, especially since Anna wasn't anywhere near Mr. Samara the last few nights. That I could see, anyway." I thought about Anna's movements. "Actually, maybe she was avoiding him. Why else would she have missed the opportunity to flirt with a wealthy and handsome man?"

"You think he's handsome?" Redvers asked.

I rolled my eyes. "I think we can objectively state that he is good-looking. But certainly not my type." I recalled how my skin had crawled at his touch, and I shivered again. Redvers noticed my reaction.

"You didn't care for him?"

"Something about him was just . . . off," I said. "But more important, why would Anna go to such lengths to hide these cuff links?"

Redvers didn't have any good answers.

We continued our search, but found nothing else of interest. I felt sorry for the maids that would be left to deal with the aftermath of both the murder and Anna's housekeeping.

When we finally decided to call it quits, early morning light was just beginning to brighten the darkness beyond. Redvers checked the hallway to make certain it was empty before we slipped out and I relocked the door behind us.

"Good night," Redvers mouthed silently, and I gave a sleepy nod in return. Then, shoeless, Redvers moved silently down the hall in what was the direction of his room, or so I assumed. I took a note from him and slipped off my own shoes before padding quietly in the opposite direction, cold marble chilling my feet and hurrying my steps. The lack of sleep was making me less cautious, and I was grateful that no other guests seemed to be up and about yet.

When I reached my hallway, I once again hid Anna's room key in the potted palm, covering it over. No reason for the police to find that in my room, should they decide to search it again. I let myself into my own room and changed back into my nightclothes. Then I dropped onto the bed, exhausted.

Yet, tired as I was, I couldn't help thinking that I knew very little about Redvers. He was still something of a mystery—by his own design. Banking was clearly not his line of work. And other than a gut feeling, I had very little indication that I could actually trust the man. I still wasn't even sure whether "Redvers" was his first name or his last.

Past experience had taught me that members of the opposite sex were not to be trusted at all—a lesson I was ignoring at my own risk. Then I remembered something else.

Redvers had taken the cuff links.

Chapter Thirteen

I can't say I felt refreshed when I dragged myself out of bed midmorning, but I certainly felt determined. My first order of business, after coffee and sustenance, was to track down Redvers and demand the return of those cuff links. They were currently my only hope for clearing my name—surely the police would see them as evidence of a wider pool of suspects. I needed them back.

I also intended to ask Amon about his relationship with the late Miss Stainton. I doubted it would be a pleasant conversation, and I would have much preferred to avoid the man altogether, but I couldn't see any way around it. I hoped a quiet breakfast would give me time to figure out how best to approach him.

A quiet breakfast wasn't on the menu, however, as I spotted Redvers right away, dining peacefully in a corner of the room. I marched over to his table and caught him with a forkful of eggs halfway to his mouth.

"You stole my cuff links." I glared at him, fists on hips. I hoped my look was fierce enough to compel him to turn them over without argument.

It wasn't.

"They weren't your cuff links," he said calmly, returning his attention to his eggs.

"You know what I mean. I want them back."

"I no longer have them." He sounded regretful. At my out-raged expression, he continued. "I passed them on to Inspector Hamadi."

"Oh." It was where I had intended them to go, and it did save me from talking with the man. "Did you explain who we think they belong to?"

"I did. I gave him all the reasoning. Although I refrained from including in my report that his prime suspect was the one who found them."

I digested that for a moment as I flopped, uninvited, into a chair at his table. "You told him that you searched her room alone." He nodded, and I realized he had probably done me a favor there. It was best if the inspector didn't think I was breaking into rooms and snooping around his crime scene. Even if I had been. "And he had no problem with that."

Redvers sighed. "If you must know, I sometimes work in conjunction with the police."

"As a banker?" I couldn't help but prod this sore spot. I knew this story of his was just that. A story.

He gave me a baleful look.

"You and I both know perfectly well that I'm not a banker. But I also can't tell you what I am doing here." His tone and his face told me he was deadly serious.

"Or you'll feed me to a camel?"

His face relaxed and a smile teased the corners of his mouth. "I don't think camels are carnivorous."

"The desert is a wide and scary place. It's hard to say exactly what goes on out there."

He gave a rumbling chuckle, and I busied myself pouring a cup of coffee from his carafe. That laugh had caused my heart to do a little skip, and I needed a momentary distraction.

I set aside my questions about Redvers' occupation for the time being. I would crack him eventually. "Well, what did the inspector have to say about the cuff links?"

There was a pause as the hotel staff noticed my sudden appearance at Redvers' table, and a young man arrived to take my breakfast order. When he had gone, I looked at Redvers expectantly.

Redvers put his fork down and reached for the bread basket. "The police will take a closer look at Samara. He's not exactly unknown to them, but they've never been able to pin anything on him. Just suspicions."

"What kind of suspicions?"

"I believe he is suspected of charming well-to-do ladies out of their funds. Then he disappears for a while. I would assume until the money runs out."

I thought that over. "He did give me a story about how he was related to the king's first wife and something about revolution. I wasn't really paying attention, to be honest. It sounded like he was selling me a line of goods."

"You were right on that account, although the ladies usually buy into it. That's all Hamadi mentioned anyway, and I'm not terribly familiar with his file."

"Then you're familiar with other police files?" I thought this was a brilliant guess on my part. Redvers continued as if I hadn't spoken, and I sighed. *So close.*

"You'll be interested to know the coroner believes Anna died around five a.m." He had my full attention, all thoughts about his secrets forgotten. For now. "The hotel staff reported that the last vehicle left at around three-thirty a.m., and the last of the hotel guests finally toddled off to bed around four."

If all the guests from town had already gone, that could only mean one thing. "Then, whoever killed Anna was most likely staying here at the hotel."

"Or walked back, which is possible, but unlikely," said Redvers. "It would take several hours to make it back to Cairo."

Another detail was bothering me. "Do they know where the gun came from?"

Redvers refilled his tea, and I leaned in.

"It looks as though Dr. Williams's gun went missing, possibly weeks ago, but he failed to report it."

I vaguely remembered the man from the day before as he reported to Hamadi about Anna's demise. "He's Australian, isn't he?"

"He is. The Mena House was used as a hospital for Australian troops during the Great War, and Dr. Williams was one of the medical personnel stationed here. The gun was his service pistol. It is rumored he developed some . . . habits . . . that made him keen to stay here in the Mideast rather than return to Australia. The hotel was accommodating and hired him."

"I can imagine what type of habits he might have acquired." And I could. Opium was readily available here, and I speculated that the doctor had fallen in with the pipe. "Does he have any kind of motive? Any connection with Anna?"

Redvers shook his head. "None that they know of. Doesn't mean there isn't one, of course. Anna knew a lot of men at the hotel." He paused. "What about her father? Colonel Stainton."

I was somewhat shocked at the suggestion, but then took a moment to consider. "I really don't think it was him. He seemed genuinely devastated when I broke the news to him." I sagged a little at the memory. The man had been absolutely heartbroken, hadn't he? I shook my head firmly against the doubt. It couldn't have been him. What could compel a father to shoot his own child? I felt a pang of guilt for even considering the possibility.

"Is the colonel still here? I haven't seen him since we found her." Of course, I wasn't surprised—I imagined he was grieving in private.

"He's still here. The body won't be released for another week at least. The government moves slowly at the best of times. Then I imagine he'll make arrangements to have her shipped back to England."

I nodded and we sat in silence for a moment. "We need to talk to Amon," I said.

Redvers stared at me for a moment. "*We* do? You realize the police will be taking care of that."

"Of course, but I would feel more comfortable if we did as well."

Redvers raised an eyebrow. "Don't trust the local constabulary?"

I shifted uncomfortably in my seat. "Well, not really, to be honest. And it's my neck on the line."

Without a word, Redvers' eyes flicked to the part in question. A flush immediately began creeping up, and I cursed my inability to control it. His eyes met mine again, and I fought to maintain a neutral expression. It was impossible to tell how successful I was.

"I'm fairly certain he's down at police headquarters now," Redvers said. For a moment, I couldn't remember what we were discussing. "It will be some time before we can talk to him."

"And what are your plans until then?" I asked.

"Do you have some for me?" There was a distinct twinkle in his eye.

Is he flirting with me? I gave up the battle against blushing, and wondered if I should work on a sunburn as a permanent cover for them. Especially since it seemed they were becoming a permanent affliction.

Casting my eyes to the sky, I shook my head. "I was just wondering if you would be heading downtown again."

"I do, in fact, need to head back into town. If you're lucky, I'll dig up more information on the police investigation."

I hoped I would be lucky.

Chapter Fourteen

After we finished breakfast, Redvers boarded the electric tram that stopped at our hotel and ran into Cairo several times a day. I marveled that a country so steeped in ancient history had such modern conveniences. I was still hoping to get the chance to experience both.

Since Amon was still in police custody, I thought about what my own plan for the day should be. I doubted Millie would be looking for my company, since I was still a suspect. I hadn't seen Charlie and Deanna at breakfast, but I could use the boost from their cheerful company. I would look for them at the pool later.

Before that, however, I decided to pay an impromptu visit to the house doctor. Perhaps I could learn something about the man and his missing gun.

As I neared the lobby, I clutched my stomach and moaned, slowing my walk to a near crawl. I drew up to the desk and held on to it as though my life depended on it.

"Ma'am! You seem unwell!" The poor lad at the desk looked alarmed. My face was glistening with sweat, which added to my performance. Unfortunately, I was coming to accept that it was simply how my face looked in this oven-temperatured country.

"I think it was something I ate," I moaned. I was probably overdoing the drama, but he seemed readily convinced.

"You need the doctor, I think. I will call him for you." His hand reached for the telephone—I assumed the doctor had a line directly to his chambers for emergencies.

"No, no. Please don't trouble yourself. If you'll just point me to his rooms, I'm quite sure I can make it there." I started to worry I might have overplayed my hand. The poor boy looked ready to have me carried off on a litter. I straightened a bit. "See? Not so bad. Just uncomfortable."

"But you look terrible, ma'am. Are you sure I should not call him?"

I was slightly annoyed at his assessment of my appearance since I wasn't actually ill, but I let it go. His hand was still on the telephone and I hurried to appease him.

"No, no. I can make it."

"We don't usually send people to his rooms directly." The clerk was still touching the phone, fingers now tapping the receiver.

"But do you know, I think a walk will help. And I'm sure the doctor won't mind. Which way is it?"

The young man still looked doubtful, but removed his hand from the phone and instead pointed uncertainly in the opposite direction of the dining room. He told me which turns to make along the way, and I had him repeat the directions twice. The hotel had many corridors and short staircases, and it would be easy to get lost without finding your destination. The original structure had been built as a hunting lodge, and when it was renovated into a luxury hotel, numerous additions were made. The additions brought a great deal of charm, with multiple heights and wood balconies encompassing the original building, but it also made it a trick to navigate. I repeated the clerk's directions to myself like a mantra.

The twists and turns took me to a secluded area, but still

part of the main hotel. Most of the long-term staff, including the gardeners and dragomen, came from Mena Village. Small and self-sufficient, the village was tucked away from the view of the guests, but still officially a part of the hotel. Apparently, the village could be seen if you took the time to walk across the golf course—so I would probably never see it, at least not from that vantage point. I counted myself lucky that the doctor was kept closer at hand.

Once I identified his room, I stood before the door a bit uncertainly. I put a hand to my gut, which was now roiling with nerves. If the doctor wanted a listen, he would certainly hear something kicking up a fuss. I could have let the young man call the doctor to the lobby, but I wanted to see where the doctor lived—or more truthfully, I wanted to see the room his gun had been stolen from. And if I wanted a look, I would need to knock.

One hand glued to my stomach, I raised the other and gave a tentative rap.

Nothing.

I raised my hand again, this time pounding with some vigor, and I finally heard some movement. The latch clicked over and the door swung wide, revealing a stocky man in a state of undress—shirt unbuttoned and pulled untidily over a yellowing undershirt, reddish brown hair mussed. It looked as though I had roused him from bed, despite the late hour. Judging from his bloodshot eyes level with my own, he had not been asleep long. My overactive imagination filled in all sorts of possibilities for where he might have been until the wee hours of the morning. None of which had to do with his medical profession.

"Yeah." In that one word, his Australian accent was unmistakable.

"Dr. Williams?" He nodded and I continued. "I have a stomachache. I think it was something I ate. Do you have something for it?"

His eyes narrowed. "They don't usually send 'em here to me room." He paused for another moment before disappearing into the gloom, leaving the door standing open. I knew it was not an invitation to enter, but he hadn't closed it, either. I stepped inside.

It was a sitting room about the same size as my own, but the air hung thick and close. The closed shutters had a thick layer of dust, and I wondered if they had ever been opened to let the room air out. Probably not. Squinting in the dim light, I could make out that the room was quite tidy, which came as a surprise.

A rustling in the corner drew my attention, and I quickly turned my head, unable to make out the noise. The doctor was still rummaging in the back, so I crept farther into the room to get a better look. The rustling grew louder and my hands came up to chest height, balled into fists, ready to strike out.

The sight stopped the doctor in his tracks.

"What . . ."

"I heard something," I said.

He gave a bark of laughter. "That would be my quail." I squinted again, and was now able to make out a cage on the floor. "She was wounded and I'm nursing her back to health. They like the dark."

Feeling foolish, I dropped my fists. It was a silly way to fight a quail.

"Mix this powder into some water. It should help with indigestion." He handed over a small packet. "And who are you now?"

"Jane Wunderly. Thank you for this." I gestured with the packet. In the frenzy over the quail, I had forgotten my play-acting. I returned one hand to my stomach and smiled weakly. I hoped I hadn't ruined my charade entirely—I still had some questions for the doctor.

"Aren't you the one what found the dead girl?" Recognition from the previous day sparked in his eyes.

With all the activity around the discovery, I was surprised he remembered me at all. My own memories of the morning were a bit of a blur—with the multitude of officers and men swarming the scene and the multitude of questions I had been pressed into answering. I didn't remember him very clearly, although I did recall his distinct accent, and the sight of him tearing down the hall toward us.

"Yes, I am. Did you know Anna, Dr. Williams?" I fully expected him to deny it.

A leer spread across his face. "I knew her. She was out for a good time, that one was."

It took a lot of self-restraint to keep my lip from curling. A parade should have been thrown in my honor, frankly. "She did seem to enjoy a good party." I was careful to keep my tone mild.

The doctor snorted. "She knew *how* to party. It's a bloody shame she won't be doing any more of that."

This line of questioning was getting me nowhere. I already knew Anna was a bit . . . wild. I changed tactics. "I hear you were a doctor here during the war. That must have been difficult."

"You hear a lot of things, miss." His eyes narrowed, but then his ruddy face softened as he gazed past me. "It was a hard war. We lost a lot of men."

"I hear you also lost your gun." My eyes widened slightly. I couldn't believe I had actually said that out loud. I fully expected Williams to order me out, but the doctor surprised me once again.

"Can you believe that? Years I go with that service pistol, and someone nicks it from my rooms. I'd like to get my hands on the bloke that done it. I have no idea how they got in here, either." He looked around as if he expected to find the person lurking behind an armchair.

I needed to cut this interview short before my luck ran out and my mouth got me into more serious trouble. I wasn't sure I had learned anything of value—other than the doctor was unpredictable. I edged toward the door.

"Well, thank you again for this." I held up the powder packet and gave another weak smile. The closeness of the man and the thick air was making me feel ill at ease. As was the continued rustling in the corner. Standing in a darkened room with an unpredictable man suddenly didn't seem like my brightest idea. Especially since there was nothing to say Dr. Williams hadn't used that gun on Anna himself. He sounded genuinely upset at its loss, but who could truly tell?

Hand to my stomach, I finally reached the threshold and hurried back out into the light. I heard the door close firmly behind me and I had only taken a few steps before I heard his muffled voice. I looked back for a moment. The doctor was either talking to his quail or he had made a phone call. I assumed it was the latter—he was most likely taking the clerk to task for allowing me to come to his suite. It's what I would have done in his position.

I kept my pace slow and measured until I had turned the corner, safely out of view of the doctor's rooms. Then I trotted back to my own.

I had more investigating to do.

CHAPTER FIFTEEN

Back in my rooms, I gave some thought as to whom I should talk to next. Unfortunately, the list was a short one. Reviewing our list of suspects was a task that only took a moment. I didn't believe the colonel was responsible, and the police had yet to find the young man we had seen with Anna that last night. The highest person on my list was Amon, and until both he and Redvers returned from the city, I was at loose ends. Since I had no idea when either of the men would return, I decided to stick with my original plan and fritter away time by the pool. With any luck, I would find Deanna and Charlie there.

I stowed the pill packet given to me by Dr. Williams in my toiletries case and changed into my bathing costume. By the time I reached the pool, every chair was occupied and I was disappointed to see that neither of my newfound friends was in sight.

I would have thought guests would leave once they heard about the murder, but if anything, there seemed to be even more people poolside, clustered into little knots of gossip. I was finally able to snag a lounge chair by hovering in the area until a middle-aged woman wrapped in a long caftan packed up her things and headed back toward the hotel. I swooped in, immediately pulling the chair into the shade of a large umbrella nearby. No need to bake myself. I made sure my sun hat was secure and settled in for a read. I had yet to finish my novel, and despite my disappointment at not finding Deanna and Charlie, I was happy to spend some time alone with my book.

Once again, quiet reading was not meant to be. I was beginning to wonder if I would ever finish the book. Out of the corner of my eye, I saw Amon arrive and I discreetly watched him over the top of the pages. He was dressed in a white bathing costume, and as he scanned the guests gathered poolside, I wondered if he was looking for someone in particular. I had pulled my book up in an attempt to hide my face, but his eyes found me—studiously attempting to ignore him— and he made a beeline in my direction. Before I knew it, the sound of a chair's legs scraping across the patio stone greeted my ears as he pulled a chair next to mine. I wondered how he had managed to scare up a seat so quickly. A quick glance to my right told me the answer; two women were now sitting awkwardly together on one lounge chair.

Unbelievable.

"Mrs. Wunderly," he said. "I'm so glad that I've found a friendly face." Since my face was currently anything but friendly, I assumed he was speaking figuratively.

"Mr. Samara." I marked my place and put the book down. I had decided earlier that it would be best if Redvers and I talked with Amon together, especially after my episode with the doctor. But Amon had presented me with a neatly wrapped gift, and it would be foolish to waste the opportunity by discussing inane topics such as the weather. That would be a short conversation, anyway, since it was mainly just hot. Whatever I learned from Amon now, I could fill Redvers in on later.

Amon seemed preoccupied—even after he sat down, his attention continued to wander around the area as though his eyes couldn't find anywhere comfortable to rest.

"You seem upset, Mr. Samara. Have you had a trying morning?" He'd requested that I use his given name, but I didn't want him to assume we were developing a friendship. Or a relationship of any sort, for that matter, so I returned to using a formal address.

He gave a dramatic sigh. "It has been terrible, Mrs. Wunderly. I have been at the Cairo police station for hours—through breakfast and then lunch. You cannot imagine how terrible the food is." He said this last part so gravely that I almost laughed. But I also hoped that I would have no reason to find out for myself.

"I presume the police were asking you questions about Miss Stainton?" I needed to get confirmation for my hunch that he had known Anna.

"Yes, but I hardly knew the girl. There was little I could tell them."

"Really? Then why did she have your cuff links?" The words were out before I could ponder the wisdom of admitting that I knew about them, but I managed to maintain a neutral expression.

Amon looked at me appraisingly for a long moment, as though reassessing whatever assumptions he had made about me. He clearly was not expecting a woman immune to his charms. And willing to challenge him, besides.

"How do you know about the cuff links, Mrs. Wunderly?" His voice had changed—not dramatically, but enough that it was noticeable. There was now a rough edge to it, and I wondered how much of his cultured speech was a deliberate act.

"The police mentioned them while they were questioning me. And I remembered that I had seen you wearing them the other night." I was improvising. I didn't want him to know that I was the one who had found them.

"You remembered my cuff links?" He sounded skeptical.

"Well, at the dance the other evening, I couldn't help but notice them. They were very eye-catching." That much was true. "Although, I thought it was strange they had different initials than your own." Hopefully, he wouldn't realize that I couldn't have seen the initials unless I'd been at the table with him.

"You have great powers of observation, Mrs. Wunderly." He paused, and for a moment I worried I'd been caught in my lie, but he continued on. "They belonged to my grandfather—a family heirloom." It was an easy response, and I couldn't decide if he was telling the truth or was a practiced liar.

I thought it was safe to assume the latter.

"How did Anna come to have them, Mr. Samara?" I refused to let him off the hook so easily. And I sincerely wanted to know the answer, although I doubted he would give me the truth.

"I'm afraid our Miss Stainton had light fingers. She had a habit of pocketing attractive items that did not belong to her. Much like those birds that collect shiny things. Um, a magpie?"

I thought that over. I had seen Anna's personal effects, and she did not appear to want for money. It was doubtful that she would need to steal things when she could simply purchase them outright. Of course, I also knew there were people who did such things for the thrill and not for monetary reasons, but I couldn't see Anna looking for that type of excitement.

Of course, she'd had my brooch in her room, so perhaps there was a pattern after all. Although it didn't explain why she had gone to such lengths to hide the cuff links, or when she had taken them. I doubted it was as simple as her "pocketing an attractive item." Anna had to have made quite some effort to steal the cuff links and then sew them into her dress in the short time between when I'd seen Amon wearing them and the time she was killed. I decided that my brooch was a completely separate matter.

With a mental grimace, I resolved to try a more flattering

approach, letting him believe that I had finally given in to his "charm."

"Well, I'm sure it was not every day that Anna met someone as handsome as you." I nearly gagged on my own words. "Perhaps she wanted a token of yours."

His eyes softened. "Perhaps. We have known each other since she was a young woman. Anna was so lovely, and such a pleasure to be around."

I disagreed, but at least I was finally getting somewhere.

"But in the saloon the other evening, she didn't even speak to you. And you said you barely knew each other."

"Mrs. Wunderly, the truth is, we were in love. But she wanted to hide it from her father, who did not approve of the match." He gazed thoughtfully at his own hands. As I watched, he began massaging the knuckle of his index finger. "We had a quarrel about it when I arrived, and that is why she was carrying on with those young men. She was trying to make me jealous. I did love her, Mrs. Wunderly." He finally looked up and made eye contact with me. "You must believe me."

If Amon and Anna were truly an item, I doubted that making Amon jealous was the only reason behind her flirtatious behavior. And while I made noises of sympathy for Amon's loss, I wondered whether there was even a grain of truth in what he was saying.

Probably not.

"Then why did you bump into her in the bar? I saw you knock her purse from her arm."

Amon stiffened. "You must have been mistaken, Mrs. Wunderly. That was not me you saw." I made a little noise of feigned agreement. I had doubted myself earlier, but now I was absolutely convinced. Amon was the man in the white linen suit I had seen bump into Anna.

Amon cleared his throat and changed the subject, eyes drifting to the horizon. "Anna could be quite generous, you know." I'm afraid here my eyebrows disappeared somewhere into my hairline, although he didn't seem to notice. "She used to work with a Catholic orphanage, even though she herself wasn't Catholic. She would visit the children, and once a year, she would take them out to her stables to let them ride."

It was the first time in our entire acquaintance that I felt Amon Samara might be telling the truth—as surprising as the information was.

"But, Mrs. Wunderly, you never answered my question the other day. How can a lovely woman such as yourself remain unmarried? Surely you have many suitors at home."

The change in conversation was abrupt and unwelcome, but not unexpected. I should have known he wouldn't let this go. After hearing Redvers' report on the man's penchant for wealthy women, I realized that Amon must assume I was one of them, despite evidence to the contrary. Nothing I wore could lead anyone to assume I came from money, but perhaps he thought I was an eccentric. I *was* staying at a swanky hotel where the king of Egypt himself spent time—Amon could hardly know that my aunt Millie was footing the cost of the entire expedition.

Unfortunately for Amon, while other women might have found his line of inquiry flattering, I was *not* most women. And the idea of a casual discussion of my personal life with this smarmy playboy set my teeth on edge. Literally.

"Do you know, I don't like to discuss it, and this is the last time I am going to be polite about it." I gave him an angry smile. "I am developing a headache." I did not even try to hide the fact that this was merely grounds for an escape. "If you'll excuse me."

I gathered up my things and left, leaving Amon Samara with his mouth hanging slightly open. I didn't care what he thought about my rude answer and abrupt departure. If he was smart, he would avoid trapping me into conversation in the future. And I would leave any further questioning to Redvers.

Just as I passed the colonnade, I saw Deanna and Charlie coming toward me.

"Leaving already?" Deanna looked genuinely disappointed. "We were hoping to find you here."

"I'm afraid so. The heat is giving me a headache."

"Is it the heat or that weasel in a white suit?" Charlie nodded in Amon's direction.

Amon was already chatting with the older woman who had taken my seat. She was gaily outfitted in a bumblebee-striped bathing costume with matching head wrap.

I gave a genuine laugh. "You caught me. He's a bit much for my taste."

"He's a bit much for anyone's taste," Deanna said dryly, and we shared a smile.

"How about if I meet you both for a drink tonight?" I didn't want to hang around in Amon's line of sight, but I did want to spend time with the newlyweds.

"That sounds swell," Charlie said.

On the way back, I made a mental note to ask the Parkses what they thought of Amon. They had obviously formed some opinions. I would be curious to see what their impressions were, and whether they had learned something about him that I had not.

Chapter Sixteen

It was still early when I got back to my rooms. I ran a cool cloth over my face and neck and went over my conversation with Amon. Unlike my talk with the doctor, I knew that I had gathered at least one or two useful bits of information. Amon had, in fact, known Anna, whether or not that relationship was what he claimed. And I still believed it was Amon who spilled her purse, a move that I felt sure was on purpose. I considered what he had to gain by that.

Perhaps nothing. He might have simply wanted to annoy her. Or make his presence known.

I attempted to go back to my novel, but I struggled to put Amon's meddling questions behind me. His nosiness about my marital status bothered me more than I cared to admit. Another woman might have found the questions a slight annoyance, but my marriage was a chapter that I had firmly closed. I didn't like anyone trying to crack the cover. His few questions and the stress of Anna's murder meant I wasn't able to keep the dark memories completely locked away. The string of maids who quickly left our employ drifted through my mind, as did the bruises I struggled to cover and the sharp smell of the salve when there was blood.

My memories left me with a sick feeling in my stomach.

When lunch rolled around, I decided to track down Millie,

since I was supposed to be her companion for this trip. I hadn't seen her for more than five minutes strung together in well over a day. I felt mildly guilty about this dereliction of duty, despite the fact that Millie seemed to be avoiding me.

I thought about Millie's obvious aversion to the police—a mystery I had yet to find an answer to. I wondered if the discovery of the cuff links and Amon's interrogation meant that I was no longer the prime suspect in Anna's murder. I could only hope so. And if that was the case, perhaps Millie would find my company tolerable again.

I crossed the hall and knocked on Millie's door, but there was no answer. I headed to the dining room, at the same time hoping I would avoid running into Amon again. His mere presence was a headache I wanted to avoid right now. I spotted Millie and her two young companions in a corner of the dining room and started over.

Millie looked slightly anxious at my approach.

"Don't worry, Aunt Millie. They have a brand-new prime suspect. You can rest easy—the police are looking elsewhere."

"Well." She seemed to consider for a moment, and I felt a small stab that she had to even think about whether I should join them. "Please join us for lunch. We haven't ordered yet."

I managed to smile graciously, settled into the empty seat, and surveyed my dining options. I had just decided on something when the waiter arrived to take our orders. That done, Millie and Lillian resumed their conversation about the quality of the various golf courses Lillian had played on in comparison with the hotel's. Millie listened attentively, but I tuned out and took the opportunity to get a better look at the girls.

Marie was the darker of the two: darker hair, darker complexion, a touch shorter, and much rounder. It seemed she had not quite lost her baby fat, whereas Lillian was long and athletic—well suited to sports. Lillian's short auburn hair was not the fashionable bob that Marie wore—Lillian's cut seemed more for convenience than anything else. I wouldn't have been surprised to learn that she did it herself with a pair of dull scissors. But Lillian had the kind of self-confidence that often comes with natural talent, and she was able to pull off the look. Marie took more care with her appearance, but she had less naturally to work with.

I wondered if either of the girls had any hobbies outside golf. Lillian seemed entirely occupied with the sport, to the exclusion of anything else, especially if the current conversation was anything to go on. And Marie appeared entirely occupied with Lillian—she spent most of her time gazing at her with a look of complete adoration. They were an interesting pair.

At long last, there was a brief lull in the conversation, and I asked Lillian how she became so interested in golf.

Millie interrupted, surprising me. "Oh, Jane, it's a lovely story. She's such a remarkable athlete." It was a struggle to conceal my shock at the obvious pride in Millie's voice. Over a girl Millie had only just met.

Or so she claimed.

"It's not that exciting, Aunt Millie," Lillian said.

My eyebrows shot up at her use of the term "aunt."

"My father introduced me to it at a very young age. He is a passionate golfer, and you know Scotland has beautiful courses. We often vacation there to take advantage." On Lillian's other side, Marie beamed as widely as Millie did.

"And where do you and Marie know each other from?" I was genuinely curious about the answer.

Lillian shrugged in an offhand way, and I looked to Marie, who was slightly crestfallen at Lillian's lack of enthusiasm.

"We met at school several years ago," Marie finally said. I hadn't even realized that Marie was American until just then. "My parents sent me to England to live with some cousins, and I convinced them to let me stay." Her gaze returned to Lillian.

In the meantime, our meals arrived, and Lillian nodded

and applied herself to her plate of fish, rice, and vegetables. She was methodical, finishing all of one item before attacking the next. She continued in this way until she finished her meal, never once mixing her foods or allowing them to touch one another on the plate. I tried not to watch, but it was difficult.

"So, Mrs. Wunderly." I started at the sound of Marie's voice. It was so rare to hear her speak, it caught me off guard. "I hear you're the one who found the body. It's like something out of *Town Topics*." Her eyes had a strange gleam in them that I found distasteful.

"Yes, I did. Her father was quite devastated." I gave Marie a pointed look, and she cast her eyes down to her plate. "In fact, has anyone seen him recently? I feel as though I should check in on him."

Everyone shook their heads vaguely, and though I could feel her disappointment from across the table, Marie let the topic go.

As soon as our forks hit our empty plates, Lillian excused herself. She headed to the greens with Marie close behind her. I was a little surprised that Millie stayed behind, but it looked as though her newfound enthusiasm for golf didn't extend to putting practice—or whatever sports-related thing Lillian was headed off to do.

"Does Marie golf as well?" I asked.

"No, she supports Lillian and carries supplies for her."

I raised my eyebrows. "Like a caddie?"

"Well, yes. But you see, Marie is quite devoted to Lillian. And she is quite an expert at choosing the clubs."

"I see." I didn't actually, but I didn't want to know anything more about golf clubs.

I expected Millie to find another excuse to leave, but she seemed content with my company for the moment, so I suggested moving out to the terrace for a round of tea. Or a drink, if she preferred.

"I think some tea sounds lovely." It almost defied belief that Millie would forgo an alcoholic drink, and I struggled to keep the surprise from my face. I wasn't sure whether to attribute it to the heat, which seemed unlikely, or if it was just the novelty of its ready availability wearing off.

Or perhaps there was another influence altogether.

As we made our way to the terrace, I asked one of the young waiters to bring us a tea service, and Millie and I found a table in the shade and settled in. Bearing a tray on his shoulder, the young man soon brought a steaming teapot and placed it in front of us, as well as our cups and saucers. The cups were turned upside down, and I had a fleeting thought that the placement was strange, since they usually arrived right side up and ready for a pour. But I shrugged it off.

Millie asked me to serve, and I reached over and tipped her cup right side up, filling it with the fragrant tea. I set the pot back down and gave her cup milk and sugar before turning to my own setting. I ignored her grumbling as she added an extra two sugar cubes to her tea, stirring vigorously.

I flipped my cup right side up, and a shiny black insect, tail in the air, scrabbled over the side.

It was a scorpion.

CHAPTER SEVENTEEN

I screamed loudly and dropped the cup on the table. It bounced once and fell to the ground, the delicate porcelain immediately shattering into several pieces. The scorpion had narrowly missed my hand when it made its escape. I pushed away from the table as quickly as possible, chair legs scraping loudly over the stone floor, trying to put space—a lot of space—between myself and the poisonous creature.

Drawn by the commotion, the waiters and fellow diners alike came rushing to our table.

"Where did it go?" My shaking hands were pressed to my chest as I stood on weak legs. At a distance.

Aunt Millie calmly took the lid from the teapot, deftly lifted my saucer with a butter knife, and in one swift move trapped the scorpion beneath the domed lid.

"Really, Jane. Such hysterics" was her only response as she went back to stirring her tea.

"I'm not hysterical." My voice came out as a gasp. "I was . . . startled. Just startled."

Millie rolled her eyes.

Our own waiter was among those who came rushing over, and his face filled with horror when he learned what we had found. He chattered in rapid Arabic to Zaki, who had arrived on his heels and was now gently directing diners back to their tables. Zaki served as translator between our young waiter and myself—the young man's grasp of English, which was excellent, appeared to have fled in his distress.

"Madame, Hasan promises he did not know there was a scorpion under your teacup." Zaki indicated the flustered young man. "He says when he picked up the tray in the kitchen, it was already set and the teacups were turned that way." He paused as Hasan kept up the rapid-fire speech, then laid his hand gently on Hasan's arm to quiet him.

"We store the cups that way, madame," Zaki explained. "But he is not sure who set the tray. Our kitchen is a very busy area during mealtimes. He says he did not see anyone, he just brought the tray out."

I sighed. The kitchen was probably a madhouse during meals, and it was unlikely anyone would recall seeing a specific tea tray. I felt for the young man. He had tears in his eyes, and I realized he was probably concerned for his job.

"Please tell him not to worry. No one was hurt. And I'm sure things like this happen all the time."

"Not really, madame." Zaki shook his head slowly. "A scorpion is quite unusual. But I will tell him what you have said." Zaki issued orders to a small army of waiters, then led Hasan away with an arm wrapped around his thin shoulders. The army stayed behind to deal with the trapped scorpion. Watching them, I shuddered.

"I think I'll head back to my room, dear, if you are fine." Millie patted my arm absently. I noticed that she had blithely finished her tea while the excitement carried on around her.

"Yes. I'm . . . fine. Thanks for your quick thinking." I watched as she traipsed off through the small crowd, which had refused to quietly disperse.

My heart had ceased pounding, but the adrenaline surge had left me shaky. I moved to a seat at a table nearby, and sitting there, I wondered how a creature drawn to dark, quiet spaces could wind up in a well-lit hotel kitchen.

Beneath a teacup.

An hour later, Redvers found me still sitting at the table, deep in thought. I was pondering whether it was an act of nature that had put me in the scorpion's path or some type of message. And despite my craving for solitude and a feeling of normalcy, I was relieved to see him.

"I heard what happened. Are you all right?" His brows pulled low in concern.

"It gave me quite a shock. I think I handled finding Anna better than I did a live scorpion." A fresh shudder ran through me.

"I'm sorry I wasn't here." Redvers took a seat and pulled it near me. His hand moved toward my own, then stopped abruptly, instead resettling in his lap.

"I'm not sure what you could have done, but I appreciate the thought. And I must say Millie handled it quite well." I paused and wondered whether to share with him what I had been mulling over. "I've been thinking, and I have a hard time believing this was an accident. How does a scorpion find its way under a teacup? In a busy, well-lit kitchen? Millie and I are lucky neither of us was stung." I filled him in on what Zaki had told me about the kitchen and tea service.

"What did the scorpion look like?" Redvers leaned forward. I described the small black creature as best I could, sheepishly admitting that I hadn't gotten a close look at it since I had been somewhat . . . less than calm.

"Well, here's the good news. If this wasn't an accident, it was only a warning. That type of scorpion isn't deadly, although its sting would have been very painful." Redvers leaned back again. "It might have put you out of commission for several days—possibly even weeks." At my horrified look, he added helpfully, "At least it wasn't a deathstalker scorpion. They're especially deadly. I knew a chap once—"

This was a story I did not need any details about, and I cut him off with an upraised palm and a violent shake of the head. "How appalling. Thank you for that."

We both sat in silence for a moment.

"I almost forgot to tell you. I had a little chat with Mr. Samara," I said.

All signs of Redvers' earlier concern vanished in a flood of frustration. "Why didn't you wait for me? Jane, we were supposed to talk with him together."

Flustered by his use of my Christian name, I stammered a bit. "He . . . he pulled himself up next to me at the pool. I could hardly ignore him, could I?"

Redvers grunted in frustration. I decided it was best to wait to mention my visit to Dr. Williams.

"Besides, how do I know I can trust you? We only just met," I muttered. I ran a hand through my hair and pressed the heel to my temple, before sliding it down my face. "I keep forgetting, but I barely know you. I don't even know your full name."

He was quiet for some time, regarding the edge of a teacup. Then, reaching out, Redvers took both my hands in his, and I noticed for the first time how large those hands were. They nearly engulfed my own, and his long, sensitive fingers were warm and strong and comforting. He leaned toward me, and I could feel myself being pulled in, as if he had his own gravitational force.

"Jane, you can trust me."

Such a simple statement—yet, gazing into his eyes, I could feel his sincerity like a brand. I could also feel heat burning its way up from the pit of my stomach as my pulse began to race. His dark eyes probed mine.

I knew at that moment that Amon Samara had been lying—although about what and how much, I couldn't say.

But there was a stark difference between someone telling the truth, as Redvers was now, and someone telling you what you wanted to hear.

Although, I did notice that he still hadn't given me his full name.

Before the moment went on any longer and I lost all reason, a throat next to us was cleared. Redvers released my hands, both of us reanimating as the spell was broken.

I turned to the waiter standing beside the table, and my hands nervously readjusted the napkin on my lap. Several times.

"Can I get you anything?" It was young Hasan. In the past hour, he had seemed desperate to make things up to me, hovering nearby, ready to meet my every whim. Not that I'd had any, but it didn't stop him from trying to bring me something every time I cleared my throat. I had taken pity on him earlier and ordered another round of tea. I hadn't wanted anything, but I felt the need to prove to the both of us that I wasn't too badly rattled.

Redvers cleared his throat and assured the waiter we had everything we needed. I was glad he had spoken—I wasn't sure my voice would work just yet. I took a long drink of water, a few deep breaths, and continued our conversation as though nothing had happened.

"So, would you like to know what Amon said? Or would you prefer to interrogate him yourself?"

Redvers sighed, and with a glance to the heavens, told me to go ahead. I tried to keep a smile from my face as I recounted my conversation with Amon, including as much detail as I could remember.

"He's lying," Redvers said as soon as I had finished.

"My thoughts exactly. But about what parts? Or all of it?" I paused, weighing whether or not I should continue filling him in on my chat with the doctor. I decided to have out with it.

Redvers was silent until I was done. "Well, if it makes you

feel better, you appear to be having more success than the police. Someone is threatened enough to try to warn you off."

"Then you don't think the scorpion was an accident?"

"Given how many people you've irritated today, I would
say no. Not an accident."

I resisted the urge to make a face at him for suggesting I was
irritating people, and instead decided to feel flattered that I was
doing at least as well as the police, if not better. But another
thought gave me pause.

"I probably need to check my room tonight for more deadly
insects."

"That is an excellent idea."

CHAPTER EIGHTEEN

Before bed that night, I did exactly that. I spent close to an hour checking every nook and cranny of my room. I looked beneath blankets, pillows, and mattresses, shaking out clothes, all while armed with the cricket bat Redvers had found for me. Its flat surface would be handy for whacking unwanted intruders—but from a comfortable distance, since the bat was fairly long.

There was nothing to be found.

Strangely, finding nothing left me feeling more anxious than if I had found some creepy crawly to exterminate with my wooden weapon. I sighed and sat on the bed, propping the bat against the bedside table. I crawled beneath the rumpled covers and wondered if I would be able to sleep.

Despite everything, I was looking forward to the next day. Redvers had offered to escort me to the pyramids in order to take my mind off things. I wasn't sure how successful he would be—until they had someone in handcuffs, I didn't think I could shake the vaguely sick feeling I carried around. But I was ecstatic that I would finally experience firsthand some of the rich Egyptian history I had been looking forward to. Redvers seemed to think the police would have no problem with our excursion, since I would be in his company. I wasn't convinced, but decided to take a gamble that my absence wouldn't be noticed—after all, the police now had other suspects to focus their attention on. And I would do my best to enjoy our day.

We had decided to meet early, well before the sun was up. This worked out well, as I was awake long before I needed to be. I was filled with anxiety and excitement, both of which were enough to keep me awake on their own. Then my subconscious took things a step further, interpreting every small noise as death lurking in the dark—I had eventually turned the light back on and left it burning.

Rolling from bed, I dressed for a day in the desert sun— long-sleeved white linen blouse and a beige pair of linen trousers. I knew the linen would breathe well, and Redvers had assured me that long sleeves were the way to go. I also donned a large sun hat. It would both keep the sun off my face and give me an excuse not to style my hair.

Breakfast was a quick affair, and I wolfed mine down, along with several cups of coffee to offset my lack of sleep. My earlier anxiety about Hamadi's orders was forgotten; I was nearly bouncing in my seat with excitement—and caffeine— waiting for Redvers to finish his tea so we could set off.

"I've never seen anyone so excited to look at a pile of old rocks."

"And I've seen old women take less time than you this morning. Are you nearly finished?"

This earned me a chuckle as he downed the rest of his tea and pushed away from the table.

Redvers was also wearing long sleeves and pants, although his were in the form of a lightweight linen suit, which somehow managed to appear unwrinkled. My outfit, on the other hand, already looked as if I had slept in it. As we left the shade of the hotel entrance, Redvers donned a cream-colored Panama hat, and I kept sneaking glances at him—he cut quite the sharp figure.

We headed to the edge of the hotel property where Redvers had arranged for a stable hand to meet us with a pair of camels from Mena Village. Most of the camels used for transporting tourists came from the village. I eyed them uneasily, although they seemed quite docile. I had expected spitting, temperamental animals that would take off at a gallop the moment I came near, but they calmly kneeled in the sand, chewing the pile of green leaves they had been given. The larger of the two fixed a placid eye on me and continued chewing as Redvers and the handler exchanged a few words in Arabic. Redvers handed the man a handful of coins, and with a small salute, the brown-robed man headed off.

"He won't be accompanying us?" I watched the man disappear beyond a small grove of palms.

"It won't be necessary. I'm quite good with a camel." I swear the camel nearest us stopped chewing and gave him a look.

"That one seems quite taken with you." I indicated the camel.

"It must be my new cologne."

I wrinkled my nose. "I'm glad you told me. I thought maybe that was the camel."

Redvers' lips twitched at the corners, and I smiled. I wasn't concerned about offending him. He smelled like the heavens, as I'm sure he well knew.

Redvers helped me mount the smaller of the two animals, my leg swinging easily over the side and settling onto the leather saddle draped over a brightly colored woven blanket. The camel's cloth bridle was similarly woven, vastly different from the leather bridles used on horses. Instead of passing between the animal's teeth, the rope rested high over the nose, leaving the mouth free. Brightly colored balls hung from the bridle along the camel's cheeks, matching the bright stripes of the saddle pad. The effect was quite festive and matched my cheerful mood. Not even the camel's slightly musky smell could dampen it.

I watched as Redvers mounted his own camel, then gave a strange double click with his mouth. The animal awkwardly heaved itself to its feet, and I followed suit, struggling to maintain my balance as the camel rocked deeply back and forth with short grunts. I gasped when I realized how far off the ground we now stood. Even seated on the smaller camel, I would have been looking down on Redvers if he had stood next to us. The gangly animal had to be several hands taller than a horse.

I quickly picked up on how to direct the camel using the reins, one hand gripping the saddle horn, and we fell into an easy pace, loping side by side toward the giant monuments.

"The pyramids aren't far—we could easily have walked. Why did we need the camels?"

"I thought you would enjoy the experience. All visitors to Egypt should find themselves on a camel at some point. Plus, we can ride a little farther out later. There's a spectacular view from the dunes."

It was still early, and though the sun had crept above the horizon, it had yet to heat up the day, so the ride was warm, but not unpleasant. A few other tourists were visible both in front and behind us, likely with the same plan of beating the heat with an early-morning tour. Most of the small groups were led by a dragoman, the elegant local guides easily recognizable by their beautiful silken galabiehs and intricately folded turbans.

"How many languages do you speak, exactly?" I asked after a few minutes of companionable silence.

"I'm passably conversational in a few." Several beats passed, the camels' hooves rhythmically sending up little poofs of sand. "Why are you so interested in the pyramids? It seems you have a deeper interest than the average tourist."

I took a second to arrange my thoughts so I could explain my interest without revealing too much. I had been raised without the ritual of religion, and I lost my mother at an early age. When I also became a widow at the age of twenty-two, I became interested in both the ceremony surrounding death and the various theories about what comes after.

"I'm interested in how other cultures view the afterlife. The Egyptians had especially distinct ideas about what happened to them after death, as well as how to treat their dead. I find the ceremonial aspects and the belief systems interesting."

Redvers nodded respectfully. "So a bit deeper interest than the baubles they are digging up."

I laughed. "Yes, a bit. Although I would like to see the baubles as well."

He was quiet for a moment. "Well, these pyramids are certainly a testament to the Egyptian belief in the afterlife." He left it at that, and I breathed a silent sigh of relief that the topic had been dropped.

The closer we drew to the Great Pyramids, the less I was able to make coherent conversation. It's impossible to imagine the effect seeing them in person had—and seeing them up close was much more affecting than the postcard views I had glimpsed from the hotel. I was left in awe of their absolute grandeur, the impossibility of their architecture, and the simple fact of their construction some four thousand years earlier. It was almost beyond comprehension that humans created these mammoth structures so many years before—and that the only remaining wonder of the ancient world had managed to withstand the punishing desert winds for thousands of years. The achievement of the thing staggered me.

Redvers had us pause at a slight distance so that I could simply gape at the sight before me. He had obviously seen them before, but even he seemed awed.

"As many times as I've seen it, words still escape me."

"Yes," I breathed.

Redvers had arranged for another local to meet us on-site, and the man led away our camels to a holding pen while we approached the pyramids on foot. Now that we were on the ground, I could feel sand trickle into my shoes with every step, grit rubbing the soles of my feet. I felt the urge to remove them and dump out the irritants, but I knew it would be a wasted effort.

At Redvers' suggestion, the structure we headed for first was Khufu, the oldest and largest of the pyramids, known to the locals as Cheops. Built in 2500 BC, it rose from the dust and heat of the desert to an astonishing height. I had never before felt so small. The limestone casing blocks that originally covered the pyramid had long been destroyed or removed, and all that remained was the original stepped core structure, although that alone was still impressive to behold. In my mind, I had always imagined stepping easily up the side of the pyramid, like up a staircase, but each block used to build the pyramid was enormous—at nearly chest height. I could see there would be no easy skipping up the side.

We came at the huge structure from the north, where tourists were allowed to enter. The climb was quite steep, smaller steps cut into the larger blocks, and I was forced to accept Redvers' help several times when the footing became tricky from the sand and rubble coating the path.

I hadn't considered what would happen when we arrived at the pyramids—having forgotten that visitors are allowed to enter the large pyramid. Redvers gestured for me to enter the tunnel first, and I went ahead with slow, uncertain steps. The first portion of the tunnel was surprising, with rough-hewn rock creating a passageway. Instead of the smooth stone I expected, it almost looked like the inside of a cave. My chest felt a little tight, but I pressed on.

We moved through the initial passage and came to a platform. Here I could see that the tunnel we were about to enter was narrow and short, and both of us would be forced to stoop over inside it. The passage was at an incredibly steep angle, and a long board with spaced steps would hold our shoes against slipping back. I stared at the tunnel in horror and began my deep-breathing exercises. Unfortunately, I had assumed it would be cool inside the pyramids, like a cave, but it was a stone structure baking in the relentless sun. The air was hot and stale and was not having the calming effect I needed.

"Ready?"

"O-of course," I stuttered, and pushed forward into the tunnel, Redvers just behind me.

I didn't make it more than a few feet inside before claws inside my chest began to constrict my breathing. I stopped, one shaking hand on the wall, and took long, slow breaths. Beads of sweat broke out on my forehead—not due to the heat. My brain screamed for me to go back, and I fought the urge to flee.

Body and mind were at war. My entire being was in flight mode, but I didn't want to miss the opportunity to see inside the famous pyramid simply because my deceased husband had ruined enclosed spaces for me. His pleasure in exploiting others' weaknesses—especially mine—and inflicting pain had left indelible marks in more ways than one. I had only been mildly afraid of enclosed dark spaces until my husband ensured I was locked inside one. Those long, dark hours in a forgotten wardrobe with no one to rescue me had been among some of the worst in my life.

A cruel laugh echoed in my mind.

"Are you all right?" Redvers placed one large, comforting hand on my back.

"Unfortunately, I'm a bit claustrophobic," I managed to gasp out. It was something of an understatement.

"Do you want to turn back?" His voice was genuinely concerned. I shook my head, feeling deeply embarrassed that Redvers was witnessing this display.

"No." I closed my eyes and wished that I were back outside. I did some more deep breathing, and Redvers had the grace to back up and give me some space. I took another few moments to pull myself under control.

"I want to see this," I said, and he returned, leaving enough space between us that I wouldn't feel crowded. "But I think it would be better if you went ahead of me."

If he was ahead of me, I could concentrate on the fact that he was fine, and I would be as well. We backed out and reversed order so he could take the lead. Outside, my body nearly rebelled at reentering the small space. Redvers, however, reached out a hand behind him, seeming to understand exactly what I needed to continue. I grasped his hand, and I was able to force myself back inside. It was an awkward climb for him, with one arm stretched behind, but he didn't let go until we reached the top.

The next tunnel was open, and we were able to ascend while fully standing. The crush in my chest was less serious here, and I didn't need Redvers' assistance this time. Instead, I continued my deep breathing, sucking in the heavy air that smelled musty and dank, the faint smell of urine tickling my nose. I decided not to contemplate why that might be. Instead, I concentrated on Redvers' strong back ahead of me and keeping my breath slow and steady.

Redvers moved slowly, checking frequently to make sure I hadn't passed out behind him. I appreciated that he wasn't asking questions, but simply giving me quiet support. I would take time later to panic about what he thought of my little episode, and whether he would think poorly of me now, but those worries would have to wait for later.

The passage finally let off at the top, and we ducked through a doorway cut in the smooth granite. The room we entered was large, and here my breathing eased considerably, the panic that had hovered around the edges of my consciousness finally subsiding. Although the treasures from inside the pyramid had been removed and stored in various museums, I could still imagine the grandeur the vault once held, and it was enough to momentarily distract me from my body. I traced the cool granite with my fingers and walked over to the only remaining item, a large stone tomb.

CHAPTER NINETEEN

A small group of hapless tourists led by their long-suffering dragoman trailed far behind us, still making their way through the first tunnel, their peppered questions carrying up toward us. We were alone in the large chamber for the moment.

"There aren't carvings here." I had anticipated hieroglyphics, such as the ones found in many of the other tombs.

"I think this room was largely ceremonial." Redvers' deep voice echoed and bounced off the walls, humming in my chest.

Regardless of the lack of ornamentation, it was still amazing to stand within the dark granite walls. And I was grateful to have a moment of peace there before other tourists arrived.

By the time the next tour group finished the ascent, I had drunk my fill and was ready to leave. The return trip was much easier—my subconscious realizing that escape was imminent, although I had to force my feet to slow down. It would have been deadly to move quickly down that steep path.

Redvers once again asked no questions, simply offering wordless support.

Blinking into the sunlight at the entrance, I took a series of deep, gulping breaths and my heart rate began to inch back toward normal. I could see that tourists were beginning to fill the place—earnest, cheerful chatter floated up to us on the light breeze, and I was glad we had arrived early. Many people were arriving in open-air motorcars; shading my eyes, I could see parking lots dotting the landscape. It appeared some were for vehicles and others for animals, since numerous other visitors arrived by horse or camel as we did.

"Would you care to climb to the top?" We were still standing on the pyramid and Redvers pointed skyward.

I gave a little laugh. "I'm quite fine with seeing them from below, thank you." I didn't need to see the view from that height, and I didn't want to admit that my legs still felt a little weak from the episode inside.

Redvers shrugged nonchalantly. "I've already seen it. And it's getting crowded. As long as you're fine." He gave me a warm smile, and I gave him a hesitant one in return.

We started the brief climb back down.

"Thank you. For earlier," I blurted.

He paused for a moment and looked back at me. "There's nothing to thank me for."

I gave a brief nod.

As we reached the ground, I struggled with whether to address the situation further—I was embarrassed that he had seen me during a full-blown attack, and I tried to decide whether I wanted to give him some sort of explanation. But would it make me feel better or worse? I couldn't decide. Redvers was carrying on as if nothing was amiss, so I decided to follow his lead. At least for the time being.

We swung around to the other two pyramids, Khafre and Menkaure, which were much smaller in stature than the pyramid we had just exited. Neither of them was open to the public, and I was ashamed at the little tug of relief I felt.

Moving around the corner of Menkaure, the smaller of the two pyramids, brought us to the three queen's pyramids. Almost like a project to use some leftover supplies, these pyramids were diminutive compared to the pyramids of the kings, even these smaller two. It irritated me that the women's monuments should be so much less impressive.

A pair of men standing near the small trio drew my attention and I squinted in an attempt to get a better look. One of the men struck me as very familiar. He was wearing a khaki outfit complete with pith helmet and a cane, the head of which reflected bright gold in the sun.

"Does that look like Colonel Stainton to you?" I gave a nod in the direction of the men. "I believe that's his cane."

The other man appeared to be Egyptian, and even at our considerable distance, I could tell that his brown robes and turban were filthy, covered with the surrounding sand. From their body language and gestures, their conversation did not appear to be going well.

Redvers turned to look. "It does look very much like him." He reached into his pocket and pulled out a very small set of binoculars, which he put to his eyes. "Yes, that's definitely the colonel."

I stared at him for a moment, then indicated the pair of binoculars that had conveniently appeared. "More magic tricks? Where have you been hiding those?"

He gave me a mischievous grin. I shook my head and we continued to watch—Redvers with the obvious close-up advantage—as the two men began to gesture angrily. For a moment, it looked as though they would come to blows, and in my excitement, I pulled the binoculars from Redvers' hands and put them to my own eyes. In my peripheral vision, I could see him staring at me in openmouthed amazement.

"Eyes front, Redvers. You might miss something."

The Egyptian man crossed his arms over his chest and the colonel threw down his cane. "I haven't seen Colonel Stainton out of his room since his daughter died. It seems strange for him to be out here." I lowered the binoculars for a moment. "I wonder what they're arguing about . . ."

I trailed off as the colonel retrieved his cane and stomped away. I handed Redvers his glasses, perversely disappointed that the men's exchange had come to a peaceful end, despite my fondness for the colonel. Redvers readjusted the vision and followed the colonel's figure until he was lost in a crowd. Tourists mixed with local sellers, encouraging the visitors to take a short camel ride or purchase lukewarm water from their goatskin flasks. When we looked back to the small pyramid where the exchange took place, the local man had disappeared as well.

Redvers appeared thoughtful and secured his binoculars in the pocket they had been hiding in. "You didn't want those back, did you?" He sounded vaguely amused.

"No, there's nothing to see now. Do you know the man he was with?" Redvers did, after all, seem to know quite a few of the locals.

"No, but there's excavating going on at some of the outlying areas. He might be a worker from one of the dig sites."

We both contemplated that in thoughtful silence. I tried to come up with a reason why the colonel would be arguing with a dig worker in broad daylight, but eventually gave up without unearthing a convincing reason.

"Hmm," I finally said.

"Hmm?" Redvers cocked an inquiring eyebrow.

"Anna told her father that she didn't approve of the company he was keeping. She was obviously referring to me at the time, but the way she said it . . . It seemed she also meant someone else. I wonder if this was the company she was referring to."

"Hmm, indeed."

After viewing the pyramids, we came back around toward the Khufu, where we had begun, but now we approached the mysterious Sphinx holding court before it. Carved out of a solid piece of limestone, the years and marauders had chipped away at it, but its beauty was still evident.

The enormous sculpture had bricks laid over its feet, and I wondered aloud if it was an effort at preservation. Redvers agreed, pointing out some other areas where the damage was evident, and he explained how the soft stone had been eroding over the years, in some places more than others. On the nearest side, we could see where attempts were being made to cover areas of deep damage with bricks that matched the golden color. Even damaged and missing a nose, the half man/half lion seemed oddly content with its lot as a guard of the Great Pyramids.

We headed to the Khafre temple lying near the Sphinx's feet—in ruins now. It was empty, as the majority of the tourists seemed more interested in the pyramids. A quick glance up told me more than a few were taking advantage of the view from the top. Redvers disappeared around a column ahead of me and I heard a scraping noise. It sounded distinctly like rock scraping hard against rock, but I couldn't remember seeing workers near the temple, or near the Sphinx. I looked up and saw a fine dusting of sand filter down toward me, narrowly avoiding my upturned face. I stepped back and craned my head backward, holding my wide-brimmed hat down firmly on my head.

Nothing. Just crumbling pillars of ancient ruins.

Another scraping noise, this time a bit closer, and I scurried back a few feet until my back was flat against a limestone pillar, eyes fixed toward the last place I had heard the sound.

The noise ground to a halt. Then silence.

CHAPTER TWENTY

My heart gave a few quick beats. Was I simply paranoid? Or could someone have followed Redvers and me out to the pyramids? And did that person mean me harm? I wouldn't have thought so, except for my run-in with the scorpion the day before. My head whipped back and forth, looking for any signs of movement, but it seemed the noise had stopped for good. My shoes crunched sand as I moved around, seeking a better view of the pillar tops around me.

A moment later, Redvers popped his head back around a post. He noticed where my attention was still focused, took a glance upward, and then raised an eyebrow.

"Coming?"

"Did you hear something just now?" My gaze was still focused skyward.

He came more fully around the pillar, shaking his head and looking about. "No, did you?" A note of concern crept in at the edges of his voice.

I finally looked at him, tearing my gaze from the pillar tops. After the episode in the pyramids, I didn't want to give him any more reason to think I might be fragile. Or unstable. I decided not to press the issue.

"Never mind." I gave him a steady smile. "Must have been a bird."

"Most likely. There are lots of quail in the area. If you're finished here, I think our rides are ready." He disappeared around the column once more.

I took one last look around me and, shaking my head, joined him.

We reclaimed our camels from the local, who also passed a large saddle pack over to Redvers. After digging for a moment, Redvers retrieved a water skin, letting me drink first. I didn't know what kind of arrangements he had made, but I was grateful. The inside of my mouth felt as though I had been chewing on a sand cracker. Having sated my thirst—for now—I clambered back atop my camel without assistance, gave two clicks, and my camel stood, stopping Redvers in his tracks. I nearly laughed at the surprise on his face, although I still had a death grip on the saddle horn.

"Did you need some help getting on, Redvers?" I asked. "I'm more than happy to assist you, if you need it." I gave him a sly smile and he laughed, climbing aboard his own camel. We set off away from the buzz of tourists, the pyramids, and the hotel, moving farther into the vast, wind-swept desert.

"I have to thank you for taking me out here today, Mr. Redvers. I thoroughly enjoyed myself."

"You are most welcome. I always enjoy a trip out to the pyramids. Did it manage to distract you?" Redvers asked.

I laughed. "I can assure you that it did." I paused for a moment, thinking about what we had seen. "Although it was strange to see Colonel Stainton, wasn't it? I haven't seen him in days, and then to find him arguing with someone out at the pyramids as if nothing happened." My brows pulled together. "Do you have any idea what he was up to?"

"It's hard to say," Redvers said vaguely.

I sighed. "Well, it probably has nothing to do with his

daughter's murder. But I'm still curious." I shook my head. "Curiosity really is one of my worst vices."

"I'm afraid someone else thinks so as well." He paused. "What do you know about the two girls your aunt has been spending so much time with?" For a brief moment, I thought he was changing the subject; then I realized what he was implying.

"You don't think either of them had anything to do with Anna's murder, do you? They're just girls. What motive could they have?"

"That's what I'm asking you." Redvers' face was quite serious.

"Redvers! They are barely eighteen years old."

He sighed. "The murder notwithstanding, what do you know about them? They are spending an awful lot of time with your aunt. I'm a bit concerned for her."

I was touched that he was worried about my aunt's welfare. I thought for a moment, mentally putting together everything I knew about them, and then told him the little I knew.

"I don't know much else, apart from the fact that Lillian is an absolute fanatic about golf, and Marie . . . Well, Marie seems to be a fanatic about Lillian."

Redvers raised his eyebrows.

"Marie is like an enthusiastic Labrador around her," I said.

We rode in silence for a few moments.

"What about your friends from America—Charlie and Deanna?"

"The Parkses? What did you think of them?" The four of us had shared a drink at the bar the night before, although Redvers and I had excused ourselves after only one so we could get our early start.

"They were very charming," he admitted. "Although I'm

curious how a couple of roving actors could afford this kind of trip."

"I wondered the same thing. I think I heard Deanna mention something about their troupe taking up a collection for their honeymoon fund."

"Generous," he said, and I nodded in agreement. It *was* generous, but I had no reason to believe they had been lying. Besides, the pair was so likable, it was easy to believe their fellow actors would be willing to chip in toward a large wedding gift.

"I already asked them whether they knew Anna. Apparently, Charlie played cards with her a few times, but that seemed like the extent of it."

"And you said Deanna's act involves snakes? Are they poisonous?"

I shook my head. "I see what you're getting at, but snakes are very different than poisonous insects." I hated that he was planting doubt in my mind about my friends. "And what reason could Deanna have for killing Anna? They barely knew each other."

"Well, we need to explore all options if we have any chance of finding who did it."

I knew that, but it didn't make suspecting friends and family any more comfortable.

Redvers was quiet for a moment and I assumed he was still thinking about Deanna and Charlie Parks. He surprised me.

"I would like to suggest you stop poking a stick into dark holes, but I'm not going to convince you to do that, am I?" His voice was mild, but he looked serious.

I was glad it wasn't only my aunt Redvers was concerned about. "Probably not. Even if I was no longer considered a suspect, I'm afraid I just can't let it go." I had to keep picking at the loose threads to see if something—or someone—would unravel. The deeper reason, of course, went back to my nightmarish marriage. I wouldn't take the path of least resistance ever again, regardless of the consequences. That path had cost me considerably.

"Even though someone might have threatened you already."

It was a statement, not a question, but I answered it anyway. "All it means is that I'm getting close to answers. We aren't even sure it *was* a threat."

We had reached the dune, and I was grateful for the interruption. The view was stunning, and we pulled our camels to a halt to enjoy it. From this distance, you could see all six pyramids, king's and queen's alike. The tourists were dwarfed by the monuments, reduced to crabs scrabbling across the sand. It was worth the extra time in the sun to take it all in, but after a few moments, we headed in the direction of the hotel.

"What about the doctor? You know, it just occurred to me that he said something strange when I spoke with him."

Redvers looked over at me.

"He said Anna knew how to party. Do you think they were involved together somehow?"

"From what I know about Miss Stainton, I have to admit it's a possibility."

I felt foolish that I hadn't asked the doctor more about Anna, but I remembered how ill at ease I had felt talking with the man in his stifling quarters. Alone. "Could she have been involved with drugs? If the doctor is, maybe she was, too." It was pure speculation. But now that I said it out loud, it didn't seem that outlandish. "Perhaps that's the type of partying he meant."

"We don't really have any proof that the doctor is involved in drugs, either. But I'm afraid that's one area of investigation that I'm going to insist you leave to me." Redvers' voice was firm. "I can't in good conscience let you flounce into a Cairo drug den asking questions. You'll get yourself killed."

"I never flounce." But I conceded he had a point. I wouldn't even know where to go about finding a drug den, much less asking questions in one. "Do you promise to tell me what you learn?"

He promised. And even though I had no doubt he could handle himself, I also made him promise to be careful.

I refused to examine why I cared.

Instead, I turned my mind back to our pool of potential suspects. "I have to admit, I still think our best suspects are either the doctor—it was his gun, after all—or Mr. Samara."

"The doctor says he was alone in his rooms—which means he has no alibi. And our dear Mr. Samara claims he was in the gambling room until it closed, and then went back to his room with some young men to play a few more hands of cards," Redvers said. I digested this.

"That's the first I've heard of his alibi. Have the police found the young men he says he was with?"

Redvers' dark eyes looked at me approvingly from beneath his bone-white hat and I blinked at the rush of pleasure.

"They have not, as a matter of fact. He insists they were from one of the downtown hotels."

"Convenient," I replied.

"It's possible that the young men—there were apparently two of them—have already checked out and gone, but it seems unlikely."

I nodded. It did seem unlikely.

The hotel was now in sight, the green palms and lush grass beckoning us from the harshness of the dry and dusty sand. But the view also reminded me of the death in our midst—even more so than our conversation. The trip to see the pyramids had been a most welcome distraction, but now I needed to be back on my toes.

We had fallen into an easy partnership. I felt a little thrill that Redvers was finally discussing the case openly with me and asking for my opinions. Bouncing ideas back and forth with him helped clear things up in my mind.

Not for a moment did it occur to me to consider Redvers a suspect.

CHAPTER TWENTY-ONE

Back at the hotel, Redvers and I shared a light lunch. The waiters were kept busy refilling my water—I couldn't quite wash the feeling of grit from my mouth. Covering a yawn, I excused myself when we finished and retired to my room. The sleepless night and long morning in the sun had finally taken its toll and I was in dire need of a nap. I managed to remove my sensible walking shoes before collapsing directly onto the bed.

I awoke several hours later, completely disoriented. I had slept soundly, without dreams and without moving. I had a moment of heart-stopping panic when I realized that I had fallen into bed without checking it for poisonous guests first. But since I had survived the nap, I let it go, and promised myself to be more vigilant in the future.

Seeking a clock, I realized that it was nearing dinnertime, and I freshened up in my bathroom. I had enough time to take a short bath, washing off the dust and grit, before donning a navy dress with a fitted bodice and tasteful beadwork ending in a loose, flowing skirt with several layers of chiffon. I put on a pair of cream T-strap shoes with a low heel that I was particularly fond of, and headed down to the bar for a predinner drink.

Aunt Millie was installed at what I was beginning to think

of as her regular table. It was in the perfect position for her
to both observe the goings-on in the bar and quickly sum-
mon a waiter for a drink. A military general couldn't have
planned better tactical positioning. I fetched myself a gin and
tonic from the bar and joined her.

"The girls aren't dining with you this evening?" I asked.

Millie shot me a glare. "Of course, they are. But they
needed to freshen up first." She took a long swallow of her
drink. "And where did you go gallivanting off to today?"
There was never anything gained by engaging with her when
she was in a temper—it only gave her satisfaction. I wondered what had put her in a mood.

"I saw the pyramids with Mr. Redvers," I said mildly.
"And how did you spend your day?"

She sniffed. "Well, I didn't spend it touring around." But
her tone was less sharp. It was more than likely the mention
of Redvers that had mollified her. She could only be thrilled
that I had spent the day in the company of a single man.

I noticed that she kept glaring in the direction of the bar. I
followed her line of sight and my eyes rested on none other
than Amon Samara. He was holding court over a pair of
middle-aged women who were simply aflutter under his at-
tentions.

I nodded in his direction. "Have you had the chance to
meet Mr. Samara yet, Aunt Millie?" I was beginning to feel
like a broken record.

My aunt's face turned sour and she took another long swig
from her glass. She spent several moments flagging down the
nearest waiter for another highball before bothering to answer my question. "Of course not, Jane." She huffed. "We
have not been introduced and I have been far too busy to
meet everyone in this hotel."

I gave a small sigh. This was one mystery that was going to
go unsolved.

The girls chose that moment to join us. Lillian bent down

to buss Millie's cheek with a kiss, instantly restoring my aunt's good humor. I set aside contemplating my aunt's strange behavior for the moment and decided to learn more about the girls, instead.

"How are you, ladies?" I asked, noticing as Lillian sat that she looked a bit pale. Marie glanced worriedly at Lillian and then at Millie.

"I'm feeling a bit ill, actually." Lillian's voice sounded as weak as she looked. "It came on rather suddenly."

"Do you think you should be up and about?" Millie toyed with her napkin. She looked as apprehensive as I'd ever seen her. "Perhaps we should get you back to your room." Marie's head bobbed in agreement.

"Oh!" I suddenly recalled my earlier excursion to see Dr. Williams. "I have a powder for upset stomachs. It's in my room. Would you like me to grab it for you?"

Lillian nodded gratefully, and I hurried off.

By the time I returned, a thin sheen of sweat covered Lillian's forehead. I handed her the packet, which she gratefully swirled into a glass of water and sipped at delicately. Marie and Millie fluttered on either side of her, watching for any signs of discomfort from the girl.

"Marie," I finally said. I was sorry that Lillian felt ill, but I would soon go mad if all we did was sit quietly and watch Lillian drink water. It was Marie's turn to start at being addressed. "I didn't really answer your question about Miss Stainton last time I saw you. I apologize for cutting you off."

Marie looked confused at the apology, but her eyes sparked with interest. I gave her a brief sketch of how I found the body, much to my aunt's disgust. Millie spent the entire story with her lips pursed and nostrils flared. If it weren't for her worry over Lillian, I'm sure she would have stopped my story in its tracks. For her part, Marie hung on my every word, lips parted and moving slightly as though trying to capture the words from my mouth and put them in her own.

When I finished, I casually asked if she had known Anna herself. I hoped that if she had any information, she would share it now that I had told her my story.

Marie shook her head. "She was a dumb tomato. I do feel bad that she's dead, but she really thought pretty highly of herself. You could tell she looked down on everyone. Her bank was never closed, either, if you know what I mean."

I certainly did not know what she meant, and I must have looked very confused, because Lillian, even paler and sweating more profusely, came to my aid with a translation.

"She was always necking with men."

"Ah," I said. I was several years past the age to have picked up the flapper lingo. Talking with Marie suddenly made me feel rather old. I glanced at Millie, who looked slightly smug, for reasons I couldn't begin to speculate on.

"Lillian, did you know her? Perhaps from England?" I asked, but Lillian chose that moment to double over in pain. She moaned, and both Millie and Marie hurriedly pushed back from the table and anchored her on either side. Gingerly helping her to her feet, Millie shot me a glare.

"What did you give her, Jane? She's even worse!" My aunt, cool and collected all her life, even when faced with poisonous insects, sounded on the verge of hysteria now.

Lillian's glass with the white phosphorescent glow was only half consumed.

Chapter Twenty-two

"I only gave her the packet the doctor gave me! It was nothing but sodium bicarbonate!"

Lillian looked terrible, her face contorted in pain. I hadn't thought for a second that the doctor might have given me something other than advertised, but now I wondered what exactly that packet contained. Marie and Millie began helping Lillian from the dining room, causing quite the stir among the gathered guests. Before leaving the table and following the others, I pulled a handkerchief from my bag and wrapped it around the packet Lillian had torn open. There appeared to be some residue caught in the corner, and I hoped it was enough to test. I quickly placed the packet into my handbag.

Dr. Williams had been lounging at the far end of the bar, but when he caught sight of the commotion surrounding Lillian, he hurried over and took charge of the scene. I was too far behind the others to bodily stop him from interfering. I wanted to tell him to back away from Lillian until I was sure he wasn't responsible for her current condition.

But if that powder—or poison—was meant for me, surely his oath as a doctor meant he would help Lillian?

Watching him with her, I had to acknowledge that Dr. Williams was excellent in a medical emergency and seemed truly concerned for Lillian. He quickly brushed Marie aside, and taking Lillian's arm, he helped Millie haul the wretched girl from the room, firing questions at both women. I decided to keep my concerns to myself, trailing in their wake beside Marie, who was wringing her hands in distress. As we moved out of the dining room, the Parkses were just arriving. Deanna caught my eye as she and Charlie passed us, and she touched my arm.

"Is there anything we can do?" she asked.

I shook my head and patted her hand. "You're a dear, but I think we'll be fine." I gave a quick smile and continued after our small human train.

I caught up with Marie first. Tears were slowly rolling down her face, gathering steam until they were flowing in a tidal wave of impending disaster. I was soon partially supporting Marie as her steps became more uneven and her sobbing increased. As a whole, we were quite the production.

Once we reached Lillian's room, I deposited the still-sobbing Marie into an armchair in the sitting room before hurrying into the bedroom. The two double beds were neatly made, and the girls' personal items were tidy, brushes and shoes marching in neat rows.

"Has she taken anything?" Dr. Williams barked once they had settled Lillian on her own bed. Moaning, her arms clamped firmly across her stomach, she curled into the fetal position atop the bedcovers. I explained that we had given her a powder for her stomach, and with a dark look, he sent Millie running for a pitcher of water.

Meanwhile, the doctor's medical bag arrived in the hands of an out-of-breath hotel clerk. The doctor rummaged around, pulling a bottle from the depths that I recognized as a common emetic. Within moments, the doctor had efficiently cleared everyone from the room except Millie. I waited outside with Marie, who paced the hall for a few nerve-wracking moments before she leaned against the wall and slid to the floor without regard for her lemon chiffon dress. Her face was streaked with tears, and she was pale and shaking.

Tense minutes passed. Finally Millie stuck her head out of the door to brief us with an update.

"She's gotten most of whatever it was out of her system," she said, relief evident on her face and in her voice. She didn't even bother with recriminations against me this time, so I knew how frightened she had been. "She's sleeping now. I'll take the first watch." Her words were firm, and she closed the door just as firmly. Millie must have intuited that Marie would argue with her, and indeed Marie spent several minutes struggling with whether to barge in and make her case, but I finally convinced her that arguing with my aunt was futile. Marie settled for remaining in the hall and keeping her own vigil.

"I'll just wait here then, and I'll take over when your aunt gets tired," she said.

I felt a bit too wrung out to argue with her, even though her plan made little sense, and I headed back to the saloon. There was no further use for me there.

Redvers found me in the bar, nursing a much-needed drink. Charlie and Deanna seemed to have vanished once again.

"Where you go, excitement follows." He watched as I took a long drink.

"I wish that weren't the case." I sighed. "In fact, I must say this isn't exactly the relaxing vacation I had hoped for."

He agreed. "How's the girl doing?"

"She'll be fine. Dr. Williams is with her. I have to admit, for all my suspicions about him, he appears to be an excellent doctor."

"People are always complicated. He could be an excellent doctor and still have a drug problem."

"Did you get confirmation on that today?" My piqued curiosity brushed aside any feelings of weariness.

His lips quirked at the ends in response to my obvious interest. "I did. Dr. Williams appears to be a regular visitor to quite a few of the opium dens around town—and some of the seedier ones, I might add."

"I wonder how the hotel can afford to keep him on," I mused.

"They most likely aren't aware. Or they are turning a blind eye to it. As you said yourself, in a crisis, he is an excellent doctor. It would appear that his drug use isn't yet interfering with that. From what I was told, he's a regular visitor—at least once or twice a week, although no one would admit to seeing Anna."

I mulled that over while I took in the scene at the bar. I noticed that Colonel Stainton had finally joined society, although he was on the other side of the room. As I watched, he shot a look at Redvers and me. Realizing he had been caught looking, he smiled at me weakly and abruptly turned back to the bar. I frowned.

"That was strange. Do you think the colonel saw us watching him today? At the pyramids?" I turned to Redvers, who appeared to have also witnessed the exchange.

"I doubt it has much to do with you," he said carefully. "The colonel isn't exactly a fan of mine."

"And what have you done to offend him lately?" I kept my tone light, but I was more than a little curious about the answer.

"Just my usual charming self," he answered, equally as light, but I detected his reluctance to respond. I knew there was more to the story, but I wasn't at all sure how to get the full story from him. He was incredibly closemouthed about his affairs, and even if I asked, I doubted he would give me a straight answer. I pursed my lips for a moment and tried to decide how best to uncover what I wanted to know.

I drained the rest of my near-empty glass and handed it to Redvers. He looked bemused.

"I'm going to give him my condolences, and since he isn't susceptible to your charms, I think I'll go alone."

"A wise choice."

"In the meantime, it would be lovely if you could procure us a few more drinks."

He raised my empty glass in salute, and headed for the near end of the bar. I headed in the opposite direction toward Colonel Stainton.

A bubble of empty space surrounded him, as if his grief had its own weight and presence. It kept other patrons from jostling too close, despite his valuable bar-side real estate. He smiled warmly at my approach, and I felt my own face crease into a returning smile. Just as Redvers suggested, the colonel's negative reaction was to Redvers, not me. I felt a bit relieved. I reached out and briefly grasped his ruddy, square hand resting atop the polished wood cane, giving it a sympathetic squeeze.

"How are you holding up, Colonel? I'm so sorry for your loss." I knew the words held little comfort for him, but they were the only ones I could offer. He covered my hand with his for a moment, giving it a returning squeeze before I took my hand back.

"I'm doing as well as can be expected, my dear." He cleared his throat. "One can't stay in their rooms grieving forever. It's not what my dear Anna would have wanted." My mind immediately went to the exchange we had witnessed at the pyramids, but I couldn't bring myself to mention it to him. Not yet, at any rate.

"No, I'm sure she wouldn't." I paused. "I don't want to upset you further, but I do have a question. I ran into Dr. Williams earlier, and he mentioned Anna. Did they know each other?" The colonel nodded and squared his chin. "Yes, they had drinks together once or twice when we first arrived," he said. "I was disappointed when she tossed him over for some of the younger chaps. The doctor is a good man."

I was surprised that he thought so, given what Redvers had learned about Williams, but perhaps he didn't know the man well.

Colonel Stainton changed directions. "I suppose you've taken the opportunity to visit the pyramids by now, have you not? I know you were anxious to see them, so I hope you were able to do so." I blanched, wondering if he had, in fact, seen us watching him; but as I studied his face, I didn't detect anything more than polite curiosity.

"Yes, actually. I visited them with Mr. Redvers." I nodded toward the other end of the bar, where Redvers leaned casually against the polished wood, waiting patiently for our drinks. His dark tweed suit was an obvious cut above those surrounding him, and I took an extra moment to appreciate how well he wore the suit.

"Oh, well . . . er, very good." The colonel cleared his throat again. "I hope you enjoyed yourself." His smile softened. "I'm only sorry I couldn't take you myself."

I nodded. "Do you know Mr. Redvers?"

He started at my abrupt question, then glanced down the bar. "No, I haven't had the pleasure." His tone was dry.

"Oh. It seemed as though you knew each other." He shook his head, and I was left with more questions than I had started with. Was the colonel telling the truth? Had they truly never met? I supposed I was hoping he would admit to some sort of medieval feud between the two, but it was a foolish wish.

Our conversation had stalled. It was difficult to find a neutral topic, given what had happened, and neither of us wanted to continue treading the same ground of his daughter's murder.

The colonel cast his eyes quickly over the room, alighting on Zaki near the doorway at the front. "It was lovely to chat with you, my dear, but if you'll excuse me, I'm afraid I have business with one of the staff." He patted my arm and, hanging his cane in the crook of his elbow, fluidly wove away from me.

At first, I assumed this was a convenient excuse to leave our awkward conversation, but I saw him meet Zaki near the entrance. The two disappeared from view, heads bent together in conversation.

"He doesn't seem to need that cane," I muttered to myself.

"I'm sorry?" Redvers arrived at my side and handed me a fresh drink, his hand brushing mine. I was certain the touch was unintentional, but it sparked my nerve endings just the same. Flustered, I didn't repeat my earlier observation, but made a new one.

"Everyone in this place is acting strangely. I can't seem to have a normal interaction with anyone."

"Perhaps it's you," Redvers said. "Bringing out the best in people."

This time I did pull a face at him, and he smiled mischievously, transforming his handsome face from dangerous to boyish in the space of a heartbeat. It was a smile that quickened my pulse, but I'd be damned if I ever let him know that.

I worried my bottom lip. Perhaps I should stop spending time with the man if I couldn't stop myself from reacting to him. Of course, there was nothing to be done about it at the moment, so I changed the subject.

"Lillian became much worse after I gave her the stomach powder. It's the same one that I picked up from Dr. Williams yesterday. Do you think there's a chance it was tampered with?"

The smile dropped from Redvers' face and he started toward the table where we had been sitting earlier. Before he took two steps, I reached out and placed a restraining hand on his arm. "It's already been cleared." It was the first thing I had noticed when I reentered the saloon.

"Damn." His face creased in frustration.

I smiled and dug into my handbag. "Not to worry, though. I saved the packet." He cocked an eyebrow and I fought the urge to wink. "Just in case. I'm not sure what good it will do, though."

"We'll test it, of course." He looked extremely pleased. "See what exactly the doctor intended for you to take."

"Are you telling me you also have a chemistry set in your room? For late-night experiments?"

"If I did, the hotel would no longer be standing. No, I should have said, I can *have* it tested. And I know just the person. I'll take it to him tomorrow."

I was about to place the packet in his waiting hand, but I paused. "You said, '*I* can have it tested.' Surely you meant, '*We'll* have it tested'?" I wanted some assurance that he wouldn't leave me out of the loop.

"Certainly," he said. "Scout's honor."

Once again, I placed my trust in Redvers' hands, giving over the wrapped packet without further question.

CHAPTER TWENTY-THREE

Millie came back through the bar before we retired for the evening. She waved a hand at me to indicate she had seen us, but stopped for a drink before heading our way. Her shoulders were stooped with exhaustion, and worry still creased her round face.

"How's Lillian doing, Aunt Millie?"

Millie heaved a sigh. "She's sleeping now, but a little color seems to have returned to her face. We'll know more in the morning. Dr. Williams thinks she'll be just fine." She took a long belt of her drink, drawing fortification from the straight whiskey in her glass.

I touched her arm. "This must be terrible for you. I know how close you've grown to her."

Redvers nodded his sympathy.

Millie drew herself up a bit, pulling herself from my touch. "She'll pull through. She's made of stern stuff." She seemed to want to say something more, then changed her mind. "I'll head back there in a few minutes. Marie wanted to take her turn keeping watch."

I nodded. I doubted either of them would sleep in their own beds that night.

"I nearly forgot, Jane. Do you have a dress for the costume party Friday night?"

Millie's complete change of direction stunned me. I stared dumbly at her for a moment, not fully understanding the question.

"Costume party?"

"Yes, a costume party," Millie said impatiently. "There aren't masks and such like we would have at home, but we dress in clothing like the native Egyptians wear. They actually wear some beautifully embroidered pieces." She paused for a moment. "To be honest, I'm not entirely sure why they call it a "costume" party. But it hardly matters. A party is a party."

Clearing my throat, I searched the cupboards of my mind, poking around misplaced thoughts, but came up with an absolute blank regarding costumes and parties.

"I . . . I just don't recall hearing about it, Aunt Millie."

Millie sighed. "Jane, what will we do with you?"

I assumed the question was rhetorical.

"Providing Lillian continues to improve, I'll take you to find an outfit myself."

I was surprised Millie was so enthusiastic about a costume party, but then she turned to Redvers.

"And you'll escort our Jane, won't you, Mr. Redvers?" Millie flashed him a smile that was supposed to be winning, but looked an awful lot like a shark bearing down on its lunch.

I should have known she had an ulterior motive. I rolled my eyes, which Millie missed since she was busy pinning Redvers to the spot.

He cleared his throat and shot me an amused look. "It would be my pleasure, of course."

I was secretly pleased that he had agreed, even though my aunt had basically strong-armed him into it. But I didn't think it was an appropriate time to attend a party—what with a murder looming over us, and Lillian so unwell.

"I'm not sure it's a good idea . . ."

Redvers continued as though I hadn't spoken. "I believe some of the local dress suppliers come directly to the hotel."

I narrowed my eyes at him and he shrugged. He was not helping me make my case.

Millie beamed up at Redvers. "Excellent suggestion. That's even better—we won't have to leave Lillian here alone. I'll make the arrangements for everything, Jane." Millie turned to me, and her smile dropped. "And now I will head back to Lillian. I don't want her to wake up and think I've abandoned her." She downed the rest of her drink, handed me her empty glass, and bustled away.

Redvers cut his eyes to me. I sighed.

"I do apologize. Don't you wish to attend?" He didn't sound at all sorry, and I raised an eyebrow at him.

"Not particularly." The prospect of dancing made me shudder. I wondered if there was a way for me to avoid the whole spectacle. Perhaps I could twist an ankle. I brightened at the thought. Turning to Redvers, I saw that he was thoughtfully gazing where my aunt had disappeared.

"What are you thinking?"

Dark brown eyes met mine. "Your aunt . . ." He trailed off.

I knew exactly what he was referring to. "I know." I frowned. "Millie is so attached to Lillian, who is a virtual stranger, as far as I know. I haven't been able to learn any more about it. I've never seen her like this."

I felt a pang of guilt. Millie's preoccupation with Lillian during this trip had left me to my own devices. I was enjoying both my liberation and the benefit of steering clear of Millie's ever-sharp tongue. Well, mostly clear of it.

I thought back to Millie's reaction to Amon. "In fact, Millie has been acting strangely since we arrived. I've caught her glaring at Mr. Samara more than a handful of times. And when I ask her about him, she gets very defensive and refuses to answer my questions. I don't know what to make of it."

"Perhaps she fell victim to one of his . . . schemes. His specialty is preying on wealthy older women," Redvers said. "Especially those without the burden of a husband."

"I'll admit, his being a fortune hunter has been on my mind. But Mr. Samara . . . scheming . . . with my aunt? That is not a picture I want to carry in my head."

Redvers laughed, and the low timbre rumbled pleasantly through my chest.

As though we had conjured the Devil himself, Samara came into the saloon through an intricately carved wooden door, sweeping his dark eyes over the room. He acknowledged the both of us with a gracious nod, but didn't cross the room to us. Instead, he made his way to the bar and conferred with the bartender. Zaki, standing alone near the front of the room and attentively watching the interaction, now moved to the bar and joined the others. Their small conference lasted a few minutes.

Apparently satisfied, Amon smiled and retreated back the way he had come. Zaki and the bartender continued conferring for a moment before Zaki joined the man behind the bar. They began to quickly and efficiently load a tray with a variety of drinks.

"What's through there?" I indicated the door Amon had passed through. I hadn't noticed it before—there were so many beautifully carved wood panels throughout the area that the door blended rather well.

"That leads to the gaming room. They do quite a bit of high-stakes gambling in there." Redvers cocked a brow. "Thinking of trying your hand?"

"Too rich for my blood." I did not care to hand over my money for nothing in return. "But I guess it shouldn't surprise me that Samara gambles. It fits the picture."

"It does indeed."

The door opened once more, and I saw a familiar face with a distinctive cowlick pop around the corner. My eyebrows shot up as Charlie glanced around the room, missing us entirely. When his eyes landed on Zaki moving toward him with a heavily laden drink tray, his eyes lit up. With a wide smile, Charlie held the door open as Zaki passed, pulling the door shut behind them both.

"So, that's the room where Charlie has been disappearing to every night." I remembered that part of Charlie's stage act involved card tricks, and I wondered if that was in part how they were financing this trip—by working the card tables. "I wonder if Deanna is with him."

"Most likely." Redvers rubbed his ear thoughtfully. "I hope he's not getting himself into trouble in there." I wasn't sure whether Redvers meant losing what money the couple had, or winning it with Charlie's sleight of hand. Either was equally likely to lead to trouble.

The rest of the night passed uneventfully, which was a relief. I wasn't sure how much more excitement I could stand on my "relaxing" vacation.

CHAPTER TWENTY-FOUR

The next morning, I slept late—much later than I was used to sleeping. When I finally did crack open my eyes, I considered turning over again, but the sun was well and truly up and I decided I should be also. The mirror did me no favors as I splashed water on my face, and I considered hiding in my rooms for the day, simply for the chance to rest and think. It wouldn't hurt to put a little distance between myself and Redvers either. I was beginning to rely too heavily on his companionship.

The pounding on my door shattered any hopes for a quiet day.

I threw on a light robe and answered it. Aunt Millie stood before me, bright and perky as a sunflower, fists on ample hips.

"Jane, I can't believe you're not out of bed yet! I thought for sure I would see you at breakfast. The dress people will be here very shortly. You'd best get yourself ready and I'll meet you downstairs on the terrace."

I couldn't do much more than nod weakly, then went back inside to wash thoroughly and dress. I couldn't believe Millie was so . . . awake, since I assumed she was up much of the night with Lillian. If Millie was this upbeat, Lillian must be feeling much better this morning.

I stumbled downstairs and found my aunt waiting for me. Cheerfully. It was almost enough to send me straight back to my room.

"Jane, you look very tired today." Millie's powers of observation were as sharp as ever.

"How is it that you don't?" I slumped into a chair beside her. "Do I have time for breakfast?" My mouth cracked into such a wide yawn I could barely cover it.

"Probably not a proper meal—you slept very late, Jane—but I'm sure some coffee can be arranged for you while we wait." She popped up and went to the desk, where I assumed she bullied the young man into obtaining coffee from the breakfast room. For once, I didn't mind her heavy-handed methods.

"That's all arranged."

I smiled at her gratefully. "Thank you, Aunt Millie." I yawned again. "And how is Lillian doing?"

"Lillian is feeling much better this morning, although she and Marie will be keeping quiet in Lillian's room today. One really can't be too careful. I'll check in on them when we are through here."

By the time my coffee had arrived, the dressmaker had also arrived and set up in a parlor off the hotel lobby. We were not the only guests who would be taking advantage of her services, but Millie had convinced her to come earlier in the morning to accommodate our appointment. We greeted the young woman at the parlor entrance and she introduced herself as Nenet.

"Welcome." Nenet's dark eyes sparkled as she closed the door behind us. Her long black hair was thick with natural wave and she let it hang loose down her back. She was a striking woman. "I'm so pleased you were referred to my shop. I brought a great deal of inventory from my store, so I am sure we can find you both something very suitable." The proprietary way she referred to the store led me to believe that Nenet herself was the owner. I was impressed that a woman close to my age was running her own business in this country.

"How did you get it all here?" I gazed around the room in wonder. Every surface was covered with dresses—tables and chairs had become an explosion of color and texture.

Nenet laughed. "I have many cousins and uncles, and they help load my cart. I have an arrangement with the hotel when they have events, and so my family is accustomed to moving my dresses."

The selection was overwhelming, and for a time, I simply stood near the doorway and took it all in. Millie waded right into the confusion. Before long, she had an armful of dresses and was headed for the changing screen set up in a far corner of the room.

"I'll just make sure one of these fits me, Jane, and then I'll help you pick out something suitable." Millie's voice came from behind the ornately decorated wooden screen. It would be interesting to see what my aunt's idea of suitable would be.

The young dressmaker touched my arm and led me farther into the room. She sized me up and silently began plucking dresses from the many piles—she obviously knew her stock and where it was located. A small miracle.

"Ah!" Millie's voice was unmistakably pleased. "This one will be just fine." She came out from behind the screen and I smiled. It suited her. The long blue robe was notched at the top with rich geometric embroidery in silver thread decorating the neckline and the front of the robe. The slightly bell-shaped sleeves had matching embroidery at the cuffs.

"This galabieh is a good fit for you." Nenet nodded in approval. "There is a matching scarf for the head."

"I will not need the head scarf." After another trip behind the screen, Millie reemerged with the blue galabieh folded in her hands. She passed over the discarded dresses.

"Perhaps just take it with you. You might change your mind." Nenet added the scarf to her pile.

Millie smoothed her slightly mussed hair, and it was my turn. I moved behind the screen and removed my blouse and skirt, grabbing the first of the dresses Nenet had chosen for me. The first wouldn't fit over my hips at all, and I immediately discarded it. I had the same trouble with the second, and put that one aside as well. Picking up on the common problem with the discarded dresses, Nenet came around the screen with a different style in her hands. As I prepared to slide the new dress over my head, I heard Nenet gasp behind my back and I turned, eyes wide and shaking my head sharply.

She had seen the scars.

"Is everything okay?" Millie's voice carried over the screen. Her view was blessedly blocked.

"Perfectly fine," I called. "I just stubbed my toe on the corner here." My hazel eyes locked with Nenet's dark ones, and she nodded.

My lower back and rear were crisscrossed with long white ridges, reminders of my late husband's unnatural relationship with pain. This particular map was created with a leather riding crop he had been particularly fond of. I was fortunate he had kept his strikes low—I was still able to wear most clothing without displaying my shame. I clearly recalled the first time he had turned the whip on me—only two months after our honeymoon. By then, I was already flinching from his fists, but the whip took matters to another level. I'd tried to run immediately after, but didn't make it far before Grant found me and dragged me back—and my punishment had laid me up for more than a week. He promised that he would always find me, and not only would I pay, but so would anyone who dared help me. I believed him when he said he would kill me if I left—I also believed he would kill me if I stayed.

In retrospect, it was unnerving how easily he culled me from the herd and isolated me under the guise of "wanting me to himself." Anyone who might have offered me refuge was told that I was in the countryside for my poor health. Even my beloved father believed the charming lies my husband put to paper, and any acquaintances I had before my marriage faded away once Grant started refusing contact with anyone from my life before. The money I brought into the marriage, Grant merged into the household accounts with a few well-placed signatures. He then ensured I never had access to more than a few coins—not nearly enough to make an escape with. I shivered as I recalled that my only plan had been to endure things until I could filch enough money from the household to change my name and disappear for good. Sadly, the war had been a blessing to me. Grant had signed up almost immediately—he relished the idea of making his presence known on the battlefield.

To her credit, Nenet recovered quickly and helped me with the dress she had chosen. It was a very different style than the loose robe Millie was wearing.

"This is a traditional dress for dance," Nenet told me once I had it on.

"But I don't dance," I started to say, but she waved a hand and laughed.

"Do not worry. This is the dress for you. Dance or no dance. It brings out the green in your eyes." She nodded with satisfaction.

It was a deep emerald green, with two thin shoulder straps—one across my collarbone, and another along the top of my shoulder. Gold embroidery adorned the straps, working down the bodice that fitted my top like a glove. The waist sleeked down my hips and the skirt had a chiffon overlay covered with small gold coins. The effect was both exotic and sensual. Nenet wrapped a gauzy green scarf with matching gold coins around my head and shooed me from behind the screen.

Mille drew in a breath. "Jane. That is simply stunning." I glowed at the compliment—they were few and far between from my aunt. "You really must have it." She turned to Nenet. "We'll take it."

"It's too much, Aunt Millie. I really don't need something this extravagant."

Millie patted my shoulder. "I insist. It will be my treat." She nodded to Nenet, who positively beamed, and I disappeared back around the screen.

Once I was wearing my own lightweight linen dress again, I brought the green dress around, and Nenet wrapped up our purchases.

"It will be a lovely souvenir, and a dress you can wear again," Millie said.

I wasn't sure that I would find an occasion to wear it again, but for the first time since Millie had mentioned the costume party, I found myself looking forward to the event.

"Besides . . ." Millie gave me a smug smile. "I'm sure your Mr. Redvers will love it."

I gave a small shake of my head.

"He's not my Mr. Redvers," I mumbled, but she ignored me.

There would be no arguing with her on the topic of Redvers—I would never be able to convince my aunt that I was not interested in remarrying, and her not-so-subtle attempts at matchmaking were a waste of everyone's time. It didn't help that I was spending so much time with the man. It was surely giving my aunt the wrong impression, but I didn't think she would be keen to learn that we were trying to smoke out a murderer, either. My relationship with Redvers might be friendly, but it was still strictly business.

The business of solving a murder.

As we parted from Nenet, I let my aunt take the lead and I turned back to give Nenet another look of thanks. She smiled and nodded in return. Catching up with Millie in three long strides, I said a small prayer that disaster had been avoided— the last thing I wanted was for Millie to start asking questions about my scars. It could only lead to an unwanted conversation about her late nephew, the sadist I had been married to.

I could still recall the small stirrings of hope I'd felt when I saw the telegram from the army. It took several readings, but when I finally understood that Grant really wasn't coming home, the dam had burst and the flood of relief had carried me away. The telegram clutched in my hand had been liberally wetted by the tears of joy streaming down my face. I was finally free.

I had not mourned his death for a minute.

CHAPTER TWENTY-FIVE

Though we had been with Nenet for less than an hour, the sleepless night finally seemed to have caught up with Millie.

"I think I'll just lie down for a bit, Jane." Millie stifled a yawn.

"I think that's a lovely idea, Aunt Millie."

"After I check on Lillian, of course."

"Of course."

Restless, I went in search of Redvers. Millie and I hadn't been occupied with the dresses for very long, but I was still worried that he had set off for town and his mysterious chemist without me.

Instead of Redvers, the first person I ran into was none other than Inspector Hamadi.

"Mrs. Wunderly, a word if you will." The inspector pierced me with his gaze, a bug pinned under glass.

"Inspector. How is your murder investigation coming along?" I managed to keep my voice calm and steady, although I felt anything but. The man had a way of unsettling me, even though I knew I had nothing to hide.

His mouth tightened. "Why don't you leave the investigating to me, Mrs. Wunderly."

"So you haven't come to make an arrest, then." I couldn't

seem to keep my mouth under control this morning. I was obviously in need of a nap as well.

The inspector took a step closer. "Do not worry. You will be the first to know if I am ready to make an arrest."

I unconsciously gulped, and his smile of satisfaction grated on me as I cursed myself for showing weakness. Hamadi struck me as the type of man who fed on it.

"I understand you visited the pyramids yesterday, Mrs. Wunderly."

"Yes, well, Mr. Redvers assured me that it wouldn't be a problem." I immediately felt guilty for throwing Redvers to this wolf. I straightened my back. "Yes, I went to the pyramids."

The inspector's face darkened. "Don't leave the hotel again, Mrs. Wunderly. I don't care who with."

"Of course not, Inspector. I wouldn't dream of it." I gave him a wide smile and saw anger flicker briefly in his eyes. I had not made an ally in the inspector. He spat on the ground next to us, and as my lip curled, his own smirked.

But then his gaze softened a bit and I went immediately on my guard. "I heard about the incident with the scorpion."

"Yes," I said. "It was a bit shocking."

"It's fortunate that no one was injured." The inspector gave a curt nod. "We are looking into the matter. I'm confident you will have no further issues, although I would ask you to be careful. If you are not in the hotel, we cannot assist you if something further were to happen."

My eyebrows shot up, and I nodded faintly. The unexpected show of sympathy from the inspector confused my notions about the man, and I now wondered whether his command to stay in the hotel was because I was a suspect, or due to something entirely different. Like an impulse to protect me?

Either way, I was relieved when he turned on his heel and moved off in the direction of the tram line. I fervently hoped he was heading back into town; I preferred to avoid any further run-ins with the man.

Agitated now, I paced the hall adjacent to the front lobby as I tried to figure out my next move. It didn't seem like the police were making a lot of headway in the investigation, despite the inspector's confidence. On the one hand, it boded well that I hadn't been arrested and interrogated again. And even though it seemed the inspector no longer considered me a likely suspect, it also meant that they were no closer to finding the killer. I needed to know more about Amon Samara, and I needed to find someone who worked at the hotel willing to give me information. I made a decision and headed off, my legs moving with purpose now that my feet had found a direction.

The clerk at the front desk looked relieved as I passed by. I was muttering a bit to myself as I paced, and he had been shooting me worried looks.

I found Zaki readying the dining room for the next meal. "Zaki, have you seen Mr. Redvers?"

Zaki seemed to be an observant fellow, and with his position, he probably knew a lot about what went on in the hotel. He stopped his straightening of the tableware and looked at me. "Yes, Mrs. Wunderly. He and Mr. Samara left together this morning after breakfast. They took the tram into town."

This gave me pause. "Did they have breakfast together? Mr. Redvers and Mr. Samara?" I asked. I wondered why Redvers had suddenly decided to become friendly with Samara.

"They did, ma'am. And they left on the tram together." He cocked his head slightly at me. "I understand you met my betrothed, Nenet, this morning."

His sudden change of topic left me unbalanced for a moment.

"Oh, Zaki, I didn't realize she was your fiancée. She's lovely."

He beamed at me. "Yes. Nenet and I live in Mena Village, where all our family lives. She often brings dresses here to the hotel."

It was obvious he was proud of his fiancée, and he had every reason to be—both Zaki and his soon-to-be wife radiated warmth and good cheer. It was easy to see them as a happily married pair one day.

"Well, I can see why you would be proud." I hoped I sounded as sincere as I felt. "She did an excellent job finding me a dress."

His chest puffed even more, but a new concern cropped up. As far as I could tell, there was no hint of pity or interest lurking in the depths of his bright, direct gaze, and I crossed my fingers that Nenet would not feel compelled to share my secret with her fiancé. The last thing I needed was to become a topic of gossip among the staff at the hotel—any more than I already was, that is. Anna's death was enough fuel to the flames.

Zaki had managed to distract me momentarily, but I remembered why I had originally sought him out. "Just between you and me, Zaki . . ." I started to say, and then trailed off.

"Of course, Mrs. Wunderly." He seemed mildly offended that it even needed to be said.

I paused, considering the wisdom of what I was about to do, since it could lead to an entirely different type of gossip, but then I barreled ahead. "Well . . . umm . . . do you know what room Mr. Samara is staying in?"

Zaki sized me up for a moment, his thoughtful scrutiny making me fidget. "Mrs. Wunderly, you are not the type of lady who goes to a man's room alone."

"No, Zaki, not if that man is in his room." I hoped he wouldn't ask any questions about why I would go to Amon's room while he *wasn't* there.

He nodded. "I hear you are asking questions about Miss Anna."

I nodded slowly, wondering just how obvious I had been with my intelligence gathering if the staff had noticed.

"I think this is a good thing to do, even though Miss Anna was . . . different. So I will tell you. Mr. Samara is staying in room 21."

"Thank you, Zaki. I trust you will keep this to yourself."

"Please be careful, ma'am." I smiled and thanked him again, walking thoughtfully toward the lobby. I realized I had forgotten to ask if the men had mentioned when they might return, but when I turned back, I found that Zaki had disappeared from sight.

Shrugging, I headed to my rooms. If I was going to break into yet another room, I would need something to get through the door with. And a pair of light gloves. I had no idea how skilled the local police force was with fingerprint collection, and I had no desire to learn first-hand.

One could never be too careful.

CHAPTER TWENTY-SIX

I scoured my room for something to open a lock with, finally grabbing a pair of hairpins I didn't mind sacrificing to the cause. I slipped into the hallway and headed for Amon's room. I kept an eye out for nosy guests, but the hallways were blessedly empty. Most were either enjoying the sights or taking advantage of the hotel's activities. It wasn't quite noon, so the day had yet to reach peak temperatures. Early afternoons were for hiding from the sun, and around lunch, foot traffic would begin to increase. I would have to move quickly.

I pulled up to Amon's door, hoping I would prove to be a quick study at picking locks. I knocked twice, and listened carefully to make sure Zaki hadn't given me bad information about Amon's trip into town. Hearing nothing but silence, I pulled on my gloves, retrieved my makeshift picks from my pocket, and prepared to give them a try. A little voice in the back of my mind suggested that I try the knob before going to any great trouble, since I had no training or experience in working a lock open. The door pushed in easily, and in my surprise, I nearly tumbled into the room.

Catching myself on the doorjamb, I slid into the room more gracefully than I had been about to, and closed the door quietly behind me. My heart was racing—from nearly falling on my face as much from the fear of being discovered creeping into yet another room. Wearing gloves, no less. I was also terrified that Amon himself would be back soon—the thought prompting me to turn back and lock the door behind me. It would give me a few extra moments of time if I heard him unlocking the door.

The air in his room was thick with the smell of cologne, and as it hit the back of my throat, I nearly gagged on the taste. This would have to be a quick search. And I would probably need a bath when I finished.

I was surprised to realize that he wasn't staying in one of the larger suites, like my aunt Millie's. Instead, Amon was staying on the inside of the hotel, same as myself, without the stunning view the larger outside rooms offered. I thought it was likely Amon's funds weren't as extensive as he would have the ladies believe—or perhaps he was conserving them for his late-night gambling.

I glanced around the tidy room, and was surprised to find that he didn't have many things with him—clothes or otherwise. I remembered his multiple suitcases when he arrived, and wondered where all the contents were stashed. What I could see wouldn't even fill one of the bags he had carried in. I poked through his careful selection of clothes, unsure what I was expecting to find. I noticed that the few suits hanging in the closet were of fine quality, but upon closer inspection had been mended several times. I rifled through the dresser drawers, and found the same was true of his small selection of shirts. They were excellent quality, but the cuffs and collars had been replaced; it was impossible to tell how many times. As my fingers moved through his things, I made a concerted effort to leave things as I found them—I didn't see any need to alert Amon that his room had been searched.

My eyes fell next on the ornamental couch along the far wall. The carved wood was inlaid with ivory, and the graceful lines drew the eye. I noticed something small and white standing out starkly against the sumptuous red brocade upholstery. It was the corner of a paper, secured beneath the cushion.

"Could he have been more obvious?" I muttered to myself as I headed for the couch. I lifted the cushion and retrieved the small cache of papers hidden there. I narrowed my eyes at them as I quickly flipped through the short stack. At a glance, it looked as though I held a list of payments, with varying amounts and initials next to each entry. The handwriting was feminine, but I wasn't surprised that the meticulous Amon would have a somewhat effeminate hand.

The next paper appeared to be a list of artifacts. At the top, it listed a dig site that I knew to be within easy distance of Cairo—I had researched local sites before we departed in case I had the opportunity to visit one while staying at the Mena House. One item on the list was circled, and I skimmed the description of the small ivory statuary.

Something tickled at the back of my mind, but before I could get a grasp on what my brain was trying to tell me, I heard footsteps in the hall. I froze, the blood pounding in my ears as loudly as the noise outside. My eyes flew around the room for a hiding spot should those footsteps stop at Amon's door. The closet was likely my best bet, but it would leave me trapped—or discovered, should Amon need to change his clothes after a day in the city.

The footsteps continued down the hall.

I took a moment to start breathing again, was reintroduced to the thick cloud of cologne, and with a covered cough went back to examining the papers in my hand. The last item in the stack was a copy of an English birth certificate for a baby girl. The date was nearly nineteen years earlier, but I sank onto the couch in shock when I came to the name of the mother.

Millicent Stanley.

As far as I knew, Millie and her husband had been unable

to have children; yet I held in my hand proof that Millie had given birth in what appeared to be a rural hospital in northern England. The father's name was left blank.

Even through my fog of shock, I realized that I had spent more time in Amon's room than was safe or healthy—my nose and lungs still protesting at the smell. I grabbed the birth certificate and pushed the rest of the papers back under the cushion where I had found them. I listened at the door; hearing nothing, I unlocked it and scooted back out to relative safety. I nearly ran back to my room, stripping off my gloves as I went, the paper clutched tightly in my damp palm. I had no idea how to approach Millie with what I had found, but it explained why she had acted so strangely around Amon— her initials had screamed at me from the list of what I could only assume were blackmail payments.

I had pegged Amon Samara as many things—none of them flattering—but a blackmailer wasn't one of them. I needed to reexamine everything I thought I knew about the man.

The papers also cast my aunt in an entirely new light—one that I had not yet begun to process.

As I reached the safety of my room, it occurred to me that with a stash of incriminating papers hidden in his room, it was incredibly foolish of Amon to leave his door unlocked.

And those papers had been awfully easy to find.

Chapter Twenty-seven

Once inside my room, I considered options for a hiding place. I needed to stash this paper, and I wouldn't be able to use my trusty potted palm in the hallway. The paper was entirely too precious. I remembered how the police had missed the cuff links secured in Anna's clothing and thoughtfully regarded my own wardrobe. My eyes fell on one of my sun hats. A wide ribbon wrapped around the band. I folded the paper lengthwise several times until it was only about an inch wide, slipped the paper behind the ribbon, and replaced the hat on the shelf. From a distance—and even up close, I hoped no one would notice the slight bump. Especially if that someone was a man.

Despite the growing heat of the day, I went for a long walk, after double- and triple-checking the security of my pilfered paper. I was already damp from my criminal excursion and I decided I might as well work up a real sweat. There was too much to think about, and I had nervous energy I needed to burn off. The paper I found held enormous ramifications for my family. I couldn't decide whether I should confront Millie, or if I should be respectful of the secret she had obviously kept quiet for so many years.

It took more than an hour of wandering in the heat, but I

eventually came to the conclusion that I would leave it alone. I had my secrets, and my aunt was entitled to her own as well.

By the time I returned, Redvers was enjoying a cup of tea on the terrace. He stood as I approached, and I pulled up a chair next to him at the blue-and-white–tiled table.

"You look a bit . . . heated, Mrs. Wunderly. What have you been up to?"

"Just out for a walk." I lifted the brim of my hat slightly and swiped some sweat from my forehead with the back of my hand. He cocked an eyebrow and I ignored him. I wasn't overly concerned with social niceties at the moment, nor with how unappealing my display must be. "Where did you disappear off to this morning?"

"Just a quick trip into town. You'll be happy to know that the doctor did not try to kill you—the powder was just that. Stomach powder."

I glowered at him. If looks could kill, there would be another body for the coroner to deal with. "You went and had it tested without me." The disappointment I felt at the news of the doctor's innocence wouldn't sink in until later—I was entirely too busy fanning the flames of my anger at Redvers.

"Well, I do need to keep some of my contacts confidential, Mrs. Wunderly."

"But you made a promise."

"Actually, I gave you my Scout's honor, and I have to admit that I was never a Scout."

"That is one of the most ridiculous excuses I have ever heard." I was well and truly heated up, and in that moment, I decided to keep to myself what I had found in Amon's room. It was childish, but I wouldn't forgive him any time soon for leaving me out. I also knew that I was overreacting, but I wasn't ready to examine why just yet.

I simmered in my seat for a while, nursing hot coffee that

left my tongue singed. Redvers picked up the copy of the *Egyptian Gazette* he had been perusing, and let me be. He occasionally peered at me over the top of the newspaper to judge whether I had cooled off, and then returned to his reading, languidly turning the pages now and again.

"Did you learn anything else? I hear you had breakfast with Mr. Samara." I was still irritated with him, but my curiosity eventually won out over anger.

Redvers put the paper down and smiled at me. I did my level best to keep that smile from winning me over. "I didn't learn much, frankly. At least not from Mr. Samara."

I decided not to pursue why they had been dining together like old school chums. "That sounds as though you learned something from someone else."

"Yes, but I'm afraid to bring that up again." His face was very serious, but a twinkle in his eye said he was teasing me. I made a show of rolling my eyes.

"So your mysterious chemist told you that the powder was innocent?" I couldn't resist a slight jab.

"That appears to be the case." He wisely ignored my parry.

"And that would make the whole affair a coincidence of timing—Lillian was ill on her own, without any extra help from the powder." The doctor *hadn't* been trying to poison me. I wasn't entirely sure whether I felt relieved or disappointed. If the powder had been poisoned, it would point the finger definitively at him, and we would be close to having answers.

"Yes. It appears that if Lillian already had a potassium deficiency, the sodium bicarbonate would have caused her to vomit. And that seems likely, especially given how active she is." I nodded. "Although it doesn't let the doctor off the hook entirely. It was still his gun that was used to kill Miss Stainton."

I hadn't been satisfied with the doctor's explanation of the gun's theft, so he was still high on my list of suspects. Right behind Mr. Samara, our resident blackmailer.

At the thought of Amon, it crossed my mind that Redvers may have a more nefarious reason for meeting with him at breakfast, but I banished it immediately. If Redvers was being blackmailed by Amon, he was unlikely to have a civil meal with him. And as irritated as I was with Redvers over breaking his promise to me, I simply didn't want to believe that Amon had found out anything about Redvers that he could use for blackmail.

It troubled me that not only had I grown attached to the man, but I also didn't want to examine any scenarios that included him in the role of a culprit. I reminded myself that I was usually a good judge of character—the exception being, of course, my first husband. But I had learned from that lapse in judgment. I would know instinctively if I had made a mistake in trusting Redvers so easily.

Wouldn't I?

He might deceive me with the little things, like a trip to the chemist, but he wouldn't lie about any larger involvement. Surely, I would know.

"Incidentally, how did you learn about my breakfast with Samara?"

I realized I had been frowning into my cup as I thought about the men in my life. Something I had truly hoped to avoid since my marriage years earlier. Yet, here I was, irrationally angry that a handsome man I barely knew had broken his word to me. A man I should not—*was not*—interested in.

Insidious things, men.

"Zaki told me. I asked him earlier if he knew where you had gone."

Redvers gazed thoughtfully toward the dining room. "Helpful chap."

CHAPTER TWENTY-EIGHT

I spent the afternoon watching Deanna and Charlie play tennis, each cheating terribly and without shame as they laughed and batted the ball and banter back and forth. I wasn't sure how they had talked me into accompanying them, but I found myself enjoying the distraction of their company. Millie was still sequestered with Lillian, who by all reports was feeling much better, so Redvers and I joined the Parkses for dinner that night. He and I both laughed loud and often. It was a welcome distraction from the events of the days prior, and for an evening, I managed to forget the growing list of things I was worried about.

When morning came, I found that I had slept better than anticipated for once and that I was actually looking forward to the evening's events, despite the inevitable dancing. As much as I enjoyed a party, I had never found dancing to be a pleasant way to spend my time. I wasn't entirely uncoordinated, only when it came to finding a beat—I had an absolute inability to keep or maintain a rhythm. But I looked forward to playing dress-up and enjoying my friends' company.

I spent the day unwinding, drinking tea, and lounging about my room. It was the most relaxing I had done since we arrived, and exactly what I needed to reestablish my equilibrium. After a late afternoon nap, I decided to take a long soak in my tub. I finally put the delicious jasmine-scented bath salts to good use, occasionally refilling the warm water, only getting out once my fingers and toes were wrinkled beyond recognition.

I took extra time with my makeup that evening, not bothering to fuss over my hair since the head scarf would cover most of it. I slid on the dress and was thankful for my aunt and her generosity—something I needed to tell her once again. I chose a pair of silver heels that were a bit higher than I normally wore, but were perfect with the dress.

I set off toward Millie's room, having agreed to assist Millie with her own primping, but I found that someone else had already beat me to it, and my help was completely unnecessary.

"Millie! You look lovely," I said as I took her in. Lillian and Marie had styled Millie's long gray hair in as much of a modern style as was possible, with marcel waves along the side of her face and a low bun at her neck. It took ten years off her age. Her makeup was carefully done and the dress she had chosen suited her well. She grumbled at my compliment, but looked pleased all the same.

The two girls were wearing similar dresses, in the same style, but differing colors—Lillian opting for a bright orange-and-red number, and Marie in a sedate cobalt blue. Both dresses were loose and flowing, but with sparkles and beading galore. Lillian still looked a bit wan, although cheerful, and Marie was positively sparkling. The excitement of the night brightened her features, and I felt buoyed by the girls' energy as we headed down to the terrace.

The party was in full swing when we arrived. It was obvious, judging by the number of people in attendance, that guests of the posh hotels in Cairo had been invited to join the revelry. White-robed waiters moved among the large crowd, passing out drinks, and through the swell of bodies, I caught a glimpse of Zaki directing his staff's traffic. A large area of the terrace had been cleared for dancing, and a small musical ensemble was crowded at one end, providing the music. Lively jazz floated out over the crowd. I recognized the song they were currently playing, "Everybody Loves My Baby."

Redvers appeared behind me, nearly causing me to jump yet again. Instead of opting for the traditional Egyptian galabieh, which most of the men wore, Redvers was devastating in a simple black tuxedo. His dark chestnut hair shone in the moonlight and his dark eyes glittered.

"You really need to stop sneaking up on people," I said.

"You should learn to be more observant." He gave me a dangerous smile. I would have had a sharp reply, but he handed me a drink and gave a wink to Aunt Millie. I took a tentative drink. It was a lemon gin fizz, my favorite.

"You look simply stunning, Mrs. Stanley."

Millie seemed entirely charmed by Redvers, and instead of giving him the harsh reply I expected, or taking him to task for not dressing in one of the native "costumes," I was shocked to see a becoming flush stain her cheeks. My aunt was actually blushing like a schoolgirl.

"You don't mind if I steal your niece away, do you?"

"Of course not, Mr. Redvers. Have a wonderful time." Mille gave me an encouraging smile and turned back to the girls. The trio headed off to the bar, happily chattering among themselves.

Redvers turned his attention to me and I felt my own face begin to redden.

"Would you care to dance, Mrs. Wunderly?" Redvers asked.

Even with my heels, he had to lean down to speak into my ear, sending an electric jolt down my spine. The noise level even in the open air was just short of deafening, and I blamed that as the reason for his sudden closeness.

I shook my head. "I'm afraid not, Mr. Redvers. My dancing skills are somewhat suspect." I hoped he would leave it there, but my refusal only made him look more determined.

"I'm afraid I can't accept that as an answer this evening, Mrs. Wunderly. I'm going to have to insist. You look absolutely ravishing in that dress, and it would be a shame not to give it a turn around the dance floor." His breath moved the hair near my ear once again.

I stumbled around in my head for a response. "Thank you." Was that coherent? I wasn't sure. It suddenly felt like I had a wool sock in my mouth.

Suddenly feeling shy, I peered into my glass, which was already half empty. I wondered where the first half of that drink had gone to. I looked at the ground. Had I spilled it? I couldn't possibly have drunk it already.

Redvers plucked the suddenly fascinating glass from my hand, and, handing it to the nearest waiter along with his own, led me toward the dance floor. I suddenly remembered why I said no in the first place.

"I really can't dance, Mr. Redvers." I tried my best to hang back.

"Nonsense," he said. "I think you just haven't had the right partner." I shook my head. He swung me into his arms and led me in a graceful arc around the floor. His arm was strong and sure against my back.

"See? You dance beauti . . ." He wasn't even able to finish his thought before I accidentally trod on his foot. "Never mind." He shook his head. "Forget I said anything."

"I tried to warn you," I said. "I haven't any rhythm. We can stop anytime you would like. I would hate to see you crippled."

"No, no." He grimaced. "This was my idea, and I fully intend to see this to the end . . . of this song, at least." We spun again and my heel connected with a man behind us, who immediately reached down to the fresh wound on his calf, hopping on one leg as his dance partner looked on in confusion. Redvers quickly maneuvered us away from the poor soul and I couldn't help but laugh—Redvers' face was priceless.

"Those shoes are sharp."

"I'll keep that in mind, should I need a weapon."

"They'll do as one." He glanced over my shoulder. "I hope you didn't draw blood from that poor bloke." Redvers soldiered on to the end, and barely even limped off the dance floor when the song finally came to a close.

I flagged down another waiter and procured us two new drinks, one of which he gratefully took from me.

"I thought you were exaggerating." He took a long drink from his glass.

"I was not."

"I'll never doubt you again." His smile was warm, even after the spectacle he had just witnessed. My own lips tipped up in return.

"But for everyone's safety, perhaps we should stand even farther away." I laughed and we moved closer to the bar.

It was hard to talk without raising our voices, but Redvers stuck close. So close that after a bit, I decided I needed to give my galloping heart rate a break. I caught sight of Millie and the girls and decided to see how they were doing.

"I think I should check in with my aunt." I pointed in her direction with my chin.

"I'll just grab us another drink," Redvers said. "And maybe I'll take a walk through the crowd and get a sense of where all the players are tonight."

He had been such a distraction that I had nearly forgotten I was supposed to be investigating a murder and keeping an eye on our suspects. I found myself squelching a feeling of disappointment that he still had a clear head about him and wasn't as equally distracted by my proximity. Then I gave myself a stern lecture on the dangers of letting a man close to me again.

I moved through the press of bodies toward where I had last seen Millie, but before I had gone five steps, a hand caught my elbow.

Chapter Twenty-nine

"**M**iss Wunderly!" The colonel was decked out in a navy blue galabieh with matching turban, and he moved in the foreign outfit as though he was at home in it. His ever-present cane marked out a bit of space around him. "You look lovely, my dear."

"Thank you. You look well yourself, Colonel." I was about to comment on his robes, when I was jostled from behind. I turned to find myself nearly nose to nose with Dr. Williams.

"Ah, Mrs. Wunderly." The doctor seemed neither pleased nor troubled to see me.

"Major Williams," the colonel said cheerfully, and they clasped their hands together in a friendly handshake. It seemed the two men were better acquainted than I thought. When the colonel had spoken to me about the doctor, I assumed that the men had a mere passing acquaintance. But upon further reflection, both were former military, and Dr. Williams had been called to the scene of Anna's death. There were a number of places they could know one another from, and the hotel wasn't so crowded that they would not have met on more than one occasion.

"Are you enjoying yourself, Major? Or are you on duty this evening?" the colonel asked.

The doctor gave a short bark of laughter. "It's a good night, and I happen to have it off, for once. Heading to the tables, Colonel?" The doctor bounced lightly on the balls of his feet.

"I am, I am. But not those high-stakes tables you seem to prefer. Too rich for my blood."

My eyebrows crept up. I was surprised that the colonel would spend the night gambling after the death of his child only days before, but I reflected that he probably needed a distraction. Stewing alone in grief wasn't the healthiest option for anyone.

"Are there many women in the gambling room?" I found myself asking.

"Well, of course, there are," he replied as the doctor shrugged. "My Anna caught the gambling fever from me, unfortunately. She spent quite a few nights in there, before . . . well . . ." He stopped and the doctor clapped him on the shoulder, shooting me a dark look that I found myself resenting.

It wasn't as if I had meant to bring up his daughter—although I did recall that Charlie had mentioned Anna's skill at the table. And since my curiosity about the young woman had prompted the question, perhaps I was in the wrong, after all. I gave the doctor an apologetic smile.

The colonel gave a shake of his head and changed the conversation in a direction that left me agape. "Have they found your service weapon yet, Major? A damn shame."

Given that it was the weapon that had killed his daughter, I was shocked he would bring it up. I was also surprised he didn't seem to hold the doctor responsible in any way.

"Not yet, although I'm not sure they would tell me if they had. Hamadi isn't the most helpful of chaps under any circumstance."

At least my initial impression of the inspector seemed universal.

"Do you know how they got hold of it?" The colonel's voice was mild, but his eyes were sharp.

"I'm pretty sure it was in my rooms. I didn't carry it with me at the hotel or when I was in the city. Didn't want it stolen." The doctor's mouth twisted at the corners in a wry smile.

"You mean at the opium dens?" I heard my voice ask. My eyes widened slightly in shock. My mouth had gotten ahead of my brain again.

The doctor's eyebrows drew together and I prepared myself for whatever he meant to dish out, when he threw his head back and barked a series of laughs. "No, I would never take it to the dens, Mrs. Wunderly. Too much trouble there."

The colonel nodded sagely in agreement. "The major does a lot of good in those places, but they are a bit rough." He gave the doctor an approving look, and I looked back and forth between the two of them in confusion.

"He tries to pull as many former soldiers from those dark holes as he can and get them cleaned up. Too many good men lost to their memories of the war and the pull of the pipe," the colonel explained.

My mouth opened and closed a few times like a guppy. I finally closed it and gave both men a weak smile.

The doctor clapped a hand on both our backs as though the three of us were old war chums. "Now, I see a young lady over there who could do with a turn around the dance floor. She looks much better, I see." I followed the direction of his gaze and realized he was talking about Lillian. She did look rosy-cheeked, and was conversing gaily with Marie and Millie.

The colonel grinned his approval. "If you'll excuse me as well, Miss Wunderly. I'm afraid the tables call." He turned his smile to me. "But it was a delight to see you, as always."

I smiled at him and he gave a small salute as he departed. I watched him move expertly through the crowd, and I edged forward to keep him in my sight line. He easily slid back inside the hotel and continued across the saloon before pausing to speak to Zaki. With a smile, Zaki slid a hand into his robes. He withdrew his hand quickly and appeared to pass something to Colonel Stainton in a handshake—although with the distance, it was impossible to tell. The colonel returned the smile, clapped Zaki on the back, and the two men moved off together in the direction of the gaming room.

I muttered a curse. If Zaki had passed something to the colonel, it had been small. I was very curious about what it could be, but I also knew there was no easy way to find out. With a small sigh of defeat, I moved off on the trajectory the doctor had taken, toward my aunt and her young charges.

By the time I reached the ladies, the doctor was out on the floor with Lillian. Marie was glaring at the pair, arms crossed and a petulant look on her face. Millie seemed indifferent. I stepped to the far side of Millie, away from Marie.

"You don't object to this?" I motioned with my head toward the doctor and Lillian on the dance floor. "He's quite a bit older than she is."

"Nonsense, Jane. It's just a dance." Millie sipped contentedly at her highball. "She was merely being polite when she accepted. Besides, the doctor does a lot of good work in this community."

I shook my head. It seemed that either Redvers had gotten bad information from his contacts, or he had fed me bad information intentionally. All outside reports were pointing to a different picture of the doctor than we had put together.

I spotted Charlie and Deanna on the outskirts of the festivities and decided that some gaiety was exactly what I needed—everyone else was confounding me, and I didn't want to spoil the evening with too much thinking. The farther away from the bar I moved, the easier it was to hear, and I was relieved that they had situated themselves where we might actually be able to hear one another without shouting.

Deanna was decked out in a similar costume to my own—a dress for traditional dance, instead of the looser galabieh robe. Hers was a shimmering number that reminded me of the night sky as it hovered between black and blue. Her eye makeup was dramatic, and I could easily imagine her captivating an audience from the stage. Charlie wore a red galabieh with a matching turban. I saw his hand reach up to smooth his cowlick and stop short when it found fabric, instead.

"Jane!" Deanna cried when she saw me, sweeping me into a hug. I guessed that she was several drinks into her evening, but I didn't mind the burst of affection. Charlie grinned at me.

"Are you having fun?" I already knew the answer to my question.

"It's smashing, isn't it, Charlie?" Deanna wrapped her arm around Charlie's waist, and he gazed down happily at his new bride.

"Only because you're here, my love." Charlie planted a kiss in her hair, and I smiled at them both.

"And where's your handsome gentleman?" Deanna asked me with a wink.

"Oh . . . well, he's not . . . I mean, we're n-not . . ." I stammered.

"Well, he should be." Deanna's grin grew even wider.

I changed the subject. "Will you be disappearing to the tables tonight?"

Charlie grinned. "Because of the party, there aren't supposed to be any card games. Although, I'm sure a few of the more dedicated among us will find a way later." I wondered where the colonel was really headed if the tables weren't open. And then I reminded myself to relax and leave the thinking for later.

We spent nearly an hour chatting over drinks, but when the band started up with "Somebody Loves Me," Charlie and Deanna excused themselves to take a turn around the dance floor. They gazed into each other's eyes as Charlie gracefully swept her along, and I found myself turning away with a small twinge. I looked over the crowd. The mood was positively ebullient—it was easy to forget that a tragic murder had happened not even a week before. The guests were outfitted more brightly than any exotic bird, and the happy chatter and riot of color was a relentless crashing of waves against the senses. I began to tire and moved out onto the dark grounds for a breath of fresh air.

"Are you having a good time?" Both the low rumble and the silent approach were becoming familiar to me. Redvers and I continued walking out until the noise of the party was little more than an echo.

"I am. It's a lovely night. Everyone seems to be having a good time." I shivered a bit. I had forgotten to bring my wrap with me. Redvers noticed my chill and removed his jacket, draping it across my shoulders. I was grateful for both the gesture and the warmth.

"Thank you." I pulled the lapels close around me, and the smell of clean soap, pine, and something spicier wrapped around my senses. "And how about you? Are you having a good time?"

"Even better now." His voice rumbled low and warm. We had stopped far from the crowds and he gazed into my eyes. My body began to tremble again—not from the cold this time—and I knew what was coming. My instincts for self-preservation, honed to a sharp knife's point since my husband's death, warred with my desire to let this handsome man take me in his arms and kiss me senseless.

He leaned toward me, and I put a restraining hand on his chest—self-preservation winning out, even as I felt disappointment drop into my stomach.

"I can't."

He straightened. "Can't or won't?"

"Doesn't particularly matter which." I was speaking to the ground, my hand still resting on his firm chest. "It comes to the same conclusion." I dropped my hand, removed his jacket, and passed it back to him, immediately missing both the heat and the comforting smell. Damn the man.

"Jane," he started.

"We are friends." My voice sounded firm, although I felt anything but. I finally raised my eyes to his. "And only friends. You will have to respect that."

His eyes were clouded with confusion and frustration as he watched me leave, jacket now slung over his shoulder and his hands stuffed into his pockets. I wrapped my arms around myself as I headed back to my rooms, feeling cold and very much alone.

He didn't try to follow.

CHAPTER THIRTY

I tossed and turned that night. I had made the right decision, I felt fairly certain of that. But the other side of the coin—the possibilities and the pleasure had I not turned Redvers down—well, that kept me from sleep. In fact, the lack of sleep I was getting on my so-called vacation was becoming ludicrous.

When daylight finally broke, I dragged myself down to the breakfast room, taking no notice of the excited buzz on my way. My priority was coffee. Only when I reached the area did I realize there was a large number of policemen milling about, and guests were whispering anxiously all around me. I closed my eyes for a moment while I debated waiting until after breakfast to discover what had happened, but as always, curiosity won out. I headed toward the greatest concentration of officers.

I got as far as the saloon before I was restrained. I craned my neck around the swarthy policeman, but I could see very little besides the backs of other uniformed officers. I eyed the policeman before me, deciding it was unlikely that I would be able to get around him, so I was both relieved and anxious when I heard a familiar voice at my back.

"Trying to sneak a look?" Redvers regarded me warily, hands in pockets.

I turned to face him full-on, and took in the bruised circles under his eyes. It seemed as though I was not the only one who had spent a sleepless night.

"Of course. What's happening in there?"

He gazed at me for a long moment without answering. "Are you just going to pretend that nothing happened last night?"

"Yes. That is exactly what we are going to do." I sounded much braver than I felt. Redvers' mouth opened, but nothing came out.

"Excellent." I kept my voice brisk to hide the tremble I felt. "I'm glad you agree with me. Now, what's going on back there?"

He muttered something under his breath that sounded an awful lot like "This isn't over yet," but I couldn't swear to it.

"Mr. Samara was killed last night."

I actually gasped out loud. Although, given what I had learned about Mr. Samara in the short time I had known him, and having learned about his clandestine blackmailing operation, it shouldn't have been such a shock.

"Where? How?" My caffeine-deprived brain felt foggy and I wasn't quite capable of forming more intelligent questions yet.

"In the gambling room. He was found lying facedown on the table by a member of the staff early this morning when they arrived for work. He'd been shot."

"Can I see him?" I asked.

"Why on earth would you want to see him?" Redvers' mouth was agape, and I felt a small thrill of pleasure that I had surprised him. "And this coming from the woman who nearly fainted at the sight of a scorpion?"

"Really," I huffed. "I did no such thing. And it was an enormous poisonous insect I had trouble with, not a dead body." I might have been exaggerating the actual size of that insect. Somewhat.

He shook his head and looked at me, brows drawn to-gether. "I'm not sure I can convince them to let you near, es-pecially since you are still technically a suspect in the last murder."

I just looked at him with raised eyebrows, and he gave an-other shake of his head, this time in defeat. I fought back a smile as Redvers glanced around. Seeing that no one was paying us any mind, he took my elbow and led me deeper into the room past the numerous officers as he attempted to shield me from view. It was unnecessary. The police had ig-nored the both of us, once Redvers took charge of my atten-tion.

We got as far as the doorway without being molested, and I poked my head in. It was just as Redvers had said. Samara's cheek and left arm rested in a dark pool of blood on the ma-hogany table. His eyes were closed, and I was grateful that I couldn't clearly see the damage that had been done to his chest. A discarded cushion from a chair at the table had been tossed on the floor, feathers sprouting from the gaping holes. Matching feathers were sprinkled across the scene—the killer had obviously used the cushion to silence the sound of the gunshots. In the same way as Anna's killer had used a bed pillow.

I took in as much of the scene as I could in a matter of mo-ments. I didn't want the milling officers to wonder why I was gawking at the body, and I certainly wasn't keen to run into Inspector Hamadi, who was doubtless nearby.

Once I had seen enough, I backed away from the doorway and headed purposefully back to the breakfast room, Red-vers trailing in my wake.

"That was quick."

"I just wanted to take a look, and I certainly don't feel like having a tête-à-tête with Inspector Hamadi before my morn-ing coffee." Just the thought of that hot, caffeinated beverage nearly made me drool with desire.

A fresh-faced young waiter greeted us at the door and led us to a table.

"Where's Zaki?" I asked the young man. I was accustomed to seeing Zaki's smiling face before every meal.

"He has the day off, ma'am."

I nodded. Zaki had been busy with the party the night before and I imagined it had been a late night for him.

Once we were settled into our seats, and I requested an entire pot of dark coffee, I turned to Redvers. "I noticed the feathers—they used a cushion again to silence the shots. Do you think it's the same killer?"

Redvers grunted. "It's too soon to tell. Although, so far, it appears that way, and I'm sure the police will be considering it as a possibility. It would seem that the same caliber gun was also used."

"Is there any way to know for certain?"

"Not without finding the gun first. That's why the hotel is inundated with police. With a second killing, Hamadi can't afford to let this go unsolved. Or he will be the one coming under fire."

"I wouldn't mind that," I muttered.

"Yes, well. Hamadi is a bit . . . rough about the edges." I rolled my eyes. *Rough* didn't even begin to cover it, in my opinion.

"Do they have any new suspects?"

"From what I can tell, they're looking at the gamblers first."

I pondered that for a moment. "I wonder if Charlie is going to become a suspect. He's a regular at those tables. I certainly hope not."

"It's a possibility. Although they would also look for a connection between him and Anna." Redvers' face was neutral.

At the mention of Anna, my mind suddenly spat out a

thought that had been nagging at me, but had been dancing out of reach.

"Do you remember the night she was killed? The man we saw with her?" My words tumbled ever faster as I went. "Doesn't Charlie remind you of him?"

Redvers thought for a moment. "It did occur to me that he had the same build as that young man. And they never did find anyone fitting his description at any of the other hotels." He sighed. "For that matter, they never found the two men responsible for Samara's alibi that night, either."

Three missing suspects that the police couldn't find. Of course, two of them might never have existed in the first place. I shook my head to clear it and took a long drink of coffee.

"Well, I hope it wasn't Charlie. He and Deanna are so happy. She would be devastated." I fervently hoped that Anna's beau that night was some other young man, and not an unfaithful Charlie Parks. Deanna had provided his alibi for the evening; so if she was lying for him, I felt sure that lie would be straining their relationship, and their relationship seemed anything but strained. If I suspected my new husband was cheating on me, there was no way I would be able to carry on with him as happily as Deanna did with Charlie.

A new thought occurred to me. If Deanna had lied for Charlie's alibi, it meant she didn't have one, either.

As I worried about the Parkses' possible involvement, another confusing memory reared its head. "Is there any way you may have been wrong about the doctor and his issue with drugs?"

Redvers raised his eyebrows. "What brings that up?"

"I heard some interesting things about him last night, and I wanted to check them against what you told me." I shared with him what both the colonel and Aunt Millie had said about the doctor, and Redvers mulled that over.

"A number of places confirmed that he was a regular."

"But not necessarily that he had been using the drugs?"

"Well, no. Outing their best clients seems bad for business."

"So, why did they even confirm that he had been there?"

"Well, a few of the . . . establishment owners . . . indicated that they knew him, but not how or why. I assumed they didn't want to confirm his patronage for obvious reasons. It appears I need to revisit some places and ask some different questions."

We were both quiet for a moment. I trusted that he was telling the truth and hadn't been feeding me bad information—he seemed genuinely surprised by what I told him. Once again, my gut told me I could trust Redvers. He played close to the vest, and skirted the truth occasionally, but when it came down to the big questions, I didn't think he would lie to me.

I tried to stop thinking about what his lips would have felt like on mine.

I shook myself. It occurred to me that now would be a good time to share what I had learned when I searched Amon's room. I thanked the fates that I had had the good sense to wear gloves for my break-in, since the police would certainly be going over the room with a fine-tooth comb today.

"It might be a good time to tell you what I found in Amon's room."

Redvers went very still. "When did you go through his room?"

"A couple days ago."

He exploded. "And you didn't think to tell me?" He practically spat the words out, eyes flashing dangerously.

"I think you might be overreacting." I watched as his eyes grew round and he sputtered. His burst of anger caused my body to stiffen, poised for flight, the response instinctive. But after observing him for a few moments, I took a deep breath and forced my body to relax. He was upset, but he wouldn't harm me.

A refill on my coffee had arrived in the meantime, and I took some time to enjoy the fresh rush of caffeine as Redvers' fingers thumped the wicker armrests of his chair. I gazed around the terrace and enjoyed the warm sunlight while I studiously ignored him. It was a bit of role reversal, and I had to admit that I was enjoying having the upper hand this time. My exhaustion had been temporarily chased away.

When his fingers stopped tapping, I raised my eyebrows at him, and he stared up into the sky. "Go ahead."

"Excellent." I proceeded to describe for him the papers that I had found.

"I don't suppose you kept these papers, did you?" Redvers looked hopeful.

"No, I put them back where I found them. Well, all but one." He furrowed his brow and I explained about the birth certificate with Millie's name listed as the mother.

"The payments? I assume they were some sort of black-mail." I said.

He nodded.

"Millie's initials were on that list."

"You realize that . . . this makes your aunt a suspect." The words were drawn out, and I could tell he regretted what he had to tell me. "She has a motive just as compelling as any-one else they may consider."

I had considered that fact at length. It would never have occurred to me before to consider my aunt a suspect, but it was clear there was plenty I didn't know about the woman. Was she capable of murder? I simply wasn't sure anymore. In fact, the entire scenario made me more than a little uneasy, especially since I had stolen the most damning evidence of my aunt's motive. Evidence that was currently hidden in my room, and not all that ingeniously.

"I realize that." I shifted uncomfortably in my chair. "But

I'd like to see what we can find out before I go turning anything in to the police."

He looked as though he was thinking about arguing with
me, but then decided against it.

"Would you at least give me the paperwork to hide? It will
look terrible for you if it's found in your room."

I considered that for a moment, but then shook my head.
He had absconded with evidence before and then turned it
over to the police—I wouldn't entrust Millie's fate to him
just yet.

He looked at me for a few beats, then sighed. "You realize
that paper gives you motive for this murder as well."

Now that was a thought that hadn't crossed my mind. My
eyes widened in horror. "Just what I need. Another reason
for Hamadi to harass me." I closed my eyes. It was hard to
imagine who had motive to kill both a partygoing socialite
and a blackmailer. Except for me, apparently. Or, perhaps,
Charlie Parks, if it was true that he was both a gambler and a
ladies' man.

I didn't like either of the options.

Redvers had moved on to other concerns. "Did you leave
fingerprints in Samara's room? I know the Cairo police aren't
the most efficient, but even here—"

I cut him off and gave him a dirty look. "Give me a little
more credit than that, Redvers. Of course, I wore gloves."

His shoulders sagged in relief.

I turned my mind to the other papers that had been hidden
with the birth certificate. "What do you think that list of artifacts means?"

It was Redvers' turn to look uncomfortable. "I think
there's a good possibility that someone is illegally smuggling
antiquities out of the country."

My initial reaction was one of absolute rage. Valuable artifacts should be held in museums where everyone from tourists to scholars could learn from their history. The idea that

they would instead be sold to shady collectors with deep pockets did nothing but fill me with disgust and anger. History should be preserved for those who want to learn from the past—not own it.

Although, I had once felt like nothing more than a possession to my husband—a precious trophy to be purchased and used in any way he saw fit. It doubtless influenced my feelings on the topic of ownership.

Once the initial wave of anger passed, I thought about Redvers' discomfort, and why the mention of antiquities smuggling would make him squirm in his seat. I came to the only conclusion I could, given what I knew about him—or, rather, what I didn't know about him.

"Is that what you're here for?" I cocked an eyebrow. "Are you looking for stolen antiquities?" Without giving him a chance to answer, I continued shooting rapid-fire questions. "Who are you working for?" Disgust crossed my face as something else occurred to me. "You're not working for some kind of collector, are you?" I would have broken off even a friendly acquaintance if that was the case. My feelings on the matter went quite deep.

He looked vaguely amused. "Not unless you consider the British crown a collector."

"Aha!" I crowed. "I knew you were some kind of government agent." I paused. "Wait. Why does the British government want the artifacts?"

"It's less a matter of Britain wanting to own them, and more a matter of trying to avoid an international incident. Egypt is still a country under British protection, and too many of these artifacts are turning up in the hands of private collectors or museums in other countries. If Britain isn't going to have them, they would prefer no one outside Egypt have them, either."

I gave that some thought. "Why are you finally telling me this?"

"It was only a matter of time before you figured it out on your own. Your snooping appears to have no bounds."

I ignored the dig. "Why all the secrecy?"

"It's often safer for certain factions of the government to claim more . . . everyday jobs as their chosen profession."

"Hmm." I pursed my lips as I considered him. I knew he wasn't giving me the full story yet, but I was gratified that my initial assessment of Redvers was correct—he was not the type of man content to shuffle paperwork behind a desk.

Redvers gave me a long look. "I think you need to confront your aunt. Find out what she knows."

I put my coffee down and sighed. "That's what I was afraid of."

Chapter Thirty-one

I made a concerted effort to find my aunt, but there wasn't any trace of her. I felt a tiny prickle of relief that the awkward conversation I needed to have with Millie would be postponed. For the moment, at least. I would have to confront her sooner rather than later.

After a full circuit of the hotel, I returned to the breakfast room, where I found Charlie and Deanna, instead.

"Join us!" Charlie waved me to an empty chair, and I sank into it, grateful to have found some friendly faces.

"Jane, have you been to the Cairo market yet?" Deanna asked.

"I haven't had the chance."

"You must go with me this morning. I want to pick up a few more souvenirs for our friends back home."

"She really is a killer in those markets." Charlie gazed at Deanna with a fond smile. "She can haggle them down to practically nothing." Deanna waved a dismissive hand, but smiled just the same. I paused at Charlie's use of words, but shook it off just as quickly.

"That sounds lovely. I haven't even thought about taking anything home yet." I wanted to pick up a few trinkets for my father, and since both Millie and Inspector Hamadi seemed to be occupied elsewhere, I assured myself there was no harm in taking a quick trip into town.

"You'll love it. You can find anything there." Deanna smothered a yawn and waved down a waiter.

I smiled at her. "Late night?"

She grinned. "Every night is a late night."

"You may as well bring us another pot." Deanna lifted the now-empty silver carafe and passed it to the waiter who had answered her beckon. "And another cup for our friend here."

"Aren't you eating?" I realized Deanna had nothing in front of her, and Charlie was working his way through a full plate.

Deanna grimaced. "Oh, no. I never eat before early afternoon. The thought makes my stomach turn. A cup of coffee always sets me up." She pulled a slim silver cigarette case from her bag and waved it a bit. "Do you mind?"

"Not at all." I had never picked up the habit, but I didn't mind others indulging, as long as there was enough air circulating.

Deanna lit her cigarette and gave it a draw. "And how was the rest of your night?" She gave me a sly grin as Charlie rolled his eyes.

I gave a quick shake of my head, and Deanna's eyes narrowed as she studied me for a long moment. I shifted uncomfortably. I didn't want to discuss what had happened between Redvers and me after the party.

"Well, he sure is something. If it wasn't for my Charlie, I might give you a run for your money."

Charlie rolled his eyes again and grinned good-naturedly. I could tell he wasn't in the least bit concerned.

Deanna waved her cigarette at me. "I'm just kidding, of course. And I know Mr. Redvers isn't yours." She grinned slyly. "So you've said. But you haven't seen the way he looks at you."

My eyes widened as I searched for some way to respond.

Charlie took pity on me and changed the subject. "I hear someone bumped off Samara last night." That was all it took for a quick turn in conversation and we fell into a lengthy discussion of how Samara had met his demise.

After they finished their breakfast, Charlie ambled off and Deanna and I headed toward the sleek convertible the pair had rented for their stay. It seemed such an extravagance that my eyebrows nearly popped up at the sight, but I managed to keep my face neutral as I settled into the passenger seat. The top was down, and I wished for a head scarf—my hair would be a mess once we reached downtown.

"I'll try to take it easy on you." Deanna shot me a sideways look. "With the roads here being what they are, we can't go that fast, anyway."

Deanna seemed at home in a fast car, but she was true to her word and kept her speed to a minimum. It seemed impossible to do otherwise, as we spent the entire drive dodging bicycles, camels, horses, the odd man on foot, large potholes, and donkey-pulled carts heavily laden with crops. After a particularly close call, I found my hand gripping the door and forced it to relax. Deanna was proving a very competent driver.

We found an open space along one of the wide boulevards and Deanna nimbly pulled our car in. A young boy on the sidewalk stared longingly at the shiny black finish, and Deanna offered him a few shillings to keep an eye on it for us. She handed him several coins, which quickly disappeared into his brown robe, and showed him a few more.

"You'll get the rest when we come back and our car is still here, all right?"

He nodded eagerly and hopped onto the hood, crossing his arms and steeling his nut-brown face into a glare. Deanna and I shared a smile and set off.

Soon the wide boulevards gave way to narrow streets crowded with natives and tourists alike. Deanna appeared to know precisely where she was going, and I struggled to keep up with her long legs as she moved easily through the crowd.

The crush of bodies increased the closer we came to the market. Vendors pushed brightly colored cloths and gold pitchers at us, calling out practiced phrases as we passed. "Here, pretty lady, good price" was a popular cry. A multitude of scents wafted through—cooking and animals, perfumes and unwashed bodies—all mingled together. I appreciated when we passed the vendors selling spices in large barrels, the bright colors and pleasant aromas overwhelming everything else. We passed a small storefront selling fruit, the sidewalk overwhelmed by precariously stacked oranges and barrels of dates, crates full of bananas crowded next to fruits I couldn't identify. The hat maker shop sat directly next door, round metal stands steaming as a worker deftly pressed the felt into circles. Red seemed to be the most popular choice for the tarbooshes, but there were other colors as well, pinks and blues and browns. Rickety wooden overhangs provided some shade to the shoppers perusing the goods that spilled from dark and narrow shops. The scene seemed to extend for miles.

"What is it you're looking for, Deanna?" I raised my voice above the storekeepers calling out their wares. The noise was deafening, and it was difficult to ignore the aggressive sales tactics.

Deanna somehow managed to breeze through it all, and I realized the hawkers were not pressing her nearly as hard as the other tourists. I wondered if they recognized her from other trips.

"A few more bracelets and things for my act. They have the most beautiful pieces here, if you know where to look." She gave an ominous look to a man aggressively waving a galabieh and he backed off to the shade of his store.

"You're quite good at that." I would have to practice my own cutting glare.

"I've been here a few times." She gave an easy shrug. "Whenever Charlie does well at the tables, I get a cut so I can come shopping. It's part of our deal."

We had started walking again, and I stuck close to her side. The calls were redoubled, but less items were pushed under my nose.

"Has he always been good at cards?" I didn't know how else to ask about Charlie's seemingly excellent luck at the tables.

Deanna paused and studied my face for a moment. She nodded once as though she had come to a conclusion about me. "He has a gift with sleight of hand. It's why we generally try to keep quiet about what we do back home. It keeps people from putting it together."

So my assumption that Charlie was working the tables with a magician's touch was correct. I found I wasn't nearly as outraged as I thought I might be. Although I did think it would be dangerous for them if they were found out.

"How does he keep from being caught?"

"He makes sure to lose every now and again. We were run out of town a few times, before he figured out a system that works. It's how we can afford this trip, honestly." She stopped to look at a few linens, and the crowd changed paths to flow around us instead of with us.

"Did he know Amon Samara well?" I asked.

Deanna paused and gave the question some thought. "I don't have a lot of girlfriends, Jane. It's hard to trust people."

I nodded. I generally found the same to be true.

"But I trust you." She dropped her voice and I leaned in to hear her over the busy street. "Amon approached Charlie with this wild scheme. He wanted Charlie to partner with him on running the tables. Charlie just laughed at him. Why would Charlie partner with someone and split the winnings when he was doing just fine on his own?"

"Why would Samara even ask? That's a strange proposition."

"It seemed Mr. Samara was angry that Charlie was sweeping the winnings every night. Whatever deal Samara had going on at the tables, Charlie was ruining it for him." She shook her head at the shopkeeper who had been hovering nearby and we moved on. "My guess is Samara's 'offer' was more of a threat, and Charlie didn't want me to worry."

"Oh, dear." I could easily see the implications. Charlie had a motive.

Deanna tugged at her earlobe. "Exactly. I'm worried that Charlie will be arrested if it gets out about Amon's 'offer.' He's already been questioned a few times by that terrible inspector."

My mouth twisted, and she gave a laugh. "I can see you're a fan of his as well."

"Let's just say, we'll never be the best of friends," I said.

Deanna smiled, but it quickly faded. She turned to me, eyes earnest. "Charlie didn't kill anyone. He really didn't have any reason to. Like I said, we've been doing just fine. And Samara was mad, but so what? People have been mad at us before."

I reached out and gave her hand a squeeze. Her face relaxed and we continued on.

I figured this was as good a time as any to ask whether Charlie knew Anna as well. "Did the police question you about Anna Stainton's death?"

"They talked to both of us. I guess they saw someone that night with Anna that looked a bit like my Charlie." She laughed. "But he worked the tables that night while I watched, and then we went to bed." She wiggled her eyebrows. "It's our honeymoon, you remember."

I smiled back at her, relieved that they both had an alibi for the night, even if it was only one another. As Deanna said,

I didn't have many girlfriends. It was nice to think I might have found one.

We pressed on, Deanna finally settling on some large and intricate earrings, as well as a bagful of bangles and gold bracelets. "The audiences back home love the Orient," she said. "I try to look as exotic as I can."

"I'm not sure how you pull it off with that blond hair of yours."

Deanna laughed and ran a hand over her long braid. "I manage to make it work."

We passed several stalls selling local clothing, but Deanna shook her head at each one, finally giving her approval at a tiny stall tucked between two spice merchants down a narrow side street. The quality was a step above the others we had seen, and I wondered how Deanna knew about the place. The shopkeeper obviously recognized her, so she was able to negotiate a good deal for me. I purchased several galabiehs, one in a midnight blue and another in a cherry red, deciding they would make comfortable robes back home. I also bought a men's version in a neutral tan for my father. I wasn't sure he would ever wear it, but he would appreciate the authenticity. I decided I would also pick up a tarboosh for him.

We stopped at several more stalls, but I found myself tiring, the noise and sales pressure overwhelming my senses. I said as much to Deanna, and she admitted that a drink and a cigarette would set her up nicely. We escaped the main thoroughfare, chasing down several alleys, before stumbling on a small café. We settled ourselves in at a tiny table on the sidewalk and chatted while we enjoyed the shade and some cooling drinks.

The rest of the afternoon passed in a blur. I purchased the red tarboosh and an ornate wooden box. Beyond that, I was content to follow Deanna and watch her negotiate prices with sellers. She could give classes on the art of haggling, and the shopkeepers seemed to realize immediately that Deanna was not going to be an easy-spending customer.

I couldn't remember the last time I had so thoroughly enjoyed the company of someone close to my own age, and I hoped Deanna was sincere when she said we would keep in touch. Especially since I felt fairly certain neither she nor her husband was a cold-blooded killer.

CHAPTER THIRTY-TWO

The following morning, I began the hunt for my elusive aunt Millie right after breakfast. I circumnavigated the hotel several times, stopping just short of tromping out over the eighteen holes of the golf course. She was most likely there, but I was unwilling to fight both the heat and the small projectiles. I could only manage one or the other at a time.

I finally managed to track her down just before lunch. Millie was at a table in the dining room, but Lillian and a sulking Marie accompanied her. I didn't ask, but if I had to make a wager, I would guess Marie's sour face was due to the number of gentlemen that had danced with Lillian during the party. A quick glance at Lillian confirmed that she was blissfully unaware of any trouble she had caused.

Knowing what I needed to ask my aunt, I didn't even approach the table. I doubted I could sit quietly through the luncheon small talk, so I asked to be seated at a small table out of their line of sight. I would try my hand again, either at afternoon tea or dinner.

I needed to find Millie alone.

I was also keeping an eye out for Inspector Hamadi. He hadn't checked in on me lately, and I was expecting another interrogation, even though he was occupied with the latest murder. I had one thing working in my favor with the police:

I had stolen the incriminating paperwork, and without it, they wouldn't know I had a motive for killing Amon.

Unless Redvers sold me down the river. My stomach dropped at the thought. If Hamadi came after me for Samara's murder, it would be reasonable to assume Redvers had done just that. I closed my eyes and hoped he liked me well enough to keep me from the noose.

It was teatime when I managed to find my aunt Millie unaccompanied. The girls had returned to the golf course, and Millie was relaxing on the terrace when I approached her. The afternoon sun had already turned the temperature up to somewhere around baking.

"Should Lillian be out in this heat?" I wouldn't ordinarily use the word "fragile" when referring to Lillian, but her illness had taken a toll. She looked better during the party, but it was hard to say whether that was the alcohol or a sign of actual improvement. I was relatively healthy, and the heat knocked me down on a nearly daily basis.

"She's doing much better, and she spent nearly all of yesterday resting," Millie said. "It was most likely something she ate. And I think it would take the entire British Army to keep her off the course any longer. Besides, Marie is with her, and she's only doing nine holes this afternoon."

Something had clicked together for me when I found the birth certificate and now I blurted it out.

"Is Lillian your daughter, Millie?"

Millie carefully set her cup down and glanced at me before fixing her gaze on something in the distance. I was certain she wasn't actually looking at anything.

"Why would you ask that?" Millie's voice was quiet.

I sighed. "I found some papers in Amon's room. One of them was a birth certificate, and it listed you as the mother of a baby girl. Given how attached you've become to Lillian, I just thought . . ." I trailed off at the sheen of tears in her eyes.

Millie blinked them back and cleared her throat. I had never seen her cry before, and it was unsettling to see it now.

"It's rather a long story, Jane. And I'm afraid I'm going to need something stronger than tea in order to tell it."

I nodded and waited quietly while she flagged down a waiter. She ordered a double whiskey, neat, rather than her usual cocktail. I poured myself a cup of tea from the now-abandoned pot. As a mere spectator, I didn't need anything nearly as strong.

We sat with our own thoughts until the waiter returned with Millie's drink. She cleared her throat again.

"You know your uncle Nigel and I were happy." Millie finally looked at me and I nodded. "But he was also absent quite often for his job. With the treasury, you know. We took a long trip to England one year, and I hoped the travel would allow us to spend time together, rekindle our marriage. Instead, I found myself alone in a foreign country."

Millie took a long drink of her whiskey. It would have left me sputtering, but she didn't even blink.

"Nigel spent long hours in meetings and I was left in the care of Lord Hughes. He was also lonely, since his wife was ill and rarely left her bedroom. One thing led to another, and before long, I found myself with child. I've never been the . . . smallest of women, so I was able to hide the pregnancy for some months. By the time it became necessary for me to remove myself from society, I begged your uncle for a few months by myself in the country. I told him that I wanted to spend time with your mother's family. Frankly, he was so distracted with his work he was happy to let me go. The hospital where Lillian was born is near where your mother grew up in the North of England. In fact, your mother helped arrange things for me via telegram. She never told your father, as far as I know, or anyone else. So, I retreated to the countryside where I had Lillian." Here her eyes welled up once more, and she took another healthy drink and got herself under control.

My heart went out to her. She must have felt so alone.

"Such a beautiful baby, Lillian was. But I couldn't keep her."

I didn't want to interrupt my aunt and risk breaking the spell that had her speaking so candidly, but here I couldn't help myself. "But why not? Couldn't you have pretended she was Nigel's?"

"Your uncle and I couldn't have children, Jane." Her mouth twisted. "Obviously, the problem was his and not mine, although everyone assumed it was my fault. For years, society heaped pity and blame on me, and I couldn't say a thing. There was no way for me to admit that I knew the shortcomings were Nigel's and not my own."

She finished her drink as I considered the unfairness of Millie's situation. I knew firsthand how thoughtless and cruel society could be without even trying—to my knowledge, no one knew of Grant's particular cruelties, but the speculation and whispers about our constant turnover in female servants was enough to keep me from returning to any parlor rooms. I simply hadn't found the society worth the trouble. Yet, Millie had faced the gossips down and suffered at their hands for years. In silence.

I waited, but she was quiet, gazing at the few stray drops in her glass. "So, what happened to Lillian?" I finally asked.

"Her father adopted her. We made private arrangements. His wife was too ill to carry a child, and adopting a baby, well, it managed to withdraw her from her rooms. They were able to salvage what was left of their marriage with Lillian's arrival. And Lillian and her father are quite close. They share a love of sports and the outdoors."

I nodded and felt unbearably sad on Millie's behalf. Millie was never able to see Lillian grow and mature. To salvage her own marriage, Millie had to sacrifice her only child.

I was beginning to understand why Millie drank so much and so often.

"Lillian's father sent me updates over the years. I burned the letters, but I kept the few photos. I was able to pass them off as the child of an old friend. Not that Nigel ever asked, but I had an answer ready, just in case."

"Does Lillian know she's adopted?"

"No. She believes that her mother and father are her natural parents." Millie's mouth twisted bitterly, and she flagged down a waiter for another whiskey. Once her order was placed, she continued. "I'll only ever be an 'aunt' to her. I suppose I should be grateful to have even that."

"How did she end up here with you?"

"Once I knew we would be traveling to Egypt, I made arrangements with Lord Hughes to have Lillian meet us here. Her 'mother' passed away last year, and we felt it was now safe for us to meet."

I considered how difficult it must be for Millie to refer to Lady Hughes as Lillian's mother, and my heart pinched. But another puzzle piece fell into place and spurred my mouth into action.

"Is that why you insisted we stay at the Mena House?"

"Very good, Jane. I knew Lillian would be difficult to convince—unless there was a golf course available. She takes her training quite seriously."

We were quiet for a time, Millie's eyes tracing the sea of palms and eucalyptus trees lining the edge of the terrace, lost in her thoughts about the past. I was attempting to digest everything she had just told me. But I did have more questions I needed answered. I waited until Millie had her next whiskey in hand.

"So, how long has Mr. Samara been blackmailing you?"

Millie raised one eyebrow. "I was being blackmailed, but it had nothing to do with Mr. Samara."

"What?" I was genuinely surprised at her answer.

"The letters started about a year ago. Each one demanded

that I wire money to an overseas account. But the letters were in a woman's hand, Jane."

"Could it have been a man with a woman's handwriting? Do you think they were from someone you know?" I asked. "How would they have found out about your daughter in the first place?"

Millie pursed her lips at my barrage of questions. "I'm fairly confident it was a woman, Jane. There was also something in the language that made me think that, although I can't quite put my finger on what. I remember being surprised that it was a woman." Millie paused. "And to answer your other question, Lord Hughes is a member of the aristocracy and quite wealthy. I suspect my blackmailer was looking to lighten the lord's wallet, and stumbled across Lillian's adoption. His name wasn't on the birth certificate, so the blackmailer did some research and decided to use it against me, instead." Millie frowned. "I do think the blackmailer is here at the hotel."

"What makes you say that?"

"Because the last note came on Mena House stationery and demanded that I leave money for them here on the grounds."

A lot had been happening while I was occupied with Anna's murder, apparently.

"And did you?"

"No. I have Lillian here, and there is no one to hurt with the truth anymore. Except my social position back home, and I have to say that that is seeming less and less important."

I raised my eyebrows. That was the last thing I ever expected to hear from the socially conscious Millie.

"Nigel passed, and Lord Hughes's wife is gone as well. The only one who might be upset is Lillian. And I decided before we arrived that I would no longer make payments to someone who would stoop to blackmail for their financial gain."

My mind was spinning, trying to churn out the appropriate questions to fit the remaining pieces together.

"So, if Mr. Samara isn't the blackmailer, why were you glaring at him? I asked if you knew him, and you never answered me."

Millie speared me with a look. "Jane, I simply don't care for his type. Mr. Samara is the slippery type of man who preys on women my age and bleeds them of their money. Every time I saw that vile man, he was cozied up to some middle-aged woman who was swooning over him. Remember Ethel Brennan?"

I nodded. There had been a hushed-up scandal back home in Boston, and Ethel had fled the city to live with relatives in upstate New York.

"What do you think happened to her? A man just like that—young, handsome, and after her money. He drained her bank account, and she left the city in absolute disgrace."

You had to hand it to Millie. She certainly had Samara pegged.

But that didn't answer the question of who the blackmailer was. Millie seemed quite certain that Samara wasn't responsible, yet I found the pages in his room. But I also recalled how poorly those papers were hidden and how easy it was to break in. Perhaps they weren't his papers, after all. Could someone have been setting him up?

The pieces weren't fitting together.

I needed to find out what the police had found in Amon's room after his death. But I had one more thing to discuss with Millie.

"I took the birth certificate from Mr. Samara's room, but there was a list of payments with it."

"You *took* it? Since when are you prowling around strange men's rooms taking things?"

I sighed. She was missing the point. "I took it so that you wouldn't be implicated in his murder. I was trying to protect you." I puffed another breath out. I had only done half a job there—I should have taken the payment list as well. "Your initials were on that list of payments. The police may have reason to believe that both you and I wanted Mr. Samara dead."

Millie's eyes closed tightly, as though she could squeeze out the information I was giving her. We sat in silence for several minutes.

I would have more questions once I had a chance to process everything, but I decided to let things alone for the time being. This had obviously been difficult enough for her. I wanted to offer Millie my sympathy, but I wasn't sure how to bridge the gap that stood between my aunt and everyone else.

"Millie, I'm very—"

She stopped me with a raised hand before I could manage anything more. "Thank you, Jane. I appreciate that. But if you wouldn't mind, I would like to be alone for a bit."

I nodded and stood, resting my hand on her shoulder for a moment as I passed by. Millie was a hard woman to get close to under the best of circumstances, and I didn't have the slightest idea how to extend myself to her now.

CHAPTER THIRTY-THREE

As soon as my feet crossed from the terrace into the hotel, Redvers appeared at my side.

"That was fast. Were you lurking in a potted palm?"

"What did your aunt have to say?"

I wasn't sure how much of the story I was prepared to give him at the moment. I still needed to process it for myself, and I told him as much.

"Can I just give you the highlights and fill you in later? It's a lot to take in."

He nodded, and I gave him the basics of Lillian's origin.

"But Millie doesn't think Samara was the blackmailer. She believes it was a woman—she seemed quite certain of it."

"Well, that definitely casts a different light on things." Redvers looked thoughtful.

"It certainly does. Do you think we might have underestimated Anna? Or misjudged why she was killed? I can't think of many other women here at the hotel that would have been involved in a blackmailing scheme."

Redvers opened his mouth, but I was on a roll with new theories.

"Is it possible Anna and Samara were in on the blackmail together? That would explain why he had the papers, but they were in her handwriting." I recalled how Amon had said they were in love—perhaps they were partners in more than simply a romantic sense. I liked this new theory and excitement bubbled in my veins. "What we really need is a sample of her handwriting."

Anna's room had most likely been emptied by now, so it was another request I would have to make of the colonel. I hated to bother him again—he had been so upset at the mere mention of her name. I wondered if there was a more discreet way for me to get what we needed. One that didn't involve either the colonel or the police.

"We still don't know what she wanted with Amon's cuff links. Or what the gambling connection might be—although I don't think Charlie is involved." My thoughts were flicking back and forth faster than a hummingbird's wings. "We also need to figure out who was being blackmailed for the smuggling. I'm afraid I haven't even thought about who that might be—they would have motive as well. For both murders, possibly?"

Redvers didn't say anything, his attention directed toward inspecting something on the ceiling, letting me run myself out. I barely paused to notice.

"I wouldn't have thought Anna capable of such a grand scheme. I guess it's my lesson in not judging a book by its cover—or a flapper by her clothing." I remembered we didn't have the original documents for comparison—I had left them behind. "Do you know what the police found in Samara's room?"

"I didn't ask what they found during their search, no."

"Could you find out? We need to know if they have those papers that I found." I knew Redvers would have to take care of that bit. There was no way Inspector Hamadi would tell me anything, even if I *was* inclined to strike up a conversation with the man.

"I almost forgot to tell you," Redvers said. "The police found the gun in one of the pool changing rooms. It looks as though it was wiped clean and left under a seat cushion. Almost impossible to trace who might have left it there."

"That area sees a lot of people at all hours of the day." I sighed. "You're right. It would be tough to pinpoint who might have placed it there and when."

Redvers nodded again and placed a gentle hand on my arm. "Are you all right? This has been a lot for you to take in, I'm sure."

"Thank you. That's kind of you. But it's Millie I'm concerned about."

He hesitated, then withdrew his hand, and we went our separate ways. Redvers planned to track down Inspector Hamadi. He was hopeful that the inspector was still on the grounds so he could avoid another trip into town. I wished him luck and silently hoped I wouldn't find the inspector myself.

I thought about where I might find a bit of Anna's handwriting. I was quite taken with the idea that she was the original blackmailer, but I needed a way to prove it without disturbing the colonel. If Anna was the blackmailer, and Amon was involved, it could give us an entirely new pool of suspects that didn't include Millie or myself. And perhaps we could smoke out a killer that much sooner.

I decided to talk to Zaki. Perhaps there was a request for the kitchen or a gambling slip or a hotel register—anything she might have written for the staff that might still be lying around. I hunted around the saloon and dining room, finally locating Zaki in the kitchen. His back was to me and I loitered awkwardly outside the door, waiting for someone to notice me. A member of the kitchen staff finally saw me, and muttered something guttural to Zaki. He turned and, with a smile, joined me in the hallway.

"I'm so sorry to interrupt you, Zaki."

"It is no problem, Mrs. Wunderly. You come to find me, so it must be important. What can I help you with?"

"Well, I was wondering if there were any hotel records that might have Miss Stainton's handwriting on them. I know it seems like an odd request, but . . ."

"If it is something you need, then it is not odd, miss." He stopped to think. "But sadly, I cannot think of anything that she might have written. You have asked the police for her things?"

"I would rather avoid speaking with the police if I can. And I don't want to bother her father." I bit my lip as he nodded sympathetically. "Is there a hotel register? Or perhaps she sent down a request to the kitchen that is filed away?"

Zaki nodded again. "You are a kind woman. I do not think we have any of these things, but I will ask some of my fellow workers and see if I can find an answer for you."

I smiled gratefully. "Thank you so much, Zaki. I truly appreciate it."

If Zaki came up empty, I would have to get some piece of writing—a letter or postcard, maybe—from the colonel. And when it came down to it, I would rather break into his room than mention Anna to him again. I also didn't want to explain why I needed something with his daughter's handwriting. If she was indeed a blackmailer, the colonel didn't need to know—he should be allowed to keep his fond memories of his child intact.

I walked slowly out to the terrace, going over the information in my mind. I took a seat in the shade, removed my wilting hat, and wiped my forehead with the back of my hand. When a waiter came by, I absently ordered a drink of cold hibiscus juice with a side of water. A pitcher of it.

By the time Redvers returned from his information gathering, I had yet to come up with a better plan for retrieving Anna's handwriting sample, despite the several hours I spent looking for an alternative. Breaking into yet another room seemed excessive, but it was looking more and more like the best course of action.

"The police did not find any suspicious papers in Samara's room," Redvers reported. "Unless you count a British passport as suspicious. One with the name Duke Herring right next to Samara's picture."

I gave a bark of laughter. "Duke Herring." My grin faded as I thought about the implications. "Was there an Egyptian passport as well?"

Redvers shook his head. "There was only the one."

"He was lying about both his name and his heritage. Well, that's no surprise, I suppose. It also explains why Anna hid those cuff links. She probably discovered his real name and was planning to use them as blackmail. Which means it's unlikely they were ever romantically involved."

I tapped my lip in thought, then stopped when I saw Redvers watching the movement.

"It looks more and more like Anna is our blackmailer."

Redvers nodded, his eyes still on my lips.

I covered my mouth for a moment and his eyes snapped up to mine.

"Someone must have removed the papers between the time I found them and when the police went through Samara's room."

"It stands to reason," he agreed.

Which meant that while we didn't know where they were, neither did the police. Without the blackmail link, the police had no reason to connect Millie and me with Samara's death. "So Millie and I aren't currently suspects." I couldn't figure out why someone would plant the papers on Amon and then remove them, but at least my aunt and I were in the clear. For the time being.

"Not at this point." A twinkle lit Redvers' eyes. "Although knowing you, I'm sure you can find a way to make their list again."

I made a face at him.

"Well, that should make Millie feel a bit better at least," I said.

"Do you remember what you saw on that inventory list for the dig? Would you be able to tell which piece was missing?"

I thought back to the list I had seen. "I'm fairly confident that I remember. Why?"

"I think we should pay a visit to the Museum of Cairo tomorrow. There's someone we should talk to about the missing piece."

I wanted to squeal with excitement, but managed to restrain myself. "Excellent."

Redvers' mouth curled into a small smile, and I knew I hadn't fooled him. The famous museum was high on my list of places to visit. I was beyond excited to view their exhibits—regardless of the reason for our visit. I promised myself time after our interview to look around.

"Do you think the statue has something to do with the murders?" I asked after a moment.

Redvers shook his head. "It's hard to say. But the artifact paperwork was found with the rest, and I think we should explore all avenues."

By the time we finished our discussion, the sun was creeping toward the horizon, so Redvers and I headed to dinner. Zaki was back at his post and seated us in a rather isolated area of the dining room, making me wonder if he thought he was encouraging a bit of romance. But I was soon grateful, as my aunt Millie stumbled over to our table and made herself quite at home.

"I'll have a whiskey."

Millie's first words to the waiter left Redvers and me regarding each other with alarm. The last thing my aunt needed was another drink. It was clear that in the time since

I left Millie on the terrace, she had continued to drown her memories in neat whiskey. Frankly, I was shocked she was still upright. While Millie's attention was elsewhere, I motioned to the waiter that she was finished, and he nodded before quickly moving away. Smart man. I knew there would be a scene once Millie realized she wasn't getting another whiskey, but I hoped to pour water into her in the meantime.

Moments later, Millie's face twisted into a familiar smirk and I mentally tried to prepare myself for whatever came next.

"Well, Jane, now you know all my secrets." Her words slurred slightly, but not enough to mask the venom in them. "But I'll bet your little friend here doesn't know yours. And maybe he should." I closed my eyes and willed her to silence, but Millie was on a roll. "Our Jane here married my dear nephew for his money. She never loved him, and she was glad when he died. Weren't you, Jane? I'll bet you've been celebrating ever since you got that telegram." Her bitter smile was triumphant, her eyes glassy.

Hot shame and anger rolled through me in equal measures. I could hear the blood pounding in my ears and my vision blurred as my eyes suddenly welled. I stood, managing to push my chair back without knocking it over. Ordinarily, I might be able to brush Millie's words off, but with everything that had happened in the last week, my nerves were too raw to withstand her attack. I fled the room, moving as quickly as I could without actually running. There were equal parts truth and fiction in what she said, and painful memories churned my stomach.

I headed up several flights of stairs, and off a small common room found an empty terrace overlooking the now-familiar view. I greedily drank in the cool air as I gathered myself together. With my heart pounding, the last thing I wanted was to close myself up in my room. I needed to feel open spaces while I got my emotions under control. I spent some time concentrating on my breathing, and let my thoughts float. That proved to be dangerous as my thoughts floated back to my difficult marriage; instead, I focused my thoughts on my breathing. In and out.

"I thought I might find you out here." His low voice carried smoothly across the distance between us.

I turned halfway toward him, momentarily giving up my view of the pyramids glowing a soft gold in the moonlight.

"Yes, well." Articulate as ever.

Redvers moved forward to lean against the railing. He seemed patiently prepared to wait me out, as silent and steady as the grand monuments he appeared to be considering. The sounds of dinner floated up from below, clanking knives against china and glass, and I propped my elbows on the cool marble railing, hunching into myself.

"Millie is in rare form tonight." I closed my eyes.

"Some of the staff have assisted her back to her rooms." Redvers was still looking into the distance. "She wasn't ready to go, but I convinced her."

"Thank you." I was relieved. She was my responsibility, but the last thing I wanted was to endure another scene this evening.

"Why do you stay with her?" Redvers' voice was gentle, and I was grateful that he was skirting around the bomb Millie had dropped in our midst.

"She's family," I said simply. "And family is complicated."

Redvers grunted in assent, and I wondered briefly if he knew that firsthand. He had never spoken of his family, except in passing.

"I want to make excuses for her because of what she's been through, but that isn't right, either." I sighed. "She's not always so terrible—only when she drinks."

He made a noise that sounded suspiciously like a snort.

"Yes, well, I see your point," I conceded with a small smile. "Millie can be kind at times. She's paying for this trip for me." I paused, gathering my thoughts. "My father . . . Well, he and I look after her. We are all she has left." I gave a little laugh. "Although, I suppose that isn't strictly true anymore, now that we know about Lillian."

I was quiet for a while, trying to decide how much I should tell Redvers, how much of my past I was willing to expose. "Grant was Millie's nephew on her husband's side." I continued gazing out over the view.

"You don't have to explain if you don't want to." Redvers turned and I could feel him watching me. His voice was a soft rumble.

I blew out a breath of air and gave him a weak smile before turning back to the moonlit scene. "It's fine. I was very young—not even twenty—when I met Grant and I did think that I loved him. He was very charming. It turns out he had everyone fooled—neither Millie nor her husband ever knew the truth about their beloved nephew." I could hear my voice sour on the word "beloved." "Millie still has no idea."

My stomach rolled again with shame and I took a moment before continuing. "Grant Stanley delighted in inflicting pain. He was sometimes harsh with his horses, but that was the only thing I noticed before we were married. I learned quickly, though, just how much he enjoyed pain. I believe it was the only thing he got any real pleasure from." I blew out another puff of air and continued quickly, before I could change my mind. "And the more I struggled, the more he enjoyed himself."

Redvers' jaw hardened until it could easily cut glass, but I continued.

"I know it's not the type of thing that is talked about in polite society, but there it is. We were married less than a year before he left for the war." I shivered, Grant's cruel laughter echoing in my mind. My hand drifted for a moment to my lower back and I wondered if there would ever come a day

3

3

when his voice was silenced. I screwed my eyes up tight instead, a child avoiding monsters in the dark.

"She's right about one thing. I was glad he didn't return. That's why I refused his family inheritance. I only accepted the pension from the War Department, which gives me enough to live on. I didn't marry him for his money."

"I would never have thought you did." Redvers' voice was quiet. "And I'm sorry that you were married to a monster." He reached out and gently turned me to face him.

I opened my eyes, and hesitatingly raised them to meet his. I expected to read disgust or pity on his face, but there was neither. All I found was understanding. I dropped my eyes to address his chest. "I'm sure there are plenty of men who would disagree with you. Even with the war behind us and a new age coming, women aren't much more than property in a marriage."

"Any man—or woman—who believes that is a fool." The hard consonants of his crisp accent had hardened with anger until they were tiny daggers. I was relieved I wasn't on the cutting end of those blades.

Without another word, Redvers pulled a handkerchief from his jacket. He gently wiped tears from my cheeks—tears that had been rolling free without my knowing. With that done, he gathered me against his broad chest. I wrapped my arms around him and pressed my face into his solid warmth, grateful for his presence as he simply held me. For the first time in a long while, I felt at peace.

Chapter Thrity-four

The following morning, Redvers and I breakfasted early. There was no mention of the night before, either what transpired on the terrace, or how I retired early without eating. Instead, we finished our meal and hopped onto the electric tram with a few other guests. The eight-mile ride into Cairo proper passed peacefully, the gently rocking tram car much less harrowing than my trip via convertible with Deanna. The tram even deposited us near our destination.

We walked companionably the few blocks to the Egyptian Museum, located on the tree-lined Maidan Qasr el-Nil Square, a mere stone's throw from the Nile itself. Redvers had made arrangements to meet the current curator of Egyptian antiquities, Reginald Engelbach—Rex to his friends.

"I suppose I shouldn't be surprised that the curator is a Brit, and yet I am."

Redvers caught the somewhat mournful tone of my voice and raised an eyebrow. He could communicate a lot with an eyebrow.

"I know. What should I expect with the occupation, right?" I sighed again.

We came upon the building, glowing salmon-pink in the morning light. Two symmetrical wings spread out on either side of the large arched entrance, nestled beneath a large dome—also pink. I wondered what type of stone the building was made of to achieve the striking color.

As we passed a large stone fountain, Redvers caught sight of Engelbach waiting for us at the top of the wide steps leading to the main entrance. The man came dashing down to greet us.

"Good morning." Engelbach enthusiastically pumped Redvers' hand and then mine. "I'm so glad you could come down."

I raised my eyebrows in amusement, since it was Engelbach who was actually doing us the favor. The man's fair hair wisped across his forehead and his snapping blue eyes seemed to take in everything. His tweed suit was fine, but outdated, and I sensed his mind was occupied with more important matters than keeping up with the latest in fashion.

We entered the museum and I paused for a moment to take it in. Large galleries stretched before us and to either side. The ceilings vaulted overhead, a series of large arches stretching across the second floor above us, giving a sense of movement along the marble balconies.

Engelbach led us back to his office, and along the way, I tried to take in as much as I could. We breezed past papyrus artifacts, stone statues, and ancient coins, all with small handwritten signs tucked behind glass. A dozen times or more I felt the overwhelming urge to stop when something caught my interest, but I reminded myself that I would have plenty of time to look once we were finished with Engelbach. Perhaps I could even convince Redvers to give me a proper tour.

We headed down a windowless hallway with a series of doors on either side, which I assumed belonged to Engelbach's cohorts. At the end of the hall, we stopped before a sturdy wooden door, and Engelbach pushed it open to reveal a tiny office that was nearly buried under stacks of paper. The ancient oak filing cabinet beneath the tiny window appeared unused; I would not have been surprised to learn the drawers were completely empty. But the top of the cabinet and all of Engelbach's desk space was covered with untidy stacks, each on the verge of toppling and drowning us beneath unrelenting pages.

"So, what brings you to my dusty corner of the world, Mr. Redvers?" Engelbach asked.

I liked the man immediately for getting straight down to business.

"We're looking for information about a local dig site—one near the Mena House. We're rather hoping you might have its artifact list."

"Ah! Yes. I know I have a copy of that somewhere."

I couldn't hide the doubt on my face, and he smiled at me.

"I know it seems impossible, but I have a system for this chaos." He stood and dug through a stack, seemingly at random. "Here we are. Is this what you're looking for?" Engelbach handed the paper to Redvers, who, without so much as a glance at it, passed it over to me.

I studied the list for a moment. Several of the pieces listed seemed familiar, but I wanted to be sure before I confirmed it for Redvers.

"I'm fairly certain this is it." I glanced at Redvers before returning my attention to the paper.

"Got it in one!" Engelbach smiled widely, and I wondered how a man buried beneath a mountain of paperwork in an airless office could maintain such cheerfulness. I envied him.

I returned to my perusal of the list and found the item that was highlighted on the paper I found in Samara's room. "It was this one." I leaned toward Redvers, pointing at the item. He studied the description before passing it back to Engelbach, indicating the piece.

"I was going to say it's curious you should mention this particular piece, but then, knowing you, Redvers, I suppose nothing should come as a surprise."

Redvers cocked an inquisitive eyebrow and Engelbach continued.

"Someone was in here last week with that very piece in hand, asking what I knew about it," he said.

I could feel excitement igniting in my blood. The idea that we might have yet another piece of the puzzle was intoxicating—a feeling I could easily become addicted to.

"Who might that have been?" Redvers asked.

"Miss Anna Stainton," Engelbach answered without hesitation. "She actually had the piece with her. I recognized it immediately from that dig." He looked at me. "All local archeologists have to register with my office and check in periodically with their findings."

I nodded for him to continue.

"I tried to recover it from her. Unfortunately, I was unsuccessful. She claimed she wanted to learn what the person originally in possession of the statue wanted with it. Then she promised to return with it. For a price, of course." He sighed wistfully. "I should have had security tackle her on the way out, but it seemed improper. I should never have let her leave with it."

I couldn't see Engelbach giving the order to have Anna bodily stopped from leaving, but I felt certain he had done his best to reason with her on behalf of the piece.

"So she took it from someone?" I perched on the edge of the hard wooden chair I had taken a seat in.

"That's certainly what it sounded like. It seems she discovered it in the possession of someone she knew, and was trying to get a read on what that they planned to do with it." Engelbach shook his head. "This is how we lose so many valuable pieces."

I gave him a sympathetic look. As a curator, it must be difficult to watch so much history disappear into the hands of international collectors and museums. Just a few years before the war, archeologists from Germany made off with an incredibly valuable limestone bust of Nefertiti. The current administration was now reluctant to let any German archeologists back into the country because of the loss.

"She didn't mention who that was, by any chance, did she?" A note of hopefulness crept into Redvers' voice.

"I'm afraid not. I wish I knew myself. It was only a small statuary, but even still. Every piece is valuable, and if we can't keep them in Egypt or England, we would at least like to know where they are being carted off to. I'm afraid quite a few pieces have gone missing lately, but it's impossible for my assistant and me to be everywhere at once. There are twenty crooks out there for each one of us working against smuggling. Probably more."

How disheartening. It was like throwing a pebble into the waves, only to have it washed back against your feet.

"As I said, though, it seemed to be someone she knew. That might help narrow the field a bit." Engelbach was quiet for a moment. "I'm afraid Miss Stainton didn't seem to appreciate the piece itself. Only what it might be worth."

"Well, that isn't a surprise," Redvers said.

"And where one piece goes, many more tend to follow." Engelbach's face was pinched. "I'm afraid whoever had the piece is in possession of more than just one. Please keep me posted on what you find out, will you, Redvers?"

Redvers nodded and Engelbach relaxed back in his seat. The two men chatted for a few moments longer, and then we rose to take our leave.

"Have you seen the museum yet, Mrs. Wunderly?" Engelbach asked.

"I have not, but I certainly planned to have Mr. Redvers take me through before we leave."

Engelbach clapped his hands together. "Excellent! I can give you a quick tour myself, although you will probably want to spend some time wandering as well. Just this year, we were able to put Tutankhamun's funerary mask and tomb on display. You must see them!"

Engelbach led us back out to the exhibit area where he proudly pointed out the most important artifacts, many of which he had personally ensured found a home in the national museum. It was staggering to think of the immense wealth before me, and to know that what we saw was a mere fraction of what Howard Carter had found in the young king's tomb. I stood soaking in the display: numerous statues in gold, stone, and ivory; a golden throne with lion's feet; numerous pieces of jewelry, the intricate work in gold and precious stones stunning. And so much more.

We made our way to the most guarded display room. Engelbach was correct, Tutankhamun's funerary mask was stunning. Bright gold alternated with black stripes around the youthful features of the young king, his large eyes dramatically outlined.

"It's twenty-four pounds of solid gold," Engelbach told me in a low voice. I shook my head in wonder.

We finally left Tutankhamun and moved on to other exhibits, where Engelbach expounded on the intense background examinations archeologists underwent to dig any of Egypt's ancient sites. Unfortunately, he explained, even the most honest of men felt their native homes—or their own pockets—deserved at least a few items for their trouble. Egypt was utterly leaking antiquities.

Engelbach left us after the first hour, and it was many hours before I even began to have my fill of the treasures housed there. Redvers seemed content to trail along beside me, discussing the history and the artifacts as we went. He was quite knowledgeable and I could have happily whiled away many more hours in his company there. But when a glance at my watch showed it to be early afternoon, I knew we needed to be heading back. If for no other reason than I was suddenly ravenous.

*   *   *

We stepped back into the warmth of the day and decided we had enough time for a stroll along the Nile to go over what we had learned from Engelbach.

"So, our Miss Stainton had the statue and wanted to know its worth," I said. "Do you think she was going to blackmail someone with the statue, or simply try to sell it for the money?"

"Given what we have learned about Miss Stainton, either scenario seems likely. It's possible that she planned to use it to extort money from someone. Or perhaps she thought it would be a way for her to break into smuggling herself." He sighed. "There's certainly money in the business, dirty as it may be."

"But we still don't know who she was blackmailing," I reminded him.

"That's not altogether true." Redvers gave a small puff of air, and stopped on the promenade, turning to face me. "There is a piece of the puzzle that I haven't given you yet," he said. "I'm here to keep an eye on Colonel Stainton. The British government has suspected for some time that he is smuggling antiquities out of Egypt. He's been loosely connected with a variety of pieces found across Europe."

A variety of emotions warred within me. Anger, certainly, but only a little. I already knew Redvers' story about being a banker was a cover for something else. I also should have suspected Colonel Stainton was Redvers' target all along, but my suspicions about their strange interactions had been pushed to the back of my mind by a variety of things. Like a few murders. And the fact that I had developed a soft spot for the jovial colonel.

The emotion I finally settled on was mild irritation.

"It certainly took you long enough to come clean." I crossed my arms.

"I was under orders not to reveal it to anyone. Besides, you were a suspect."

I rolled my eyes. I didn't believe he had ever seriously considered me a suspect.

"And your aunt might still be," he continued to protest.

I laughed harshly. I hadn't forgiven my aunt for the night before quite yet, and I dreaded seeing her again. If she even remembered her terrible behavior—with the amount of whiskey she'd consumed, it was possible she wouldn't recall what she'd said. "Millie may be many things, but I don't think she's a cold-blooded killer." Even though I had been forced to consider that possibility.

Redvers' revelation left me with more questions. "Does the colonel know you're here to spy on him?"

"I think he suspects me of something. He's been doing his damnedest to avoid me since I arrived."

"I guess he hasn't heard 'to keep his enemies close.'"

A sudden image of Colonel Stainton arguing with a digger at the pyramids flashed before me—was that only a few days ago? It felt like weeks. But that interaction made a lot more sense now.

I considered the other players. "Why would Anna have brought that statue in to the museum if her own father was doing the smuggling? Wouldn't she have known about it already? It seems as though it would be a difficult thing to hide from someone you're traveling with."

"It's hard to say with Anna Stainton. Perhaps she only just discovered her father's role. It's not as though most young women are interested in their father's business dealings."

"I suppose that's true."

"But she was certainly interested in how much money an artifact could bring in." Redvers sounded as disgusted as I felt on that matter.

"So, if the colonel is our smuggler, who's our killer? And

where are these artifacts the colonel is supposed to be smuggling?" I asked.

"I am afraid I haven't gotten those parts sorted out yet."

"Well," I said airily, "please let me know once you do." We started walking again, and as I enjoyed the slight breeze coming off the river, I thought about the colonel. I realized I was secretly hopeful Redvers was wrong about the man. Hadn't he said the colonel was only loosely connected? Perhaps there was another explanation.

"Why would the colonel be involved in smuggling antiquities out of the country in the first place? It can't be for money."

"I'm afraid that is precisely the case. Colonel Stainton lost most of his fortune during the war. It appears he invested poorly with some . . . suspect companies overseas. And he has been using his knowledge of artifacts in an attempt to recoup his losses. He's been dealing with some fairly shady characters."

My hopes were dashed, after all. I felt a sinking sense of disappointment, which I knew was fairly ridiculous, since I had only just met the man. But our shared excitement about the country's historical treasures now left a bitter taste in my mouth.

The disappointment in myself for misjudging his character was even more piercing.

"I'm sorry you had to find out. It's another reason I waited to tell you—I know you are fond of him." Redvers cast me a sideways look.

I gave a small smile and touched his arm in thanks. But I could not excuse anyone stealing historical treasures. And despite my regrets about the man, we had to soldier ahead if we were to clear my name—and Millie's—once and for all.

"I suppose this confirms that Anna is our blackmailer. So I can stop looking for samples of her handwriting." I was pleased I could skip breaking into the colonel's rooms, especially given what I now knew about the man. I planned to stay far from his path. "So, what's our next step?"

"I would suggest we wait and see what comes to us, but I'm guessing that's not something you'll be able to do."

"All signs point to no," I admitted.

Redvers might be content to sit and wait, but I was restless with anticipation of the end. Whatever the end might be.

CHAPTER THIRTY-FIVE

Having missed lunch, we stopped for a late meal in a small café before heading back to the tram. My mind was still buzzing with possibilities, but the rest of my body was tired. As soon as we returned, I headed straight back to my rooms.

After a long day on my feet, a leisurely bath sounded like absolute heaven. I spent nearly an hour luxuriating in cool water scented with the jasmine bath salts. After my bath, I lay down on my bed for just a moment, enjoying the warm breeze drifting through my window.

I awoke an hour later, and realized that the sun had all but disappeared from the sky, and I was late for predinner cocktails.

I dressed for the evening in a hurry; after several minutes, I gave up on mashing my hair back into place, instead adding a wide silver headband. I hoped it would weigh down the whole mess. Or at least distract from it. Falling asleep with damp hair had not been a great strategic move.

I hurried along the halls, the retiring sun casting long shadows in my path. When I finally reached the lounge, I cast my eyes around the clusters of guests enjoying their drinks, looking for a friendly face. I spotted my aunt seated at a small round table with Lillian and Marie. But when our eyes met,

Millie immediately found something fascinating on the table to inspect. I gave my head a little shake and headed for the bar. I wasn't ready to wade into those waters just yet.

Redvers and the doctor were deeply engrossed in conversation, and I joined them once I secured a drink for myself. The doctor politely acknowledged me, and I could almost swear Redvers gave me a quick wink. I blinked back at him.

"I'm sorry to interrupt, gentlemen." I wasn't actually sorry, but my arrival had brought the conversation to an abrupt halt. Dr. Williams gave a polite smile and excused himself.

"Well." I turned my head and watched him leave. "I really am sorry. Did I interrupt anything important?"

"No, we were just discussing horse racing."

"Horse racing. Really." I didn't quite believe him.

"Really. The good doctor may not be using drugs, but he is certainly putting some money on the ponies. I think we'll get to see that firsthand tomorrow." He changed directions before I could ask what he meant. "Have you spoken with your aunt?"

"I'm afraid not. I think she's pretending not to know me."

Redvers grinned. "She won't be able to for long."

I was surprised to realize that I wasn't actually concerned with Millie at the moment, and I wasn't terribly invested in whether or not she brought herself to apologize. She obviously remembered the events of the night before, but Millie was Millie, and there was very little changing her. Things would eventually get back to normal—or at least as normal as things ever were with my headstrong aunt. And after what I had learned about her forfeited daughter, I couldn't find it in my heart to hold her outburst against her.

"Now, what do you mean we'll find out firsthand? Find out about what?"

Redvers' eyes turned mischievous. "I think we both could

use a distraction, and tomorrow offers just the thing. Be sure to wear long sleeves and a sun hat again. We'll head out directly after lunch."

I was completely mystified, but I couldn't get any more of an answer from the man.

The following afternoon found me standing awkwardly in the lobby. I was dressed in long sleeves, slacks, and my largest sun hat, feeling unsure about what the afternoon would bring.

I suffered a sneak attack from behind as Deanna wrapped her arms around me.

"Are you ready, Jane?" Her voice was bubbling with excitement, and Charlie grinned at me, hands stuffed in the pockets of his white linen pants.

"I suppose so. I'm just not sure for what." But a laugh bubbled out of me. Deanna was infectious.

Redvers chose that moment to join us, and Deanna pulled me by the hand out the front entrance of the hotel. We climbed into their rented convertible and Redvers and I settled ourselves into the backseat. Charlie did a bit of a spin out from the parking lot, but was soon driving sedately in the direction of the pyramids. Redvers and I still kept one hand on our hats.

"It's easier to drive this time," Redvers told me.

"Well, I still don't know where we're going." He answered me with a smirk, and I poked his arm.

Streams of people were heading in our direction, tourists and hotel employees alike, many of whom were on horseback or camel. I wondered if anyone would be left in the hotel. It was only minutes before we pulled into a parking lot near the Great Pyramid and walked toward where a large grandstand had been set up.

"Should we sit?" Charlie asked.

"I think it's more exciting to stand along the track."

Deanna led us a little farther past the stands, and positioned our small group so we would have an open view. I could now see the crowd forming two walls of people along what appeared to be a track of sand in the center.

"Now will you tell me what this is?"

"It's a gymkhana."

I blinked several times at Redvers. "I hate to tell you this, but I have no earthly idea what that is."

Deanna laughed. "I didn't, either. Apparently, it's a British-Hindi term for what are essentially horse races." She bounced a bit on her feet.

"Camel races as well. And don't forget the donkey races—both men and women are allowed to participate in those." Redvers turned to me, a teasing smile playing across his mouth. "Would you like to enter? There might still be time."

I laughed and shook my head. The excitement of the crowd around me was palpable and soon I could feel my own blood begin to thrill. Redvers was correct—this was the perfect distraction from my troubles. He reached down and briefly squeezed my hand, sending an entirely different type of rush through my system.

Trying to ignore my response, I cast my eyes over the throng around us. It seemed I would be able to keep an eye on most of the hotel staff and residents—nearly everyone I knew was visible somewhere in the crowd. The doctor was across the track from us, and Zaki and several members of the kitchen staff stood a short distance down from our position. I spotted Aunt Millie seated near the front of the stands with Lillian and Marie. Her eyes met mine and this time didn't flinch away. Instead, she cocked her head slightly and raised an eyebrow. I paused, then gave a single nod and a small smile. Her face relaxed and her lips tipped up in return, before turning back to the chattering girls beside her.

Redvers watched the entire exchange. He cocked an eyebrow.

"Have you spoken to your aunt?"

"No."

"So . . ."

"So that was the apology."

Redvers looked incredulous, and I merely shook my head with a smile. "That's more than most would get from Aunt Millie." Things would soon return to normal between us. A tightness between my shoulders eased at the thought.

A military band began to play, interrupting any further conversation. Deanna clapped her hands in delight, and with a smile, Charlie watched her instead of the band.

The first several races were on horseback, nearly exclusively ridden by locals. I worried that the men were pushing the animals so hard in the heat, but Redvers assured me that the Arabian horses were bred for the weather and their endurance. The crowds clapped and cheered—everyone had a favorite, it seemed.

Behind the crowd on either side, I could see groups of men gathered in a circle, and I nudged Redvers' arm and nodded in that direction. Zaki now stood among them near the center.

He read my unspoken question. "That is where the good doctor is losing his money today. And, apparently, our friend Zaki as well."

Betting circles. Last night's conversation made sense to me now.

I enjoyed the horse races, but I was not prepared for the sheer joy the camel races brought me. The ungainly animals seemed nearly graceful at high speeds, and I had no idea they could move so quickly. This was the race that more tourists participated in, and it seemed not quite as serious as the earlier horse races. I laughed out loud as one camel stood stubbornly at the starting line long past when all the rest had raced off, the hapless tourist bobbing in his seat trying to convince the animal to go. No luck. The camel then decided it was a delightful time to lie down, and the man nearly fell out of the saddle as the camel collapsed itself to the ground.

Shouts and laughter accompanied the racers to the finish line. I was not surprised to see a local man had won the race—the tourists seemed mostly unable to keep the camels moving, regardless of their experience in a saddle.

When the donkey racers lined up, I was shocked to see both Marie and the doctor astride a long-eared animal. Marie's face looked grim as she glanced at the doctor, and he grinned at her in return.

At the starting pistol, Marie leaned forward and her donkey took off. My mouth hung open as she maintained her slight lead, the doctor close behind. If anything, the donkeys were even more difficult to control than the camels, but Marie held hers in steady check. I clasped my hands together when it seemed she would be overtaken near the end of the line, but with a final quick burst, Marie pulled ahead and finished first. I found myself grinning widely for her. I could see her face was triumphant, and I thought the look suited her. So did the knickers-style sport pants she was wearing; she had obviously come to Egypt prepared. I continued watching as Lillian met her at the finish line and gave her a hard hug. Marie looked fiercely proud, even as Lillian gave the doctor a polite handshake with a smile and a shake of the head at his loss.

Redvers looked at Marie in appreciation. "I had no idea she was such an accomplished rider."

"I'm shocked myself." I hadn't thought Marie had any hobbies of her own, but it appeared I was wrong. The girl had hidden depths.

It was well after five when we returned to the hotel, caked in sand but in high spirits. After a wash-up, we regrouped in the lobby and headed in to dinner together. Charlie and

Deanna regaled us with tales from the stage, and my frequent glances at Redvers showed a man enjoying himself. Warmth pooled in my stomach.

Yet after such a long day in the heat and the sun, I excused myself after only one drink in the lounge. Despite the protests from both Deanna and Charlie, and even Redvers himself, I was done in. Egypt's heat was never truly going to agree with me, it seemed, and after having spent the day awash in sound and color, I needed some quiet time to unwind.

I had just pulled back the covers to crawl into bed when I heard heated words being exchanged in the hallway outside. I couldn't tell who the speakers were, but I turned and started toward the door, grabbing my silk robe along the way. A sudden thump just outside hurried my footsteps.

I opened my door to find Aunt Millie unconscious on the floor with Redvers standing over her, a cricket bat at his feet.

CHAPTER THIRTY-SIX

I rushed to Millie's side, immediately putting my face near her own to see if she was still breathing. She was.

"Aunt Millie . . . Millie, can you hear me?"

Millie gave a slight moan but she didn't wake.

"What did you do to her?" I shouted the words at Redvers, who looked shocked at the accusation. He bent down to check Millie's pulse, but I pushed at him, and he straightened and took a step back, face grim. Several doors nearby opened, and another robed guest entered the hall. One look at the scene before him sent the middle-aged gentleman hurrying quickly toward the front desk.

"Call the doctor!" I called after him.

"I would never hurt your aunt," Redvers said quietly. His voice had a dangerous edge to it, which didn't help his case.

I refused to answer. All the lies Redvers had told and all the times I couldn't explain what he was up to flooded back to me the moment I saw him standing over my aunt's crumpled body. I had trusted this man with everything, and now I may have paid for that foolish trust with my aunt's life. Rage bubbled up and held my tears at bay. I pushed the cricket bat behind my aunt, putting myself between it and Redvers. I touched it as little as I could for fear of leaving my own fingerprints. Or smudging those of my aunt's attacker.

Redvers didn't come any closer, but I kept one eye on him. I tried to move my aunt as little as possible, but I monitored the pulse in her wrist. It was threaded, but distinct. Minutes that felt like years passed before the doctor appeared at a full-out sprint, fell to his knees, and immediately began appraising Millie's condition. I stepped to the other side of the hall to give him space. The stranger who had fetched the doctor returned, breathing heavily, and stood beside me.

"Let's move her to her rooms." Dr. Williams gestured for Redvers to assist him.

"No," I said loudly. I grabbed the stranger's arm next to me, giving him a little push toward the doctor and my aunt. He did as he was told, and Redvers turned on his heel and left. I felt a twist in my gut. If he had hurt her, would he have stayed to make sure she was taken care of? I shook my head. The police could sort that out.

But the cricket bat could not stay in the hallway. I pulled the sleeve of my robe over my hand and gingerly picked it up, bringing it into Millie's room and setting it gently on the desk.

The men settled Millie in her room and my heart continued to flutter as I paced near her bedroom door. Dr. Williams came over after a moment.

"Do you know what happened?"

"No. I heard people arguing outside my room—it must have been Millie and Mr. Redvers—and then I heard a thump, and that must have been him hitting her or maybe her hitting the floor. When I opened the door, he was standing over her and she was lying there . . ."

The words were coming too fast, and I hoped the doctor was able to make sense of them. My brain was still trying to make sense of the scene, and my fear for Millie warred with the crushing pain of Redvers' apparent betrayal.

"Will she be okay?" I held my breath for the answer.

"We'll have to see. She's suffered a serious blow to the head. But we'll do our best for her."

He gave me a look of compassion, and yet again I felt guilty for my earlier suspicions against him. He was a good doctor.

"You might as well go back to bed," he continued. "There's nothing you can do here, and I'll take care of her overnight. Come back in the morning."

I began to argue, but he gave me a pat on the shoulder and a firm shake of the head. The stranger I pressed into service was already gone.

I gazed around the room and flapped my hands uselessly against my side. "What if she wakes up and I'm not here?"

"Mrs. Wunderly, I hate to put it to you like this, but she's not likely to wake up tonight."

My watery eyes gave way to fat tears.

"You'll do her more good if you rest now."

"Will you show the police the weapon?" I pointed to the cricket bat, lying innocently on the desk.

He assured me that he would. Without touching it.

I finally gave in and left the room. I realized I would be in his way, and my anxiety wasn't of any service. The doctor needed to concentrate on Millie, not me.

Returning to my rooms, I remembered the cricket bat Redvers had given me for bug hunting, and realized that I hadn't seen the wooden bat in days. After several nights of diligent searches, I had become lax in my evening patrols. I checked around my room now, and nervously pulled at my ear. The bat was nowhere to be found. It looked as though someone had taken the bat from my room and attacked my aunt with it. The thought horrified me.

There was no way I was going to sleep, so I changed into flowing linen trousers and a matching blouse. I was going to look for some answers.

*   *   *

I slipped through the mostly empty halls. It seemed the saloon had emptied early—not even the usual late-night party-goers were out and about. I stopped at the front desk, where a concerned clerk assured me that the police had been rung. I thanked him, then pondered my next move.

I decided to head to Redvers' quarters. He had a head start, but with a little luck, I could catch up with him. If he was planning to make an escape, I would stop him.

I crept down the hallway where his room was located, but all was still. I moved to his door and pressed my ear against the wood, hoping to hear something—snoring or the sounds of packing, but the room was silent. I pursed my lips and pushed off in the direction of the common areas instead.

As I neared the dining room, I heard heated whispers again. I wasn't able to make out what they were saying, but I could tell it was two men, and both voices struck me as familiar. I looked down at my heeled shoes and realized I wouldn't be able to come much closer without being detected. I reached down and began slipping my shoes off, but then the voices began to fade. As quietly as I could, I crept to the doorway and peeked my head around the corner.

I was too late. The voices' owners were gone.

Chapter Thirty-Seven

"Damn," I whispered. I waited a moment before moving into the darkened room myself. The electric lights had been turned off, and the sliver of moon in the sky cast weak light through the tall windows. It wasn't enough to see by. I cursed a variety of people and places as I banged my right shin on a chair, and then the left—I could barely make out the shapes of furniture in my path. I put my hands out in front of me and moved a little more slowly, managing to avoid all but a few more thumps.

I was going to be black-and-blue in the morning.

I finally reached the French doors leading to the terrace, and approaching cautiously, I peered through the glass. Squinting, I could make out two figures moving across the grass. I immediately recognized the easy, loping walk of the taller man.

Redvers.

The other figure wore flowing robes and was also familiar, but I couldn't quite put my finger on who it was.

I had a moment's panic when I reached for the knob, but the doors were not yet locked for the night. I moved onto the terrace, where I was now able to see the obstacles in my way—the moonlight was dim, but brighter in the open. I was also able to follow more quickly, and I kept to the dark tree line to avoid being seen.

Following these two out into the night—unarmed—was not my brightest idea, but each time I paused, I remembered my aunt and fresh rage propelled me forward.

Before long, I realized the men were heading toward the stables. The building was deserted this time of night, since the stable hands had retired back to Mena Village. From a distance, I saw the robed figure unlock the doors and gesture for Redvers to enter before him. He turned his face, and in a brief moonlit moment, I realized it was Zaki.

I didn't have time to wonder why the men were in the horse stable together. Instead, I waited for Zaki to follow Redvers into the building, and then I slipped up and hid behind the open door, grateful he hadn't closed it behind him.

It occurred to me that the entire time the men had been walking across the grounds, I hadn't heard so much as a whisper. But once in the white stucco building, the argument I overheard earlier resumed.

"Why are you doing this?" Redvers asked.

For a moment, I was confused. What *was* Zaki doing?

"I cannot let you go. You saw what happened tonight." Zaki's voice had a ring of desperation.

The sound of restless hooves and snorting noses drifted out on the night air—the arrival of two strangers had agitated the animals. I tried to peer through the crack in the door, but it revealed nothing. I needed to get a glimpse of what was happening.

I crouched down, away from eye level, and risked a quick peek around the corner. Zaki had his back to me and was holding a small black revolver.

A revolver aimed at Redvers.

It appeared I had interpreted the events of the evening incorrectly.

"I don't understand why you attacked Mrs. Stanley." Redvers' voice was growing ever so slightly fainter and I risked another look. He was backing slowly down the center path, drawing Zaki farther away from me.

I assumed it was unintentional—he hadn't seen me yet. I slipped off my shoes, and praying fervently Zaki wouldn't turn around, I crept quietly around the door. I could not afford one false step.

Despite the tremble shaking my entire body, I went slowly, gravel piercing the bottoms of my feet, twisting my mouth into a grimace. To my right was a tack area that shared a wall with the first stall, and I pressed myself against the rough wood. I scanned my body to make sure I was out of their sight line and practiced my controlled-breathing exercises as quietly as I was able. The pulse of my blood pounded in my ears.

"That old woman is much too clever," Zaki said. "And far too nosy. She saw me enter the changing room where I hid Dr. Williams's gun. And she saw me with Samara too many times—she was always *watching*. It was only a matter of time before she put things together."

I hadn't realized that Millie saw anything, but she and I hadn't exactly been on speaking terms lately. If Zaki had hidden the gun, it could only mean one thing.

"You think she was going to put together that you killed Samara," Redvers said slowly. He was working out the pieces just as I was.

"Samara and I had a good arrangement. When I brought drinks to the gambling room, I would signal to him what cards the others had, and he would give me a cut of the winnings."

"And no one noticed you cheating?"

"No one notices the staff." Years of mounting anger set each of Zaki's words ablaze. "We are servants to you, peasants. You say hello, good morning, but you never really see us. I bring the drinks, and all you see are the drinks. You never see me, Zaki the man."

I felt a spark of shame as his words struck home. As much as I liked Zaki, how much did I ever really notice him? Had I ever seen him as a person?

It sounded like Zaki and Samara had a good system worked out for themselves. They probably made a fair bit of money—until Charlie Parks came along.

I was letting the story distract me. Right now, I needed a plan to keep Zaki from shooting Redvers. I peered around the corner, and my eyes fell on the latch of the stall adjacent to the wall where I stood. It was nearly within reach. I gave the wood next to me a small kick, and the horse on the other side startled. Fortunately, the noise was lost in the restless horse sounds around us.

"Samara got greedy when he realized how good the American man was at card tricks. He said he did not need me anymore." Zaki's voice now shook with rage. "I thought if I planted the blackmail papers in his room, your lady friend would turn him in to the police. But no."

That explained where Zaki had disappeared to after I saw him in the dining room. It also explained why he was so happy to give me Amon's room number, and why the door was left unlocked. But he hadn't counted on the papers incriminating my aunt and my stealing one of them—I could hardly call the police after that. He must not have read the papers very carefully.

The time for action was running out. I popped my head around the corner one last time. Redvers snuck a fast glance my way, and this time, I knew he had seen me. I held my breath, waiting to see if Zaki noticed.

Zaki never turned around.

Redvers maintained eye contact with Zaki after that, shuffling side to side to keep Zaki's attention trained solely on him. I went to work on the latch, slowly easing the metal clasp apart. I couldn't afford for it to make noise. The horse behind the stall door bumped against the wall and moved his feet restlessly.

"So you killed him." Redvers was trying to draw the story out and focus Zaki's attention.

"He threatened me. He said I would lose not only the money we made, but also my job if I turned him in." The gun started to shake in Zaki's hand.

The latch came apart and I swung the door toward me, ducking down behind it. The horse bolted from the stall, and Zaki turned in surprise, a shot ringing out and knocking wood splinters from the wall above me. As Zaki turned toward the massive black horse rearing on its hind legs, Redvers leapt forward and grabbed the gun, wrenching it from Zaki's hand. Just as quickly, Redvers hit Zaki squarely upside the head with the black metal weapon, and Zaki crumpled to the ground. The horse, to its credit, spied the open door behind us, and once all four hooves found the ground again, it bolted for freedom. For its own safety, I hoped it wouldn't go far.

Redvers was bent over, hands on knees, gun still clutched in his right hand. He looked up at me. "Thanks for that."

I came out from behind the door and brushed down the front of my pants as nonchalantly as I was able.

"Anytime," I said lightly. My face grew serious. "Redvers, I'm sorry I thought—"

He cut me off. "You don't have to say anything. I understand." He gave me a crooked smile. "Besides, you just saved my life. We're probably even."

We shared a long look, and I hoped he would be able to forgive me for thinking he was behind Millie's attack.

Hands on hips, I looked down at Zaki's unmoving body. "Did you kill him?"

"I think he'll be fine." Redvers came to stand beside me and gave Zaki's leg a little push with his foot. He didn't stir.

Looking closely, I could now see Zaki's chest moving slightly up and down.

"Do you think he killed Anna also?" I asked.

"I'm sure Inspector Hamadi will be happy to find out."

CHAPTER THIRTY-EIGHT

I hurried back to the hotel and called the police while Redvers watched over our prisoner. I also let the desk clerk know that someone needed to retrieve a stray horse—I didn't want it getting lost in the desert.

By the time the police arrived, Zaki was starting to wake up. The inspector was thrilled to have a suspect in hand, but he was not shy about sharing his feelings over my involvement. Frankly, he seemed disappointed that I was in the clear. He still snarled a few threats in my direction, then offered his condolences about my aunt and his hope for her recovery. He clearly enjoyed keeping me off balance.

Redvers seemed inclined to stay with the police and accompany the inspector back to the station, so I offered an awkward wave and a good night before heading back to the quiet hotel alone. It was an uncomfortable way to leave things, but I wasn't about to make any sort of apology in front of Inspector Hamadi.

I checked on Millie—no change—before crawling into bed fully clothed and falling into an exhausted and dreamless sleep.

I awoke in the morning with a heavy weight in my chest. Zaki's arrest had officially cleared my name of the murders, but thoughts of Millie still plagued me. I was also uneasy about where I stood with Redvers. I put on fresh clothes in a hurry, not noticing until I was nearly out the door that my skirt was on backward.

When I knocked at Millie's door, Dr. Williams answered. His eyes were shot through with red, but his face looked hopeful.

"Is she . . . ?" was all I could manage.

"She's doing well." Dr. Williams gave me an encouraging smile. "She came around for a bit, but is asleep again now. She had a whopper of a headache, so I gave her something for that. You can stay for a bit if you like, but try not to wake her. She needs the rest. I'm going to bed, but I'll be back again this afternoon to check on her."

I nodded and went in to see her. Her round face was pale against the pillow, but her breathing seemed steady and sure. I decided to sit with her for a while.

I wasn't there ten minutes before Lillian came knocking at the door.

"I heard what happened last night." Lillian's face was pale and worried. "When she didn't come down to breakfast, I started asking around. Oh, Jane. Will she be okay?" Lillian had moved to Millie's bedside and was fluttering, trying to decide if she should take one of Millie's hands.

I moved to Lillian's side and squeezed her trembling hand with mine. "She's going to be fine. She's awfully tough. The doctor said we should let her rest now, but she did come around for him this morning."

A great gust escaped from Lillian's lungs, and she gave me a wobbly smile.

"Could I have some time alone with her?" Lillian asked.

I was surprised, but nodded.

"I only just found her," she added.

I wondered if perhaps Lillian knew more than we thought. But rather than ask unwanted questions, I quietly exited the room. I stood in the hallway for a moment, feeling relieved that Millie would recover. I decided to check in on her later in the afternoon.

I no longer had a clear direction for my morning. After a few moments, I decided to fuel up on caffeine and headed to the breakfast room.

I paused at the doorway of the dining room, expecting Zaki's cheerful greeting before I remembered his arrest. It felt strange to miss Zaki's smiling face, especially since he was the reason for so much suffering. His post was empty for the moment, and I moved into the room.

Redvers was at a table near the windows, reading the paper. I hesitated, feeling awkward about the fact that I had recently accused him of attempted murder. But he looked up and smiled at me warmly, so I headed toward him.

"Good morning," I said softly.

"Good morning. Coffee?"

I realized that he had already ordered a full pot especially for me. I smiled gratefully, inhaling the fragrant steam as he poured me a cup.

His smile fell away. "How is Millie?"

"She's doing well. The doctor said she'll recover."

"That's excellent news." Redvers seemed genuinely re-lieved and I felt another stab of guilt for suspecting him.

"Lillian is with her now. She asked for some time alone with her."

Redvers cocked an eyebrow.

"I agree. Maybe she knows more than we give her credit for," I said.

"It's entirely possible. Hopefully you'll be able to talk with Millie soon."

I pulled a face. "She's going to be in quite the mood when she wakes up. I can't imagine the headache."

Redvers grimaced and then we shared a smile.

"I spoke to Inspector Hamadi this morning," Redvers said.

"That was fast."

"I couldn't sleep."

I looked for signs of a sleepless night on his face and found none. I came close to rolling my eyes. I could feel how puffy my own face was and it felt as though someone had rubbed grit beneath my eyelids.

"Apparently, Zaki told the inspector quite a lot. He and Samara had a whole system worked out for communicating about the cards."

I nodded. I had heard as much the night before.

"And Zaki had come to depend on that money—it was quite lucrative for them," he said.

"So why kill Samara?"

"Zaki didn't realize that Charlie had no intention of working with Samara. And with Samara out of the way, he thought he could partner with Charlie, instead."

"That makes sense." I covered a yawn. I was interested, but dead tired.

Redvers eyed me and I motioned for him to go on.

"Zaki was also afraid of losing his job if Samara talked. He had a great deal of pride in the position, and he got nervous when Samara was interrogated by the police. He was afraid everything was going to come out. So Zaki arranged to meet Samara in the gaming room that night after everyone had gone, then killed him."

"But Samara had only arrived a few days ago. How could they have worked out such an elaborate scheme so quickly?"

Redvers poured me another cup of coffee. "Amon was a regular here. He did a circuit of fine hotels and this was one of his stops. He would move on to the next if it seemed like management or other players were catching on, but then return after a month or so. Between the cards and the older ladies, Amon was quite the crook."

I shook my head and thought about Zaki. Despite everything he had done, my heart went out to his family—especially Nenet. "I met his fiancée—she was so lovely. I'm very sorry for her."

Redvers' brows drew together. "As far as I know, Zaki wasn't engaged. I'll ask the inspector, but I feel fairly certain."

"Why would he have lied about that?" I was genuinely confused. What purpose would such a story have served?

Redvers shrugged. "Who can say?"

I paused for a moment. "Did you learn anything else?"

"Well, Zaki had the blackmail papers. They were Anna's."

"So it was Anna all along." At least I had guessed correctly about that.

"She was the mastermind. Apparently, she was quite fond of spending money, and when her father could no longer afford her expensive tastes, she began looking for an income stream elsewhere." Redvers' lip curled. "Zaki admitted to stealing her blackmail materials—he was hoping she would pay to get them back. And then he hid them in Samara's room for you to find."

It made sense. Anna had been fond of beautiful things. And those things cost quite a bit of money.

"I suppose it was easy for Zaki—he had access to all the keys."

"Precisely. And no one suspected him because he was so helpful and managed to blend into the background at the same time."

I sighed, suddenly remembering the weapon used to assault Aunt Millie. "Did he take the cricket bat from my room as well?"

Redvers nodded. "Apparently, he took it a couple days ago. He was looking for something to incriminate you with and found the bat in your bedroom. He thought it might be useful."

It made me sad that he had been trying to cast guilt my

Erica Ruth Neubauer

way. I had genuinely liked the man and he seemed so earnest. But I also felt uneasy that someone had been in my rooms and I hadn't noticed.

"Do you think he's the one who planted the scorpion?" Thoughts of the little black insect sent a violent shudder through me.

"Most likely. He saw you talking with all the major players that day. He was probably trying to warn you off. I should mention it to Hamadi and have him ask about that as well."

"I'm lucky he didn't try again and plant one in my room. I stopped searching after a few nights."

"I think he was merely trying to scare you with the first one. Putting a scorpion in your bed would have meant a bite for certain. And alone in your room, you wouldn't have been able to call for help."

I let my good fortune sink in for a moment.

"Last night . . ." I paused. I was apprehensive about bringing up last night's attack, but I needed a few answers. "How did you get there so fast?"

"I was worried about you, so I had my things moved into the empty room across from yours."

"When was this?"

"Two days ago."

Redvers' concern was touching, but it had worked against him. Because he was on the scene so quickly, I assumed he was guilty of the attack.

Then I wondered whose door I had been listening at when I had been searching for him.

"I was going to retrieve a note from the front desk, and I heard your aunt and Zaki arguing. I wasn't in time to stop him from hitting her. And then he managed to slip into the adjacent hall just as I came through my door."

I had been across the room when I heard the voices and stopped for my robe, so I had missed Zaki's escape and found the aftermath, instead. "I'm so sorry." I wasn't sure I could ever apologize enough. I reached out and grasped his hand on the table.

He shook his head and covered our clasped hands with his other strong hand. "Nothing to apologize for. It looked terrible, and I should have been more truthful with you all along. I also should have let you know that I relocated."

We shared a warm smile.

Colonel Stainton chose that moment to approach our table, and we pulled our hands apart.

"Good morning, Miss Wunderly." He sounded more like his cheerful self. He acknowledged Redvers with a cool nod, but it seemed not even Redvers' presence could dampen his spirits.

"How are you, Colonel Stainton?" My tingling hands were back in my lap. Redvers was like lightning for my nerve endings.

"I hear that things are all wrapped up with that waiter's arrest. It's capital news. It means my poor Anna will be released and I can take her home."

"When will you leave?" I asked.

"First thing tomorrow." He tapped his cane against the ground. "I must say, when things finally do get rolling around here, they really do get rolling."

"Well, that must certainly be a relief for you."

"Yes, thank you, dear." He cleared his throat. "I must go now. I just wanted to say good-bye in case I didn't see you again. I have much to do before tomorrow. Lots of arrangements to make."

Redvers and I both stood up from the table. I gave the colonel my hand and we shook good-bye as I wished him the best of luck.

He turned and stiffly shook Redvers' hand next.

"Good-bye, Colonel. Safe travels." Redvers' voice was polite, but lacked any warmth.

"Thank you, Mr. Redvers."

The colonel nodded once more at me and then hurried away.

I watched him leave. "He said things have been wrapped up and they are releasing Anna's body. Hamadi must be convinced that Zaki also killed Anna."

"It looks that way, although last I heard, Zaki was still insisting he had nothing to do with it. He claims he was home in bed when her murder happened. But the same caliber gun was used, and Zaki had easy access to it."

"The keys," I said.

"The keys," Redvers agreed. "He was able to enter the doctor's room undetected and steal the gun."

"I feel like there's something we're missing. Why wouldn't he just confess to Anna's murder as well? He's already admitted to killing Samara and trying to kill my aunt."

Redvers shook his head; he didn't have the answer to that.

"And what about the smuggling? Does this mean the smuggling had nothing to do with anything?" It felt like something still wasn't fitting together. I just couldn't put my finger on what it was.

"Well, we know who was doing the smuggling, just not the how." Redvers nodded after the colonel. "And now it appears I have a very short deadline to find that answer."

"Before he leaves tomorrow."

Redvers nodded.

CHAPTER THIRTY-NINE

After breakfast, Redvers went on his way and I checked back in with Aunt Millie. She was awake, but just barely. She gave me a weak smile before closing her eyes again. Her head was still in a lot of pain, and she was sleeping most hours of the day, but I was relieved to see her awake for even that short time. The doctor was continuing to monitor her progress, and Lillian barely left her side, making sure she was eating and drinking a little something during the times she was awake. I offered Lillian a break from her vigil, but she quietly shook her head.

With Millie taken care of, I was at loose ends and feeling restless. Redvers had gone in search of evidence to sew up his case against Colonel Stainton—alone. I tried to sit by the pool and read, but my mind wouldn't stop tumbling over facts and faces, so I soon gave that up. I wandered aimlessly through the corridors until lunch, where I dined alone, picking at the delicious meal that held no appeal for me. I only managed to choke down a few bites.

After lunch, I decided to take a walk on the grounds. It was hot, but getting the blood circulating might help me think things through—or exhaust me enough that I could actually rest. I had not gone far when it struck me that I should find out where Mena Village was located. A chat with the lovely Nenet might answer some of my questions about Zaki's lies, and my mind would have fewer things to worry at. I turned back toward the lobby.

I asked at the front desk where I could find the workers' village, although it earned me a strange look. The young man assured me that the quickest path would be to set out across the golf course, but it would also put me in the way of fast-moving golf balls, even in the scorching afternoon sun. People's devotion to the sport never ceased to amaze me. I decided to take the long road out around the edges of the property, but since it was quite a hike, I decided to save my feet and ride there, instead.

I walked leisurely to the stables, yet again going over the events of the night before. I couldn't come up with a motive for Zaki to have killed Anna that fit with everything I knew. I wanted the case closed as much as the inspector did—even more so—but I wasn't convinced we had all the answers.

Once the building came into view, I was reminded of last night's episode. The white stucco building looked completely different in the daylight, cheerful and busy, with guests and stable hands scattered about. None of the menace remained and I found myself breathing out anxiety I wasn't even aware of.

At my request for a horse, a quiet young man sized me up and headed into the depths of the stable. He returned with a small, docile-looking chestnut mare named Bibi. As he saddled her, I stroked her velvet nose and she snuffled at my hands, looking for a treat.

Bibi and I headed out slowly. I didn't want to overtax the horse in the heat, even though she was doubtless more accustomed to it than I was. It didn't take long for me to feel comfortable in the saddle once again, those long-ago riding lessons coming back as if they were yesterday.

As we neared the village, I could see low mud brick buildings scattered in a random pattern. Geese wandered about, occasionally splitting the quiet afternoon with a honk, while

livestock sought refuge from the sun under low overhangs. I realized I would have to ask where Nenet lived, and hoped she would be home. It just occurred to me that she might be in town tending her dress shop—what most shopkeepers would be doing this time of day.

Small faces peered at me from open doorways as my horse plodded toward the main square. I spotted a well near the center of town and dismounted, grabbing the reins and leading Bibi toward the water. As I pumped at the handle, several of the children dared to come near, and one held the community bucket for me as I pumped. I gave Bibi the fresh water, then turned to the curious faces staring at me.

"Do you speak English?" I fully expected no response.

The children looked one to another, and finally one small boy with dark hair flopping over his forehead, stepped forward.

"Little." His eyes were dark and serious as he regarded me.

I had no idea if these children were educated, and remembered what Zaki had said about wealthy tourists ignoring the locals, treating them as servants. I felt shame creep up my neck, and I promised myself to learn more about the people of the country I was visiting.

"What's your name?" I asked him.

"Kadir."

"Kadir, do you know Nenet?"

He nodded solemnly.

"Where does Nenet live?"

The children conferred in chattering Arabic, and I waited for the results of their conference from their spokesperson.

"We show you," Kadir said.

One small girl took Bibi's reins from me and walked next to me as I led a small parade of children to Nenet's house. We wound through a number of dusty alleys before coming to a stop before a small, tidy mud brick house. It didn't look as if anyone was home.

The children looked at me expectantly, and I realized it

would have been wise to bring some sort of gift with me. I checked my pockets and pulled out a few Egyptian coins. I wasn't sure how best to distribute the funds, so I looked to Kadir and told him to share. He nodded his understanding, and though he kept the largest amount for himself, he seemed to disburse the rest of the money fairly amongst his compatriots. We shared a nod, and I stifled a laugh at his solemn little face. Within moments, all the children scampered off, their entertainment for the afternoon over.

At the darkened doorway, I called out for Nenet, but there was no response. I didn't feel comfortable entering her home with no one there—which was frankly surprising, given how many hotel rooms I had broken into lately. Instead, I walked my horse around back, looking for some shade where the both of us could rest. There was a large overhang at the back of the house, most likely used as a small porch, and I led Bibi into its shade.

I tied her reins to one of the supports, hoping she wouldn't get any ideas about pulling the whole thing down. It took several moments of struggle with the hardware, but I finally figured out how to remove her saddle. I pulled away the colorful pads underneath, soaked with sweat from the ride, and used one to wipe down her back. I rubbed her soft nose for a moment before stepping away, and she soon closed her eyes, tail twitching periodically to swat away flies. One of the children had carried a bucket of water with us, and I set it within Bibi's reach.

I was beginning to think that my plan to turn up unannounced had been a foolish one. There was no telling how long I would have to wait for Nenet to return home, if this was even where she lived. The children could have simply parked me at the nearest vacant house, although the front stoop was well swept and the yard neatly tended. I felt hopeful I was in the right place.

I looked around for a place in the shade to sit. Bibi was taking up most of the space under the overhang, and I didn't think taking a seat near her large hooves was the best of plans. She was a sweet girl, but if something spooked her, I would be crushed. Avoiding the sun wasn't worth the risk.

A large tree beckoned me from the corner of the yard, and I sank down against its trunk. I adjusted my large-brimmed hat and tucked my limbs in, out of the sun. I must have fallen asleep, because when I next opened my eyes, I could hear someone moving around at the front of the house. I stood stiffly and brushed myself off. I checked on the peaceful horse before walking around the side of the house.

"Hello, Nenet." The sound of my voice startled her and she whirled around.

"Mrs. Wunderly!" Nenet put a hand to her heart. "You surprised me. What are you doing here?"

"I just wanted to talk with you a bit. I have some questions about Zaki, I'm afraid." She nodded, somewhat sadly, and motioned me into her house.

It was simple but clean. The centerpiece of the room was a beautiful fabric wall hanging and I found myself glancing at it frequently. The woven design was intricate and the light from the window caught flashes of gold thread intertwined with the bold reds and oranges. It was stunning and I wondered if it was a family heirloom, or something she had made herself. A wooden chair sat opposite a worn bench with upholstered cushions that had been recently re-covered. Despite the sparse furnishing, the room felt cozy and lived-in.

"I heard about Zaki. We all heard. It is very sad." Nenet gestured for me to sit down.

"It is sad," I agreed. "I liked him very much."

Nenet nodded.

"But he told me that you were to be married."

Nenet rolled her eyes. "I was very fond of Zaki, but I was

not going to marry him. I was married to a man called As-wan, but he died during the war. It is how I came to own the shop."

I nodded. I knew plenty about losing a husband during the war.

"Zaki decided that he was going to marry me, and asked me about it frequently. But I have no intention of marrying again. And if I do, it will be for love." Nenet shrugged. "It was very annoying, his constant courtship. He would not take no for an answer. But it's hard to believe he killed a man."

"Yes." I sighed. "But he did confess to Mr. Samara's murder."

"What about that young woman? Did he kill her as well?"

I shook my head. "He claims he did not. But he does not have an alibi."

Nenet nodded. "I see her father—he is a military man? He is here in the village quite often."

I went very still. "Do you know why he is in the village so often?"

"No, but he meets with a man who lives several houses down." Her face darkened. "He is called Radwa."

"You look as though you don't care for him very much."

Nenet shook her head. "We all work very hard here in Mena Village, but this man, he does not work at all. Radwa has been in much trouble, ever since he was a young man."

That sounded like someone who would be involved in a smuggling racket. I couldn't believe my extraordinary luck. Of course, Mena Village was small enough that everyone probably knew everyone else—and everyone else's business. But I was excited to be so close to the answers Redvers was looking for.

Not, of course, that I wanted to see the colonel locked up. But if he was involved in stealing artifacts and selling them to wealthy collectors, I had no problem turning him in. As much as I liked him, I truly felt that antiquities smuggling should be stopped.

"Can you show me which house he lives in?" I asked.

"Of course," Nenet said, and we stepped back outside. She pointed to a house several doors down. "It is the one with the trash in the yard." She wrinkled her nose. "We ask Radwa to clean up, but he does not."

The house was in a state of disrepair—I could see where corners of the foundation had begun to crumble, and the roof looked the worse for wear. I was sure a rainstorm of any size would cause an indoor flood. Stray bricks and other building materials littered the side yard.

We went back inside and chatted for a few more minutes. Nenet invited me to stay for dinner, but I declined. I didn't want this kind woman to go to extra trouble simply because I had been nosy enough to appear on her doorstep. I did take her up on her offer to find a bit of grain for Bibi, after I explained that I had parked my horse in her yard. When I asked if I could leave Bibi for a while longer, she said it was no trouble. She even offered to take her back to the hotel for me, but I assured her I would return.

I just needed to wait until nightfall to go poking around Radwa's house.

When Nenet realized I intended to stay in the village but had no destination, she insisted that I stay for dinner. I finally gave in, but on the provision that I help her in the kitchen. Together we made a delicious dish of grilled chicken, stewed vegetables, lentils, and flat bread. The spices were delicious, and I made a mental note to pick some up at the market to take home with me. We ate and chatted and had a lovely time together. Nenet was very easy to talk with, and the time slipped quickly away. By some unspoken agreement, we avoided mention of our marriages, and I was grateful she never brought up the scars she had seen.

Darkness fell, and I wished Nenet a warm good night. She wished me the best of luck. I could tell she was concerned about my plan for the evening, but she did not ask what it was. I left Bibi tied where she was, and Nenet promised to take good care of her until I returned.

A dim light shone from Radwa's front window, so I moved around to the back of Nenet's house and crept through her neighbors' backyards. I was lucky no one kept a dog—the only animals I came across were a few disgruntled chickens, and they clucked their irritation at being disturbed from their roosts.

I slowed my steps as I neared Radwa's house and kept to the dark angular shadows. The backyard was just as cluttered and unkempt as the rest of the yard, and I had to place my feet carefully to avoid tripping and making noise. The back windows beckoned, and I carefully sidled up beneath them, the area mercifully free of the debris and crates littering the rest of the yard. I positioned myself below a window and listened for several minutes.

The house was silent.

I popped my head up quickly, and, seeing no one in that first glance, I carefully poked my head up again to peer inside. I was looking into a room that was obviously used as storage. I could see through the kitchen to the front room—the setup largely the same as Nenet's house. The room I stood outside of had several tall stacks of wooden crates, but I couldn't see what was in them, or if there were any markings. The light was too dim and I wished I had thought to bring a flashlight.

A noise in the yard behind me dropped me into a crouch and I froze there, blood pounding. A brown chicken strolled by, contentedly scratching and clucking, and I breathed a sigh of relief. My pulse began to slow and I went back to peering through the window, straining to see.

The blow from behind came quickly and turned everything to black.

Chapter Forty

Icame to slowly, my eyes opening to complete darkness. In those first few moments, I worried that I was now blind, but as I tested my limbs, I realized I was tied up. And in a tight, dark space. My body immediately flew into a panic, and I struggled against the ropes that held my arms behind my back. My knees were near my chest, and my ankles were bound as well. I was curled into the fetal position and I could feel rough-hewn wood against my limbs—a packing crate. I'd been stuffed into a packing crate. Sharp slivers pierced my exposed skin as I struggled against the close walls.

Tears rolled freely down my face as I gagged against the rag packed into my mouth and tied behind my head. I continued to struggle for several moments as I rode the waves of panic that washed through me. I prayed my body would soon exhaust itself from pumping adrenaline into my system. After a time, I was able to clamp my eyes shut and direct all my focus to forcing long, slow breaths through my nose. My breathing eventually slowed somewhat, although my panicked thoughts continued to race, and it still felt as though something enormous was crushing my chest.

If I was going to survive, I needed to regain control.

It felt like an eternity, but was probably only half an hour before the adrenaline dump started to slow and I was able to start pulling myself together. I was still frightened, but I was able to order my thoughts, and I repeated calming phrases to myself like a mantra.

Footsteps.

As they drew closer, I could hear an argument taking place between two men, and I appeared to be the topic.

"What are we to do with the girl? Now that you have knocked her out?" a deep male voice hissed.

At least they hadn't realized I was awake yet. I continued to take long, slow breaths as I considered whose voice it was. Judging by the thick accent and where I was found lurking, I guessed it was Radwa.

A sigh. "We'll have to get rid of her. She was a delightful girl, but I'm afraid she knows too much." I recognized *that* voice at once.

Colonel Stainton.

I felt a pinch somewhere around my heart. Apparently, I had still been harboring some hope that Redvers was wrong about the colonel. And smuggling was a far cry from assault and murder—it rocked me back to think he was capable of murdering me in cold blood.

At least he sounded regretful that he was planning on disposing of me.

"I don't want to be part of another killing," Radwa said. My heart stopped for a moment. *Another* killing?

"You had nothing to do with the first one," the colonel sneered. "I took care of that on my own."

"Your own daughter," Radwa spat back at him.

I stopped breathing for a moment as my brain tried to process that bit of information, then started my long, slow breaths again. When the colonel said that I knew too much, I had assumed he meant the smuggling operation. Was Radwa really accusing the colonel of killing his own daughter? I waited for him to set the man straight. I wasn't convinced that Zaki was responsible for Anna's death, but someone else must have been.

"The little bitch got too greedy. Just like her mother. If she had gone on any longer, she would have ruined us all." The colonel's voice was cold and clipped. "Don't get any ideas yourself."

If it weren't for the gag in my mouth, my jaw would have fallen open. The news that the colonel killed his own daughter did not bode well for my own fate—he would have no compunction about killing me if he could murder his own child. All the cheerful friendliness and warm feelings I had felt toward the man now left me cold. I never once suspected him capable of such a thing. Perhaps he had missed his calling on the stage, after all—he had given the performance of a lifetime as the grieving father.

The panic returned twofold—this time compounded by my imminent death. Tears rolled down my face, soaking my hair and shirt. My breathing became more and more shallow as the pressure increased on my chest, and then there was nothing.

When I awoke this time, it only took the span of a heart-beat to realize the men had loaded my crate onto some sort of vehicle. I could hear the loud rumble of an engine, and I felt the bumps and jostles of a pot-marked road. Fortunately, the panic stayed manageable this time—my body had either exhausted itself of adrenaline, or I was becoming used to my confinement. I pushed with my legs, praying that the noise of the engine would be enough to drown out whatever noises I made. Now was the time to see how well this crate was built.

I kicked as much as I was able—which wasn't a lot. I was wedged in pretty well and lying on my side, but I thought I could feel some movement of the wood as I violently bashed my knees into the slats before me. I paused between blows to gauge whether or not my captors could hear me, but the vehicle continued bouncing on. Blood soaked my pants where my knees were making contact, but I continued slamming them against the rough slats for all I was worth.

The next time I paused, I heard a scrape above me, and I froze, mouthing a silent prayer that my luck had held and my escape attempts hadn't been noticed.

Luck was not on my side.

I could hear the creaking of my crate's lid above the rumbling engine. The vehicle hadn't so much as slowed, but I didn't have time to wonder who might be waiting outside my wooden prison. Instead, I tried to position myself so that I could throw a good kick at them—whoever they were—but I couldn't quite swing my legs free to make the turn onto my back.

The lid swung open, and I steeled myself for whatever came next.

It was Redvers.

My eyes filled with tears of relief, and a few slipped free. He pulled me into a crouch, and then quickly pulled down my gag, allowing me to suck in great gasps of air. My muscles had cramped in the box, and Redvers had to hold me steady for a moment so I didn't fall back over. Once he was certain I was steady on my own, he went to work on the ropes binding my hands and ankles. As each was freed, I flexed them in relief as blood rushed back to my tingling extremities. They weren't just asleep, they were in pain—Redvers had to help me stand and step out of my cell. Blood ran from my knees, and my entire body ached, but as soon I was free of the crate, I wrapped both arms around Redvers and squeezed hard— surprising myself nearly as much as him. I had never been so happy to see another person.

"We have to be quiet," he whispered in my ear as we jostled against each other.

I wanted to tell him that he was the only one talking, but I was too relieved to argue with the man.

Now that I was free, I could see we were on the back of a

small truck—it looked like a Model T. A small cab perched in front, where I assumed Colonel Stainton and Radwa were riding. Redvers and I were in a midsized bed with sturdy wooden slats on either side. The numerous crates stacked high behind us obscured the men's view—my crate had been loaded last, allowing Redvers easy access to it.

"How did you find me?" I whispered, leaning close to his ear.

"I heard you banging in there. I've been following the colonel all day, and after they loaded the truck and started to drive, I managed to run up behind and climb on without them seeing me."

"What were you going to do when they stopped?" I asked.

"I guess we're going to find that out together."

We were both crouched awkwardly beside my former cell. Redvers looked me over and pulled a handkerchief from a pocket of his dark robe. He wore a native galabieh instead of his usual suit, and as he handed me the handkerchief, I cocked an eyebrow at him in question. He motioned at my knees, and I took the cloth and did my best to mop up the bloody mess. The knees of my thin linen pants had torn away, and my ragged wounds were exposed. His handkerchief nearly soaked through before I decided it was a losing battle. I would have to deal with my numerous slivers and cuts later. I tossed the handkerchief over the back of the truck.

"Hey!" Redvers' voice was a low, indignant whisper.

"Did you really want that back?"

He stared at the sky for a moment before shaking his head. I didn't think he was answering my question.

"Do you know what's in the other crates?" I asked.

"More antiquities would be my guess." He moved to the other side of my crate, away from the end of the truck, and gestured that we should replace the cover.

We did our best to put the top back on and secure it, moving slowly to keep our noise to a minimum. I was surprised the men hadn't heard Redvers cracking it open, but our luck had held there. When we were finished, Redvers returned to my side.

I took a moment to take in our surroundings as we bumped back and forth. We were heading into Cairo, and since it was the dead of night, very few people were out and about. As we reached the city limits, the truck slowed, and despite the improved roads, the truck continued to jostle us back and forth. Redvers moved to the very end of the truck bed and climbed over the back gate, motioning for me to do the same. My eyes widened, but I followed him. I was already bleeding from my cuts and scrapes, and I supposed a few more wouldn't hurt. Whatever Redvers' plan was, I knew it was going to be painful.

"When we take the next corner, jump," Redvers said. "Bend your knees and try to roll."

I gave him a look that told him how enthusiastic I was about his plan, but I prepared myself just the same. When the truck careened around the next corner, crates sliding to the left, Redvers let go of the truck, dropped to the ground, and rolled across the road behind. I gave a brief look to the heavens before doing the same, launching myself from the back of the truck.

I wasn't nearly as graceful as Redvers, and felt my pants give way in a few more places. I lay on the road for a moment and evaluated my person—nothing broken, but a multitude of new bruises and abrasions. When this was over, I wouldn't be able to move for days. The truck continued on, the darkness of the street covering our escape.

"Are you okay?" Redvers helped me to my feet, looking me over.

Every part of my body cried out in pain. "I'll live." I tested my legs and evaluated my pants. More tears, but still not indecently. "Where are they headed?"

"To the docks, I believe." He strode off in the direction the truck had disappeared, and I struggled to keep up with him, my battered body slowing me down. He glanced back at me, face softening, and slowed his pace, catching my elbow when I stumbled over my own feet.

"What's your plan once we get there?" I asked. "To call the inspector? For once, I would like to talk with him—I heard the colonel confess to killing Anna."

Redvers stopped short and I stumbled again, catching myself on his arm, but I continued talking. "We need to let the inspector know what I heard. Or maybe you should tell him. The inspector is not my biggest fan."

"Colonel Stainton killed his own daughter?"

"I heard him tell Radwa."

"Did—did he say why?" Redvers asked. He looked as disturbed as I felt about the matter. We were standing on a deserted sidewalk, and his words echoed slightly as they bounced off the mud brick buildings around us. "And who's Radwa?"

"I think Radwa is the man we saw the colonel arguing with out at the pyramids. I was at his house when they captured me—that's where they were storing the smuggled artifacts. I wasn't terribly clear on why he killed Anna, but he mentioned that she had gotten greedy."

Redvers sighed as he cast his eyes around us. "We need to find a telephone." I cocked an eyebrow. "I thought we were going after a man who was simply a smuggler. But if he killed his own daughter, he's much more dangerous than I thought."

"It doesn't seem like anything is open." I surveyed the block myself. We had dropped into an area near the docks that was primarily businesses. Businesses that were closed for the night. Nothing but darkened windows to greet us. "How far is the police station? Perhaps we could make it there and bring the police back?"

Redvers considered the possibility. "It's probably a thirty-minute walk from where we are now." He eyed my torn pants. "Are you in any shape to make it that far?"

My answer was interrupted by the crate-laden truck careening around the corner toward us.

We had spent too much time debating our next move, and those precious minutes had given the colonel and Radwa time to discover that the first crate on their truck bed, the one that I had been bundled into, was now empty.

There would be no time for phoning the police.

CHAPTER FORTY-ONE

A shot pinged off the building nearest me, and Redvers and I both ducked, heads turning toward the sound. The colonel was hanging out the window of the truck, gun pointed decidedly in our direction. The truck came to a screeching halt and the colonel fumbled his door open as we ran for the dark alley running between the squat buildings. I nearly ran headlong into a wooden cart parked just around the corner. Redvers caught my arm as I stopped short and tried to keep my feet under me.

"Where is everyone getting these guns from?" I hissed.

Redvers ignored me. "Get under there. I'll draw their attention."

There wasn't time to argue as I tucked myself beneath the cart. He took off at a brisk jog, continuing farther along the shadowy alleyway, dodging obstacles as he went. I tried to make myself as small as possible in the darkness behind the sturdy wooden wheel, and I held my breath as I watched two pairs of men's feet sprint past. They slowed slightly when the first pair tripped over something metal, a large crash and a shout bouncing off the narrow walls.

They continued away. Radwa and the colonel were close behind Redvers, but not so close that they realized we had split up.

I appreciated the gallant effort Redvers was making on my behalf, drawing the men away from me. However, if he thought I would wait quietly while these two men killed him and then doubled back to look for me, he was mistaken.

When the footsteps sounded suitably distant, I unfolded myself from beneath the cart, feeling every bruise and ache from the day. But I had no time to baby my injuries.

I had two choices as I saw it; I could go after the men, or try to find a phone and contact the police.

Finding a phone would take too much time.

I moved in the direction the men had gone, looking for something I could use as a weapon. The alley appeared to be a dumping ground for broken bits and pieces of trash. Discarded crates with vegetable remnants and broken glass littered the ground, and when I stepped in something wet and decidedly squishy, I closed my eyes rather than look at what it was. I would add my shoes to the list of lost causes.

I started to feel frantic. I couldn't find anything to use as a weapon, even though the farther I moved down the alley, the more trash I was stepping through. I expected to find a bit of pipe or a piece of metal I could wield, but no such luck. I headed back the way I came, hoping that Redvers was faster on his feet than either Colonel Stainton or his compatriot.

I came back to the corner where the cart sat, still hunting for a makeshift weapon. I poked my head cautiously around the corner—I had seen both men run after Redvers, but I was still nervous about their whereabouts.

The street was deserted.

But the truck was still parked at an angle blocking most of the road.

As I hurried toward the truck, the rumble of the engine made me weak with relief. In their hurry, Radwa had failed to turn it off. While I'd had rudimentary driving lessons at home, I had no desire to start this truck by myself and have my arm snapped off by the hand crank. I hefted myself up into the driver's seat and used the foot pedal to put the car into reverse. I slowly pushed the gas, trying to gauge how sensitive the pedals were, and the truck shot backward.

Sensitive gas pedal, then.

I pushed the third pedal down to the floor for first gear and eased the gas, praying I wouldn't kill the engine. Then I pulled the truck into a wide arc, crates careening wildly to the opposite side of the truck bed. I winced, hoping the antiquities would survive whatever happened next.

I had no idea which way the men went, nor whether the alley they had traveled down had an exit. I hoped for Redvers' sake that we hadn't hurried into a dead end. I took an abrupt left, crates sliding, and for a long moment worried that the change in weight would tip the truck. I wasn't certain how well it was built. But all four wheels stayed on the ground, and I accelerated down the street in the direction I thought the alley would let out.

None of the men were anywhere in sight, so I slowed and put the truck in neutral for a moment, trying to listen for sounds over the truck's substantial rumble. There was no way for me to kill the engine and listen—I would never get the thing started again. I thought I heard voices to my right, so I took the next turn, but a vacant street greeted me once again. Frustration wrinkled my brow. I was beginning to fear that my theft of the truck had been an ill-advised plan, when I heard what was definitely a shout. I put the truck into first and held on to the large steering wheel with both hands as I pushed the truck toward the sound.

As I rumbled around the next corner, I nearly hit Redvers. His reflexes were fast and he dove out of reach of the truck's tires at the last moment. The colonel wasn't nearly so lucky. The brakes on the truck were not nearly as sensitive as the gas, and I wasn't able to stop before he bounced off the right side of the truck's grill.

I felt an uncomfortable bump.

Radwa was close behind the colonel, and even as I mashed the brake to the floor, the truck knocked Radwa straight over and he disappeared beneath the front of the vehicle. I grimaced as I felt another bump under the right wheel. The truck finally ground to a halt and I killed the engine.

The sudden stillness was a sharp contrast to the rumbling and shouts of a moment before. The street was silent except for the ticking of the truck engine—and the groans from the colonel as he lay on the ground. Redvers was disarming him before I could even dismount from the truck.

"Does Radwa have a weapon?" I called to Redvers. I squatted beside the front left tire and attempted to peer beneath the truck. If Radwa did have a weapon, I hoped I could get behind the large tire before he could get a shot off.

"No, I only saw one on the colonel here." The offending weapon was now pointed unwaveringly at the colonel. "Doesn't mean he doesn't have one, of course."

I nodded even though Redvers couldn't see me. I didn't hear any noise from beneath the truck, and I decided Radwa was either biding his time or had been knocked unconscious by the impact. I was guessing the latter. I stood, brushing myself off, even though I knew it was a lost cause. My entire outfit was bound for a trash receptacle.

I walked on shaking legs over to the colonel and looked down on him, hands on hips. He was rocking back and forth in the dirt and gravel, moaning as he tried to reach his lower leg. The first bump I felt had obviously been the truck rolling over his leg. Or possibly his foot. It was hard to tell which, but I was overcome with the urge to kick him and find out exactly where he was hurt.

I restrained myself.

"I suppose he really will need that cane now." I could hear my voice shaking slightly. I wasn't nearly as calm on the inside as I hoped I looked on the outside.

Redvers grinned at me. "He certainly will."

CHAPTER FORTY-TWO

We needed a phone.

I volunteered to find one, despite my lack of Arabic, since I was too shaky to hold a gun on our captives. I might accidentally shoot them or someone else. Although I wouldn't have been terribly upset about either of our two criminals.

I walked two blocks over to a street where the buildings were taller. Small balconies with wrought-iron railings decorated the walls above my head, and the laundry hanging from several of the windows indicated that families lived on the floors above the ground-level shops. I pounded on several doors until I managed to wake someone. The man who finally came to the door was disheveled and highly aggravated, but with a series of hand motions, I managed to indicate that I needed a telephone. I could tell he was thinking about slamming the door on me again, but he grudgingly led me a block over where he himself pounded on a peeling wooden door. Another sleep-addled shopkeeper answered, and I smiled politely as the two men gestured angrily back and forth. Finally, the second shopkeeper stood aside and allowed me the use of his telephone. I managed to indicate to the operator that I wanted the police by repeating Inspector Hamadi's name several times—the operator's English was as bad as my Arabic, but Hamadi was well known enough that I was put through.

The police arrived minutes later, and things moved quickly after that. Hamadi refused to acknowledge that I might have been helpful in any way, ignoring me as he praised Redvers' quick thinking in apprehending the two men. I rolled my eyes behind Hamadi's back—frequently—and Redvers accepted the praise with indifference as he passed the colonel's gun over to the inspector.

Redvers was happy to turn over custody of the colonel to an eager cadre of officers. A handful of others pulled Radwa from beneath the truck. He was a bit tattered, but not that much worse for wear considering he had been run over by a truck. Radwa had indeed been knocked unconscious by the impact of his head against the packed-dirt road, and his leg was definitely broken. Probably some ribs as well.

Once the adrenaline that had been pumping through my system stopped, my body started to shake and I found a place nearby where I could sit down. Hard. Redvers left his post next to Hamadi and came over to me.

"I'm sorry I don't have a jacket to offer you this evening." Redvers indicated his long robes.

"It's quite all right." I marveled that my voice sounded so calm and normal after yet another harrowing evening. "I'm not actually cold. I think I'm just in shock." I tried to smile, but it was more of a grimace.

Redvers took a seat next to me, his back against a stucco wall, long legs stretched out before him. "Well, the police seem to have this in hand," he said. "I'll see if I can arrange us a ride home."

"Not the truck?" I asked. "I've become quite fond of it."

Redvers smiled. "They will need it for evidence. Hopefully, all the pieces in those crates can be returned to Engelbach and he can sort out where they belong. He'll be thrilled." Redvers looked at me. "And I'm not sure I'll be letting you drive again any time soon."

"Surely you're joking. I saved your life with that truck."

"Barely. You nearly took me out with it." Then he turned serious. "I do have to thank you for coming to my rescue, yet again."

"I'm not sure how you ever managed without me." This time I managed a real smile, mirrored by his. "I have to thank you, too, for drawing the colonel and Radwa away from me in the first place. We make a good team."

Redvers agreed and took my hand in his own.

By the time we pushed our stiff bodies from the ground, Inspector Hamadi had decided that instead of releasing us to our hotel, we would accompany him to the station to make our statements. Even Redvers' complaints couldn't sway the man. Most of the officers had arrived by small motorcycle, so we were loaded into one of the few police cars and bounced the several miles to the main police station. Redvers had been right—I would have struggled to walk the distance, given the shape I was in.

The sky was growing light when we arrived at the station, and as the car came to a halt, Redvers nudged me awake—I couldn't keep my eyes open any longer. I looked around and realized we were now close to downtown and the museum. The faint morning light bounced off the light pink façade of the police station. I was quite surprised at its run-down appearance. I wouldn't have thought that the fastidious Inspector Hamadi would stand for it.

We were bundled inside and taken through the lobby to the main office area. Scarred wooden desks were crammed into the small space, with two offices at the far end. I assumed one of the offices belonged to Hamadi. I could hear the colonel being brought inside, his shrieks of pain alternating with indignant blustering. They were being none too careful with his injured leg, and I found that I didn't feel bad for him in the slightest. The officers bundled him off to an interrogation room in a different part of the building and I decided not to ask where that was. I didn't want to give the inspector any ideas about where I should be seated.

We gave our statements to an officer with a curling moustache, who was thankfully nimble on the typewriter; he made good time on the keys as we recited our tales. Redvers, ever the gentleman, allowed me to go first. Hamadi sat glowering beside the officer, interrupting me frequently with sharp questions. If it weren't for the inspector, we would have been done in less than an hour. While Redvers gave his statement, I slumped in a chair and propped my head against the wall. I was asleep within moments.

By the time we were able to leave, the sun was fully up and I was delirious from exhaustion.

The ride home passed in a blur, and I only vaguely remembered Redvers helping me stumble to my room. I crawled into bed and strong hands tucked in my covers around me. When I awoke, the sun was already setting—and judging by the clock, I was late for dinner. Yet despite the growling of my stomach, I didn't hurry. I needed to bathe and check on my aunt before heading down for dinner.

I ran a lukewarm bath and lowered myself into it. The cuts and abrasions screamed, even more so as I carefully washed each one out. I let my bruised muscles soak until the cold water and my empty stomach forced me out of the tub. I found the loosest clothing possible and dressed before crossing the hall to knock on Millie's door. I tried to steel myself for the worst in case something had happened while I was out. The doctor answered, and he gave me an up-and-down look.

"You've looked better, miss."

I nodded. "It was a long night, Dr. Williams. How is my aunt?"

He smiled widely—a genuine grin—the first I had seen

since I'd met the man. "She's a tough old bird. She was up and about today, but I made her go back to bed. She'll be right as rain in a few more days."

I smiled. I was relieved that she had continued to improve.

"Miss Lillian and that other young sheila went to have some supper, but they should be back soon. Your aunt is resting now." The doctor shooed me away from the doorway, stepped into the hall, and closed the door behind him.

When Millie was back on her feet, I was going to have a serious talk with her about making a full confession to Lillian, if the young woman didn't know already. Life was fleeting, and they both deserved the chance to spend time together without any more lies and secrets between them. But for now, I would let her regain her strength.

Dr. Williams eyed me again. "You want me to take a look at anything?" He nodded toward the cuts visible on my arms and wrists.

I shook my head. I didn't think they were serious enough to need medical attention.

"I'll drop some salve off just the same. Put it on those burns."

I gingerly touched the rope burns around my wrists and thanked him. I thought about showing him my ravaged knees, but decided against it. They looked better after I had washed them out, and there was little to be done but keep them clean and dry. I would consult him if they started to look infected.

I dragged myself to the dining room, my spirits light with the knowledge that Millie was recovering swiftly, but my body weeping in pain. I considered retiring to my room after dinner and soaking in another bath. Or perhaps I would break down and ask the doctor for a pain reliever.

A new face greeted me at the entrance to the dining room, a smiling young man, chest puffed out in pride at his new position. I gave him a smile, but his cheerful demeanor left me feeling sad as I remembered what became of Zaki. When he asked if I was waiting for someone, I shook my head and told him I was looking for friends.

As my eyes passed over the room, I saw Redvers at a table with Charlie and Deanna, and my heart lifted. I limped over to them and helped myself to a seat, even though they were nearly finished with their meals. The waiter appeared immediately and I ordered lentil stew. I needed to eat something, but I couldn't tolerate the thought of anything more substantial. My stomach was still nervous from all the excitement.

"We heard what happened last night, Jane," Deanna said. "I'm not at all surprised that you rode in to save the day. Women always do, you know."

Both Charlie and Redvers rolled their eyes at her.

"Thanks, Deanna." I smiled at her, then looked to Redvers. "What did I miss? Have you heard anything from Hamadi about what happened after we left the station?"

"Of course. I was just telling these two. The colonel finally confessed to killing Anna, although his statement was made under . . . duress."

I grimaced. I could only imagine how the inspector and his men had elicited a confession from the man. I felt a small twinge of sympathy, despite his crimes and the fact that he intended to kill me.

Redvers continued. "He claims it was self-defense, that she was threatening him."

I rolled my eyes, Charlie barked a laugh, and Deanna cocked a disbelieving eyebrow. It was difficult to see how he was going to pull that off as a defense.

"Anna was apparently going to either blackmail her father over the antiquities smuggling or kill him and take it over herself," Redvers explained.

"What a sweetheart." Deanna lit a cigarette.

"The inspector is still wondering why you ran the men over, Jane." Redvers' eyes had an unmistakable twinkle.

"He asked me that last night—several times, if I remember correctly." I shrugged. "I honestly didn't mean to. The brakes were a little stiff and I didn't expect you three to be right around that corner. Did he ever find the papers Anna was using for blackmail?"

"No, the police are still looking for those. But he did give me this." Redvers reached into his inside coat pocket and pulled out a small brooch, passing it to me.

"My scarab!" I pinned it to my blouse. "I'm glad to see it again. Millie gave it to me for my birthday last year," I explained to Deanna and Charlie.

"Speaking of your aunt, how is she?" Charlie asked.

"She's doing much better. She was even up and about today. Although, we'll probably be here a bit longer than we expected. Just to make sure she's fully recovered."

Charlie and Deanna shared a look. "That's too bad, because we have to leave soon," Deanna said.

"It's getting a little too hot for us here, now that word about cheating at the card tables is out. So we're going to move on before management asks us to." A wry smile touched Charlie's mouth.

Deanna put her hand on mine. "When you make it back to the States, let us know. I meant it when I said we should keep in touch."

I smiled and nodded. I certainly did intend to keep in touch with them both. A few minutes later, the pair excused themselves to start packing, and we said our good-byes. They planned to leave first thing in the morning.

After they departed, I turned back to Redvers. "There are still a few things I'm wondering about."

"And what are those?"

"How did both men come to use the same gun?"

"Well, that's the interesting part. Zaki stole the doctor's gun from his room before Anna was killed. Everyone assumed it was the gun used to kill Anna because it was stolen.

But Zaki was holding on to that gun at his house. The colonel used his own gun and then held on to it. He had the exact same model—they were service pistols, if you remember. I'm sure they will find it's the same gun we took from him last night."

"And no one thought to check because none of us suspected the colonel. Awfully bold of him to hold on to the thing." Then I sighed. "He seemed so devastated that day. He really would have made quite the actor."

Redvers snorted.

"I suppose it also explains why he wanted me to go in and find her body."

"It would have been more suspicious if he had been the one to find her."

"At the time, I wondered why he would try to wake her so early. There was no way Anna Stainton was an early riser. But he knew that she was already dead."

Redvers nodded sadly.

When I finished my stew, I set my napkin aside. "I'm afraid I'm headed straight back to bed. I feel as though I could sleep for a week."

"Well, you've certainly earned the right."

I took his arm and we passed through the lobby. The desk clerk smartly snapped to attention when he saw Redvers. "A telegram for you, Mr. Dibble," he said, holding out the paper envelope.

I stopped short. *"Dibble?"*

For the first time, I watched an embarrassed flush creep up Redvers' neck. He cleared his throat and moved a discreet distance away from any listening ears.

"You mustn't tell anyone about this. Under threat of death, Jane Wunderly." His voice was fierce, but his eyes begged.

I couldn't help a fit of giggles.

"Redvers Dibble is your actual name? I can see why you're discreet about it."

I was caught in another laughing fit while Redvers glared at me. He gave his head a shake and opened his telegram, reading it while keeping one eye on me. He folded it and tucked it into his inside pocket while I got my laughter under control.

Suitably somber, I regarded him. "So, good news, Dibs?" I asked.

He took a threatening step toward me and leaned down until we were practically nose to nose. The clerk eyed us nervously, and Redvers caught his look out of the corner of his eye. Straightening, he grabbed my elbow and pulled me around the corner. I have to admit I was still amused—and not in the least scared of Redvers Dibble.

"I'm going to regret ever meeting you, aren't I?"

It was probably a rhetorical question, but I answered anyway.

"Most likely." I grinned up at him.

He heaved a sigh and regarded the ceiling.

"So, what news?" I asked again.

He paused and regarded me. "Looks like I'll be departing sooner than I had expected." He had the grace to seem disappointed.

My own heart dropped into my stomach, but I tried valiantly to seem unconcerned. I had hoped he would be staying, especially since it looked as though I would be here until Millie was strong enough to make the long trip again. It would be nice to spend some time with him while our lives weren't in danger.

"Where to?"

Instead of replying, he smiled, and my stomach did a small flip.

"I'll be seeing you again, Jane Wunderly. Don't you worry."

I considered him for a moment before stepping forward. I wrapped my hand around his neck as I went up on my tip-toes and pulled his face down to mine. As his soft lips met mine, an electric spark ran between the two of us.

I kissed him. Thoroughly.

When we pulled apart, it was my turn to smile. I turned and walked out to the terrace, leaving him standing in the hall with a stunned look on his face. I thought a nice cool drink was in order. Perhaps a gin and tonic.

See him again? I wasn't in the least bit concerned.

ACKNOWLEDGMENTS

I have a lot of people to thank, and it might seem like I'm thanking everyone I've ever met, so buckle in.

I want to thank my amazing agent Ann Collette. I'm so fortunate to have you.

Thank you to my wonderful editor John Scognamiglio who has been an absolute pleasure to work with. Big thanks to the rest of the team at Kensington who have made my job so much easier and brought this book to life.

Thank you to Zoe King. Without her, I never would have sent this book out in the first place. I'm so grateful for her editing skills, her support and her encouragement. Love you, Z.

Thank you to Tasha Alexander and Andrew Grant for their support, encouragement, and advice—and for giving me a refuge to get a lot of work done. I love you madly.

Thank you to my oldest and dearest friends: Kate Conrad, Jenny Lohr, Erin MacMillan, Beth McIntyre, Katie Meyer and Megan Mueller. I love and appreciate you more than words can say.

Chris Hammond. You're pretty old too. An old friend, I mean.

Thank you to my beta readers—some of whom read some really early versions of this, and bless their hearts for encouraging me to keep going: Tasha Alexander, Susie Calkins, Dana Cameron, Kate Conrad, Jordan Foster, Carrie Hennessy, Tim Hennessy, Katrina Niidas Holm, Jess Lourey, Megan Mueller, Mandi Neumann, and Clare O'Donohue.

I count myself incredibly fortunate to have been welcomed into the crime fiction community—I have truly found my tribe. They are some of the kindest, most talented, and generous people I know. Many of them have offered support, advice and encouragement, and in some cases even blurbs, so special thanks to: Tasha Alexander, Gretchen Beetner, Lou Berney, Terri Bischoff, Susanna Calkins, Hilary Davidson, Matthew FitzSimmons, Andrew Grant, Alex Grecian, Chris Holm, Katrina Niidas Holm, Rob Hart, Linda Joffe Hull, Dana Kaye, Elizabeth Little, Jess Lourey, Jamie Mason, Nadine Nettmann, Mike McCrary, Catriona McPherson, Lauren O'Brien, Lori Rader-Day, Johnny Shaw, Jay Shepherd, Victoria Thompson, Ashley Weaver, James Ziskin. If I have forgotten someone, you probably owe me a beer. Or I owe you one.

Special thanks to Brad Parks for never reading anything I've written.

Thank you to Jon and Ruth Jordan and Richard Katz for introducing me to the crime fiction community to begin with. And to the Crimespree family: Dan and Kate Malmon, Tim and Carrie Hennessy, Bryan VanMeter and Kyle Jo Schmidt. A further thank you to the Milwaukee crew: Daniel Goldin, Rochelle Melander, Nick and Margret Petrie. Events are better with you there.

Thank you to Walid Ghonem, the warmest and most knowledgeable tour guide you could ever hope to meet. He graciously answered all my questions and showed us the most wonderful time in Egypt.

Big love and thanks to my mom Dorothy Neubauer, my sister Rachel Neubauer and my aunties Sandy, Sara and Sue. Love and thanks to the other members of the extended Neubauer clan who have been super supportive through this process: Justin and Christine Kierzek, Jeff and Annie Kierzek, and Ignacio Catral. Keep it weird, you guys.

Shout-out to my step-kids: Angel, Mandi, Alex and Andie.

Thank you, always, to Beth McIntyre. None of this is possible without you.

And thank you to my husband Gunther. His unwavering love and support keep me sane.

I got the news that this book was going to be published exactly a month after my dad, Police Chief Scott Neubauer, unexpectedly passed away. It was bittersweet for me—my dad was my biggest cheerleader and my staunchest supporter. He would have moved heaven and earth if I had asked him, and I hope that he knows we finally did it.